THE
FRAGILE
ONES

BOOKS BY JENNIFER CHASE

JENNIFER CHASE

THE FRAGILE ONES

bookouture

Published by Bookouture in 2021

An imprint of Storyfire Ltd.
Carmelite House
50 Victoria Embankment
London EC4Y 0DZ

www.bookouture.com

ISBN: 978-1-83888-896-1
eBook ISBN: 978-1-83888-895-4

To LFC Sr.

PROLOGUE

"Please can we go?" whined Tessa as she followed her mother through the living room and into the kitchen. "*Please*," she said again, pushing her blonde curls away from her eyes. "I really want to go to the swing by the creek."

"Not by yourself," countered Mrs. Mayfield, ignoring her daughter's angry stare. "We've talked about this before."

"Yes, and you said I couldn't go alone, and I'm not. Megan will be with me." Tessa's older sister was barely a year older and her best friend. Her mother began emptying the dishwasher, putting plates and glasses away in the cabinet. It was unclear if she was thinking about what Tessa had said or not, so she tried again. "I'm *almost* eleven and Megan is *almost* twelve. We're practically teenagers," she said. "Besides, Janey and her brother will probably be there."

Mrs. Mayfield laughed. "You know, you would be a good lawyer the way you make your case."

"I don't want to be a lawyer. I'm going to be a vet," Tessa said, grinning.

"Well, I know you are going to be whatever you want to be." Mrs. Mayfield laughed to herself as she slipped the last piece of silverware into the drawer and turned to face her daughter. At the sound of her name, Megan had joined Tessa in the doorway and they both stood quietly waiting for an answer. Glancing at the wall clock with a sigh, she said, "You both have to be back by four thirty, not a second later. Understand?"

"Thank you! Thank you!" Tessa said, grabbing her sister's hand in glee. Both girls were in denim shorts and pastel T-shirts with their favorite matching blue sneakers.

"Be home on time," their mom called after them.

"We will," chimed the girls.

Mrs. Mayfield heard the front door shut, followed by the sound of running footsteps.

She smiled and went back to her chores as the afternoon ticked by.

At 4:45 p.m. Mrs. Mayfield was waiting impatiently to hear the girls enter the house with a list of a dozen reasons why they were late—but the front door never opened. An hour after that, unable to wait any longer, she looked outside, thinking that the girls might be in the yard.

Debris from a croquet set littered the lawn; the wooden mallets abandoned and colored balls scattered as if the girls had been playing only moments ago. The trampoline in the corner had one of the girls' bright blue sweatshirts hanging on the edge. It swayed slightly in the breeze.

There was no sign of them.

She ran through the house to the backyard, but it, too, was deserted. No whispers. No giggles. No shrieks of laughter. The wind was picking up and whistling through the branches and leaves of the surrounding trees—almost whispering a warning.

Mrs. Mayfield pulled off her apron and reached for her coat, deciding to walk to the creek and bring the girls back herself. At this point, she was more angry than concerned, knowing how they could be forgetful when they were having fun, and often lost track of time.

But surely they would be on their way home by now? she thought to herself as her pace quickened from a fast walk to a jog. Against her better judgment, and knowing that she couldn't shelter them forever, she had crumbled and let them go down to the creek where one of the neighboring boys had constructed a swing that they loved to play on.

And now fear ripped through her body. "Tessa!" she yelled. "Megan!" Terrible scenarios shuffled through her thoughts as she tried desperately to keep her emotions on an even keel.

"Tessa! Megan!"

She yelled their names over and over until her voice went hoarse. Her chest felt strangely heavy and her vision blurred as she ran, but her strength and mother's instinct pushed her forward, down the trail leading to the creek. The trail was well-worn by local kids looking for adventure and fun. Stumbling as she ran, she frantically turned left and then right. There wasn't a soul around… She was alone. She kept moving.

Looking up at the tall pine trees, everything spun in a dizzying blur of forest and darkening sky. She squeezed her eyes tightly shut and open again, then stopped for a moment to listen.

The swing was only visible at the bottom of the path just above the creek and she could hear the water rushing below. Peering over the edge, there was no sign of them—or anyone. She kept turning, expecting to see her girls everywhere she looked. They weren't there. All around her were discarded candy wrappers and remnants of fast food containers. Proof that children played here often.

There was no sound apart from the whisper of the trees. No children laughing nearby.

"Megan! Tessa!" she yelled again, but there was only silence. She ran all the way up the trail to the street, still calling their names in a full-blown panic.

Mrs. Mayfield turned her attention up the road, her mother's instinct in high gear. Something blue lying beneath a bush caught her eye and she ran towards it.

She leaned down and her hand trembled over the light blue canvas before she forced herself to grab the abandoned blue sneaker.

"No," she said, barely breathing.

Written on the side tread of the shoe with a thick black pen was one word: *Tessa*.

CHAPTER ONE

Two years later

Tuesday 1945 hours

"I'm so proud of how far you've come, and really impressed at how hard you've been working to tackle your anxiety," said Dr. Carver, her calm voice and serene expression beaming through the computer screen.

"I'm finally feeling like I'm in control and not the other way around. I can actually say that a weight has been lifted," said Katie Scott as she took a deep breath and tried to visualize her worries and fears leaving her body as she'd been taught. She then readjusted herself on the couch with Cisco, her jet-black German shepherd, at her side.

"I want to insert a bit of caution," said Dr. Carver.

Katie didn't want to hear anything negative to take away how great she had been feeling recently, but she knew that Dr. Carver had been right about many things so far. She braced herself and listened.

"This process will sometimes involve great steps forward and then surprise you with unexpected setbacks, but I don't want you to become discouraged. Okay?" The doctor continued to makes notes just out of view, pushing her dark hair away from her face to concentrate.

"I understand," said Katie.

"Do you still have nightmares?"

"Sometimes, but they are becoming less frequent." The truth was that she had disturbing dreams a couple of times a week, but she'd had them so long that she only really counted the truly terrifying ones. They'd become such a familiar part of her life.

"That is common—so don't worry. And taking into consideration your job as a cold-case detective and its unique stresses, it's best to be alert, calm and prepared for what your next case will bring," she said, and smiled. "There might be some setbacks, but it won't take away all the hard work you've put in. You are in a much better place now."

It was true. Katie had come a long way since she arrived home a little more than a year ago from two tours in Afghanistan as an army K9 handler. She glanced down at Cisco who was snoozing beside her. Not a day would go by where she wasn't grateful for being able to bring home her partner with her. "Thank you, Dr. Carver." She smiled. "I know there will be tough days ahead, and my past experiences will haunt me from time to time—but I've never given up on a fight."

"And that's when all your new skills and knowledge will kick in, and you'll be much better prepared."

"I know now that the first case I took on after I came home from the army caused me more distress than I realized. The image of the graves of those little girls will never leave me."

"I know, but now you can use the fact that you overcame your demons and solved the case as a strength. Don't forget what we've talked about; how you stay focused and in the moment, counting to ten with each breath. As simple as it sounds, it's more difficult when you're in the middle of an attack."

"Yes. I have several images that help to calm my mind," she said.

"Well, look, our time's up for today. And I think that we can meet again in two weeks?"

Nodding, Katie said, "Definitely."

"You know you can call me anytime, if you need to speak before then. Okay?"

"Thank you."

"Good night."

"Good night," said Katie as the screen went blank, before the screensaver kicked in with a photo of her and Chad—her childhood best friend and now boyfriend. It was amazing how they had found each other again, and on this occasion the timing was right. She smiled, remembering everything they had been through growing up together, and then finding each other again at the perfect moment.

Slowly shutting her laptop, Katie mused that things were falling into place at last. Perhaps for the first time since leaving the army she felt it was possible to be a police detective and lead a normal life. There were things that she had seen that would never be erased from her mind, but she was learning how to live without panic attacks and anxiety paralyzing her. She was learning to forgive her past, and herself.

CHAPTER TWO

Wednesday 1015 hours

Detective Katie Scott left the Sequoia County courtroom where she had been called to testify for a case she had worked involving a missing person, which had turned out to be a murder. She was surprised that she was only questioned for about half an hour and then excused. She would probably be recalled for the defense.

Katie passed a few familiar faces as she descended the marble stairs, heading back to the main entrance. The old Californian courthouse building, originally built in 1895 and named the Muir Building, was still as stunning as it would have been all those years ago; detailed crown moldings and rich, polished mahogany transported you back in time.

Trailing her hand along the wrought-iron railing, Katie stepped off the stairs and hurried to the large wooden doors where Deputy Sean McGaven stood waiting for her. It was difficult to miss him, since he was about six foot six inches tall, and with his cropped light red hair, brown suit and white shirt; he looked official and handsome as he towered over people.

"Hey, Gav," said Katie as she greeted her partner. "What's up?"

"Oh great, you're out already," he said.

"What's the hurry?"

"The sheriff wants us to meet him in his office—like, ten minutes ago."

"What's it about?" she asked, wondering why he hadn't texted or called her. Sheriff Scott, her uncle, never held emergency meetings unless there was a very important reason. Her mind began to search through the cold-case files she had been investigating recently—it most likely had something to do with one of them.

"Don't know."

"And you drove over here to tell me in person?"

"C'mon, I'll race you back," he said. "Let's go."

Katie had finally purchased a new car after her old one was totaled in a high speed chase. She took almost two months to decide what type she wanted. McGaven clearly wanted to check out her new wheels.

"Nice..." he said, as she led them over to a black Jeep SUV and disengaged the lock.

"This was the only car I really liked."

"But more importantly, how does Cisco like it?"

Katie laughed. "He likes it just fine." A minute later she followed McGaven out of the county parking lot, and headed to the sheriff's department a few blocks away.

As soon as she was parked up, Katie grabbed her briefcase and got out of the vehicle.

Jogging up to her, McGaven said, "We don't have time to stop at the forensic lab first."

"What's the hurry? What do you know that I don't?" she asked, hurrying to keep up with McGaven's long stride.

"Nothing, I swear."

They quickly entered the building, but instead of going to the forensic lab where their cold-case office and files were located, they went straight up to the administration area where the sheriff and top supervising personnel had their offices.

It amazed Katie that whenever she went to the sheriff's office her heart still beat just a bit faster. Her uncle was the one who stepped up to raise her after her parents died in a car accident when she was a teenager, and he was the only family she had now—but he was a strict boss. They had been through a lot together, and had their differences, but they had always managed to work them out and their bond had only become stronger.

Katie reached the sheriff's office only to find the door was shut, which seemed strange. He usually had the door wide open when she arrived for a meeting or an update on cold cases. There were low voices and some laughter coming from within, which made her wonder even more about what was going on.

Hesitating, she raised her hand and knocked twice, McGaven waiting behind her.

"Come in," came the familiar authoritative voice from the other side.

Katie took a deep breath and opened the door, taken aback for a moment when she saw the group that was assembled inside. She glanced to McGaven, seeing the same confused expression on his face.

Sheriff Scott, Undersheriff Dorothy Sullivan, the new Mayor Brendon Brown, and two casually dressed men that Katie didn't recognize stared back at them.

"Please, Detective Scott, Deputy McGaven, come in and take a seat," said the sheriff. With close-cut gray hair and his immaculate uniform, her uncle looked strong, distinguished and authoritative. Katie felt her stomach drop. Was one of her cold cases coming back to haunt her, or was it just her anxiety kicking in? She sat down next to McGaven.

"Mayor Brown has asked a favor from the department, and I'm inclined to grant it," the sheriff said.

Favor?

The sheriff continued. "Detective Scott and Deputy McGaven, I would like for you both to meet Matt Gardner and Emir Patel. They are part of an award-winning documentary team—Wild Oats Productions."

Katie and McGaven nodded politely and glanced at each other.

"Matt is the director and Emir is the camera operator and assistant director," Scott explained.

Katie was still clueless as to what a film company had to do with her.

"Detective Scott, it would be helpful for everyone involved if we all work together," piped up the undersheriff as she looked at Katie.

"Maybe I can explain." The mayor spoke up, noticing Katie's and McGaven's confused expressions. He was newly appointed, younger than any previous mayor, and extremely ambitious. "I'm familiar with Matt's film work—which is extraordinary, I might add. They approached me because they want to film in our city and county areas for a new documentary—actually several areas around California. They want to explore how so many of these great cities and towns wouldn't exist if it weren't for the early settlers, and the decisions they had made. Basically, separating facts from stories passed down—filming from a different angle. I think it's fantastic because we have such rich history, and some unanswered questions from the past, which will make for great cinema and bring a lot of tourism to the area."

"I'm sorry for interrupting, Mayor," said Katie as politely as she could, thinking about her next cold case getting colder by the minute. "That sounds great but I don't understand why McGaven and I are here?"

"Well," Mayor Brown continued. "The production company has requested a guide to give them a tour of some of the more rural areas, especially those surrounding the sink holes and near the ghost town of Silo."

Katie felt her nerves tingle and her stomach tighten, suddenly realizing where all this was going. The mayor kept talking, but she only heard white noise as her mind recalled previous events…

"So I thought, since you had worked the Chelsea Compton case, and of course are quite familiar with the area, you'd be the perfect person to show them around. I understand that the trails are a bit tricky to navigate, but you grew up here—it's no problem for you." He forced a politician's smile. "What do you think?"

Katie only heard the name Chelsea Compton. Her heart had practically stopped. It was her first case after she had been discharged from the army. The experience had almost pushed her over the edge—even before she was promoted to detective. She could still see the delicate little body of ten-year-old Chelsea in a carefully crafted coffin with her arms wrapped around a teddy bear. She had moved on from all the experiences surrounding that particular investigation, especially the geological sink hole that had almost taken her life, and she didn't want to go back. It was a harrowing experience that was a defining moment in her life that she didn't want to repeat.

Sheriff Scott spoke up. "It would be a short tour to get them started, just something to help them scout some good locations and know where to stay away from. You have the most hiking experience of anyone I know. And quite frankly, we don't have anyone else right now that I could send and feel confident about their abilities."

Katie still didn't answer. She looked from her uncle to the two men waiting expectantly for her response. "I don't know what to say," she said, hoarsely. "We have cold cases to process."

"McGaven can hold down the fort. You can take a day or two to show these gentlemen around our great county," said the sheriff, to Katie's dismay.

How could Katie say no, with everyone staring intently at her, waiting for an answer?

"Of course," she stuttered.

"Fantastic," said the mayor. To the filmmakers, he said, "Katie is great and knows all the best spots and the best ways to get there. She can answer any questions you might have."

"Thank you," said the director, Matt, to Katie. "I promise we won't take up any more of your time than absolutely necessary."

Katie stood up, grabbing her briefcase. "I appreciate that. Well, I guess let's meet here in the parking lot at 0800 tomorrow morning. That's eight a.m. Wear hiking shoes and appropriate clothing—layers." She smiled.

The director and assistant director both thanked her, as they also made to leave.

"Do you have four-wheel drive vehicles?" she asked.

"Yes, one, will we need another?" said Matt, scratching his neatly trimmed beard.

"Probably not, but it's still a good idea in case you have any car troubles. You can rent one from Karl's Rentals on Huntington Street if you need to," she said.

"Thanks again, Detective," he said.

As everyone filed out of the office, Sheriff Scott called Katie back. She waited until everyone had left and then shut the door and sighed.

Now with a softer tone, her uncle said, "I know this is about as appealing as going to the dentist for you, but it's good PR and frankly we need it—I don't need to remind you about previous incidents we've had here with the child murders and… the murder of your aunt Claire. Our beautiful county has been a little slow on the tourism and this will help."

Katie sat down. "Yeah, well, I just hope that we don't have everyone and their grandmother coming here to see the 'sink holes' or thinking we have some haunted ghost town to explore; that's more than this small department can handle."

"I know, I thought about that and we've been in contact with the proper county and state authorities to make sure that the fencing is properly maintained well beyond the geological dangers—and to keep a watchful eye on any erosion."

Katie let out another sigh.

The sheriff laughed. "I know that look from when you were a teenager and you didn't want to clean your room."

Katie couldn't help but smile, remembering all the good times with her uncle—even after the death of her parents. "This is totally different, and you know it."

"Just think of it as a little break. You've closed all your cases so far—take a time out. Besides, you love the woods and hiking—so try to enjoy yourself. It'll be over in a day, or two, tops."

"I know you're right, but you do realize that Mayor Brown is trying to appeal to the community, so he has to hit this one out of the park?"

"Maybe, but he's a good man. A bit green, but he has the right ideas about Pine Valley and Sequoia County."

Katie stood up to leave. "Do I need to write a report?"

"Yes. Nothing too detailed, but I like to keep updated on anything that has to do with the department. Make sure you give me the exact locations. Should make for some interesting reading. Oh, and take Cisco with you."

"Okay. I guess it will give me a chance to break in my new Jeep."

Sheriff Scott stood up and hugged his niece. "See, things are looking up already."

"I hope so."

CHAPTER THREE

Wednesday 1300 hours

Katie stopped to grab a cup of coffee and see her friend Denise, the record's division supervisor. Looking around at all the hustle and bustle, she realized that she was lucky to work downstairs in the forensic tomb or just "the tomb"—as many people called it. It was quiet, but that suited Katie just fine.

"Katie! Nice to see you," said Denise, a petite woman with short dark hair. Her twinkly eyes and upbeat personality were infectious.

"Hi, Denise," Katie said, feeling her mood instantly lift. Denise and McGaven made such a great couple Katie couldn't help but be happy for them.

"What brings you out of the tombs?"

"Just had a meeting with the sheriff, but I'm on my way down to pore over more cold-case files soon."

"Hmm, is something bothering you?" Denise said studying her friend's expression and quiet attitude, always able to sense when something was weighing on Katie's mind. "Sit down for a moment." She gestured to an office chair next to hers.

Taking a seat, Katie explained. "It's no big deal, but they want me to babysit some documentary crew for a day or two."

"Sounds like fun…"

"Yeah, but they want me to take them to where the sink holes are, and give them a tour of Silo."

Her friend frowned, which was unusual. "I get it. That's the last place you want to go, or be reminded of."

"Exactly."

"You know what? The crew is looking to you for ideas, right?"

Katie nodded.

"Why don't you just think of it as a fun opportunity to explore? Take them where you wanna go. I bet they'll name you in the acknowledgments at the end of the movie," Denise said, and smiled.

Katie stood up. "You're right, and I could use a bit of a break, to be honest. Thanks, Denise."

"I want to hear all about it."

"Absolutely. Look, I'd better get back and do some reading. I need to see which case we want to investigate next."

"Lunch next week?"

"Sure," said Katie.

"I was thinking just us girls."

Katie smiled. "You bet."

She hurried down the long hallway, and took the stairs instead of the elevator to the lower level. She passed a couple of deputies and exchanged hellos. Just before exiting to the parking lot, she stopped at an unmarked door.

Above the doorframe was a small round camera pointing downward at whoever stood at the door. Katie glanced up at it, wondering if the forensic supervisor, John Blackburn, or one of his two technicians, ever watched the security camera—either in real time, or from the computer recordings. She swiped her card, waiting a second for the mechanism to disengage, and then pushed the door open. No matter what kind of day she was having, every time she entered the forensic lab it had a calming effect on her. This place felt like home to her and she never grew tired of walking by the labs and into the depths of the building.

She slowed her pace as she passed John's large examination room and saw him at one of his many computers examining and comparing something she couldn't quite make out—possibly the grooves of a bullet from a firearm. He was dressed in jeans and a black T-shirt which showed his numerous tattoos from his Navy Seals days. His handsome rugged looks, dark wavy hair, green eyes, and the fact they shared a military background, always made Katie notice him, but her heart belonged to her childhood sweetheart Chad.

She smiled to herself, not wanting to disturb him at work, and moved on down the hallway to the offices that had stood empty before Sheriff Scott decided to move the cold-case unit here when Katie came back home from her tours.

Katie stopped at the office door on the right, which was slightly ajar, and pushed it open. McGaven was in his usual spot, sitting up straight in his office chair poring over some case details.

"Hey," he said cheerfully.

Katie dropped her briefcase on her desk and shed her jacket, slipping it over the back of her chair. "You sound upbeat."

"And why shouldn't I be?"

"No reason." She shrugged, still thinking about the meeting.

McGaven gave a fake frown for Katie's benefit. "I know why you're grumpy."

"I'm not grumpy—honest. *Confused* would be a better word. I'm fine with the tour and I have made peace with it."

He swiveled in his chair to face her. "I know it probably feels like you've been demoted or something."

"The last thing I want to do is babysit a group of wannabe Spielbergs, especially when there are cases to solve and families that need answers and closure."

"Or maybe take a chill pill and try and have fun with it?"

Katie sat down in her chair. "I know… I know… sorry for being such a complainer. Let's move on." She looked at his computer screen with keen interest. "What are you looking at?"

"Oh, well, I thought I'd just take a look at this Wild Oats Productions and see what they are all about."

She raised her eyebrows. "And…? Don't keep me in suspense. Did you run police background checks yet?"

"Haven't had time. Not sure it's completely necessary." He saw Katie's expression. "I'll have Denise run some preliminary stuff. Just perusing their website and checking out their films…"

"And?"

"Actually, some awesome footage. I think they will be able to bring a lot of interest to the area. Good for everybody, like the mayor said."

Katie let out a breath.

McGaven laughed. "It's not *that* bad."

"How many are in the crew?"

"From what I can see," he said, reading the credits, "besides the director and co-director we met today, there's a sound guy, Keith Cooper, a grip, Butch Price, and a writer/researcher, Ty Windsor."

"The lucky five," she said with sarcasm.

"Check this out. They've filmed in the Galapagos Islands and Iceland. Amazing shots. And that famous guy who does those insurance commercials did the narrating—professional stuff."

Katie leaned over and watched some of the trailers. "OK. It is nice. But do the due diligence, please do backgrounds on all the players. It would make me feel better to know they're decent guys. And what I'm up against—if anything. I don't want any problems. Or surprises."

"Done."

"I know it might take some time, but if anything stands out, text it to me tomorrow."

"Roger that."

"Okay, now to more important stuff." Katie opened some files. "I read through some interesting cold cases last night—some the sheriff has notated and others that I've flagged myself."

"What do you have?"

"I have two cases for missing persons from 1963 and 1974 that might be linked."

"Okay, I'm guessing we start with the newest case and then work backward since the trail would have gone stone cold on the earliest one?"

"Not necessarily. If cases are too old, say twenty and even thirty years, many things can change. People change and might give or remember information that they didn't originally when the report was filed. Or, sometimes enough time has passed for people who weren't willing to talk to come forward." McGaven nodded and began reading over her shoulder. "But, I agree with you. We should begin with the cases that we can bring closure to quickly."

"What's the Stanton case?" he said reading the label.

Katie opened the file and pulled out the missing person's poster, the report filed by the family, and statements by friends and family. "This is it." The photo was of a young teen with brown hair and dark eyes.

"Not much to go on," he said, skimming the report.

"Jared William Stanton, just turned eighteen, had an argument with his parents, walked out of the house about six months ago and went missing. No one has heard from him since."

McGaven read from the report. "It says the argument was about attending college. Jared wanted to take a year off and his parents wanted him to attend right away."

"And note, his keys and cell phone were left behind," Katie said grimacing. "Not jumping to conclusions, but how many teenagers would even leave the house without their cell these days?"

"Detective Alvarez spoke to the parents several times, but they vouched for each other and there were no other witnesses. And Mr. and Mrs. Stanton have stayed strong and consistent with their story. With no other leads the case went cold," read McGaven. "What do you think?"

Katie skimmed through the statements from friends. "There was some speculation that he was hiding out with a new girlfriend, but that doesn't seem likely since the police talked with her several times and no one had seen Jared. We will have to reread every statement."

"And I think we need to check some background more thoroughly before we start making visits."

"You're right. Check the parents and the two best friends and see what else shakes out. And if you can find out anything about the girlfriend." She leaned back in her chair and looked at her watch. "Looks like we have a couple of hours for background and alibis, and then I'm going to be getting ready for my fieldtrip tomorrow."

CHAPTER FOUR
Thursday 0630 hours

Katie woke to the sound of light rain tapping on her farmhouse roof. By the time she had finished loading her car with rural maps, extra clothes, an extra pair of hiking boots, bottles of water, energy bars, and her usual law enforcement duffel bag filled with gear, it had turned into a steady downpour. She also tucked in behind her seat a small ice box with two turkey and cheese sandwiches, two bottles of iced tea, and a couple pieces of fruit.

The temperature was cool with a brisk wind blowing. It was unclear if the weather would hold, or become a full force storm—the local weather channel didn't say one way or another. Katie made sure Cisco had his lightweight rain harness and packed him some doggie snacks and water too.

As she stood in her driveway zipping up her navy windbreaker, gazing at the overcast day, she thought about the Jared Stanton case and wondered if he was truly alive and had just run away to escape his parents. She knew McGaven would be hard at work finding out information so that they could move forward with the case once she was done with the film crew.

She watched Cisco in the front yard, sniffing the bushes and plants, working his way from one to the next, and then made ready to go as he approached the Jeep.

Suddenly deciding that she should be ready for anything, Katie doubled checked her Glock in its holster inside her jacket. It was a usual precaution when she travelled, and whenever the anxious soldier inside her would arise. It was better to be prepared than not. Glancing at her watch, she saw it was time to get to the sheriff's department.

As Katie backed down the driveway there was a rumble in the distance, low and long, but she ignored it as she made her way along the winding road. The rain pounded her Jeep, like an omen. But the storm clouds seemed to be moving south, and, if she had to estimate, the weather would clear within the hour and shouldn't be a problem during the trip. She wondered how the film crew would cope with the hike in this weather.

The rain subsided a little as she turned into the sheriff's department's parking lot. She slowed as she approached the crew from Wild Oats Productions, counting five men next to a large white SUV. Some were dressed for the Andes Mountains, while two were only wearing lightweight shirts and blue jeans.

She swung into a parking place and cut the engine, muttering "Be nice, Cisco" before pulling up her hood, her hiking boots hitting the pavement.

"Hi, Detective Scott," said the director.

"Hello, everyone," she said, trying to sound upbeat while moving slightly to stay warm. "Please, call me Katie."

"Okay, Katie," he said, turning to his crew. "You already met my camera operator Emir Patel. And that's Keith Cooper, our sound guy. Butch Price, grip and grunt. And our writer and researcher, Ty Windsor."

"It's nice to meet you all," Katie said. "Okay, a few things before we get started. First, everyone needs to dress in layers. Fall here can be unpredictable, even on a day like today—raining one minute and then steaming sun the next." She pointed to Butch. "You need to layer up with a sweatshirt and lightweight windbreaker." Pointing to Keith, "You need to do the same, and change your shoes. Your feet will be killing you in those leather work boots within an hour."

Both men went back to the large SUV and began rummaging through their luggage.

"Sorry to be blunt, but trust me, we've got a long hike ahead and you don't want to be uncomfortable. Okay?"

"No problem, Detective—I mean Katie," said Matt. "I think our four-wheel drive is sufficient, but we have one problem."

"What's that?" Katie kept her patience in line and reminded herself that they were a film crew and not a combat military team.

"Our other car won't handle any type of off-road conditions. With all our gear, there's only room for four people to fit comfortably."

"That's fine. One of you can ride with me and Cisco."

Matt smiled. "I would love to, but unfortunately I'm allergic to dogs."

Katie looked to the others and there was an awkward silence. She wasn't sure if it was because she was a cop or that Cisco was a jet-black German shepherd staring intently out the window at them.

"I'll ride with you," said Ty as he walked up to Katie.

"Okay!" she said, hurrying back to her Jeep. "We're going to drive up to Rifle Ridge and then cut on to Hidden Trail, which will be bumpy and slow going for about an hour, especially if the rain starts up again. Don't worry, it will take us up to an area about a mile and half from the first location by the town of Silo."

"And?" asked Butch.

"And then we hike."

"Okay, sounds good," said Matt.

"Any questions before we go?" she asked, looking to each one.

"Yeah, when do we eat?" said Butch.

Everyone laughed.

"I hope you've packed some provisions," said Katie. "If not, we can stop before heading up the mountain; otherwise, you're going to get very hungry and thirsty before we make it back."

"No, we packed food and water," said Keith, the sound technician. "We're all good."

"Good," she said. "We're ready to go."

Katie climbed back into her Jeep and Ty took his place riding shotgun. He hesitantly slipped his backpack behind his seat as Cisco watched his every move. The dog's black coat, wolf eyes and alert ears made the researcher move cautiously.

Katie sat with the Jeep idling while the rest of the crew got settled in their SUV. She couldn't help but notice that the four men gave each other some rolling-eye expressions as they took their seats. Matt was driving, beside him was his assistant director Emir, and Keith and Butch squeezed into the back seat around their equipment and packs.

"Don't mind them," said Ty as he fiddled with a little charm around his neck.

"Why do you say that?"

"They can be jerks and say stupid stuff—it's best to ignore them. It's been tense recently because we're on such a tight schedule and there are budget issues. I've done the best I can at scheduling new locations."

"I think you'll find some areas of interest in Pine Valley," she said, smiling.

Katie watched as Matt gave her the thumbs up, a low growl coming from the back seat.

"What's that mean?" said Ty.

"It means that he's ready to go. That's Cisco, by the way."

Ty turned and looked directly at the dog. "Hey, Cisco, nice to meet a war dog."

Katie glanced at Ty and realized that he must've done his homework on her. Since he was the writer and researcher for the film company that made sense. He seemed to be fairly relaxed as he gazed out the window, even with Cisco in the back. His waterproof jacket was expensive and his hiking boots were top of the line—she was grateful that he, at least, had arrived prepared. She guessed that he came from affluence and cared about how he presented himself to others. His wavy dark-blond hair, clean-shaven look and almost perfectly pressed clothes made him appear more like a catalog model.

Katie eased the SUV out of the parking lot followed by the film crew and was soon lost in her own thoughts. She didn't mind that Ty was quiet as well, and it wasn't long before they turned onto the gravel road that led to Rifle Ridge.

"What's that sound?" said Ty, looking up with some apprehension.

"Don't worry. It's just the truck shifting into four-wheel-drive mode. Believe me, we're going to need it where we're going."

"Oh," he said, turning around to his satchel and pulling out a slim laptop. Moments later he was tapping away. Katie drove for almost half an hour with only silence from her passenger, which gave her time to reflect on the cases she was working on, and what leads she should pursue next.

A heavy roll of thunder shook the ground. She slowed down to let the film crew catch up with them.

Ty looked up from his laptop. "What's up?"

Katie surveyed what she could tell were layers of worse incoming weather. "There's a storm ahead."

"So… it's just a storm, right? It'll pass?"

"Yes and no. Those clouds," she gestured through the windshield, "those are cumulonimbus clouds, and they're very heavy with frozen water. See how they are vertical in areas? Looks strange, right?"

"Yeah."

"They're holding large pellets of frozen rain."

"Hail?" he said.

"*Big* hail. I've never seen such dense clouds and so many of them. We need to get to shelter if we don't want to do serious damage to our vehicles."

Ty fidgeted in his seat, eyes glued to the clouds. "Well, where's that?"

"Can you get Matt on the phone?" she said.

Ty hit a memory button on his cell and. Matt answered immediately.

"Hey, Matt," said Katie. "We've got some serious weather coming our way. We need to find shelter and wait it out."

"What do you suggest?"

"There's a ranger sub-station not far from here and they have a covered area where they keep some of their all-terrain vehicles."

"How far?"

"It's close, about a quarter of a mile, but we have to access it from an old fire trail off this road. It's a little dicey. You up for it?"

"Do we have a choice?" he said, with slight cynicism.

"I would say no," she laughed. "Okay, keep your steering steady, and try to keep up."

"Copy that," he said and ended the call.

Katie pressed the accelerator and the Jeep lurched forward, bouncing side to side. "Sorry, Ty, hang on."

Cisco had been standing up behind Katie ever since the thunder started. Now he gave a low-pitched whine, pacing back and forth in the seat. Eventually he settled down and braced himself, with his back against the rear door.

Ty closed his laptop down and grabbed on to the armrest. His eyes were wide as he stared at the road ahead. Katie glanced in the mirror as Matt kept up with the pace in the large SUV.

Then the rain began to pour at such a velocity the wipers were barely able to keep up. Katie gripped the wheel tighter and felt the temperature drop—even inside the vehicle. She kept glancing at the sky as the charcoal vertical peaks grew denser and attached themselves to the thunderheads. She hoped that they would make it to the small station in time.

Turning the Jeep sharply, she heaved the car onto the path, not knowing whether or not it would be washed out already. Thunder hammered above their heads, rattling the car. The accompanying wind burst through the trees, bending branches to breaking point.

"Is this normal?" said Ty, trying to keep his voice even.

"Does this happen? Yes. Is it a *normal* occurrence? Not really," she said, steadying her voice. Katie had seen some severe storms growing up, but she had never been in the middle of one, or been responsible for the safety of others during one. She glanced again in the rearview and was relieved to see that Matt was handling the terrain well.

Cisco let out a whine.

"It's okay, boy, we've been through worse."

Ty glanced at her and he seemed, from his expression, to remember that she had been in the military and no doubt seen much worse than a storm.

"You okay?" Katie asked as she fought against the slippery roadway, gripping tightly to the steering wheel.

"Uh, yeah," he replied.

"We're almost there," she said. "In fact, there it is." Katie was relieved to finally see the small compound surrounded by chain-link fencing tucked back in the heavily wooded area. There were two wooden structures inside, along with several parking places and a large metal building. Heavy tarps covered some of the county's equipment.

At the entrance, she jammed her Jeep into park and dared to open the driver's door—erratic wind and heavy rain instantly battering her—but she pushed forward and slammed the car door with all her weight.

Pulling her hood tightly around her face, she fought to keep her eyes open as the rain pummeled her. The temperature had dropped at least ten degrees, making it feel like ice needles were stabbing her eyes and cheeks.

She grabbed at the gate in relief, only to realize it was securely locked with a bulky chain and two padlocks. She didn't have any keys or way to get inside. Razor wire lined the top of the barrier for extra security, so jumping over wasn't an option.

Katie turned around in despair, blinded by the headlights of her Jeep and the film crew's large SUV. The ground beneath her feet was sodden as the rain was pooling fast, she felt like it could collapse beneath her at any moment.

CHAPTER FIVE

Thursday 1045 hours

Rattling the gate hard out of pure frustration, Katie knew that there was no getting in without a key. The storm was ruthless, but as she pushed water out of her eyes she suddenly realized that she had a pair of bolt cutters in the trunk. It was smaller than the average set, about eight inches, but would hopefully do the trick.

She ran back to her Jeep and rummaged furiously through her tool kit until she found what she was looking for. Returning to the gate, her feet dragging through the rising water levels, she opened the bolt cutters wide and clamped down on the first lock with all her strength. It wasn't enough. She continued to struggle as gusts of wind forced her body back and forth, making it difficult to hold her balance.

She thought she heard Cisco barking over the wind and rain.

"Let me try!" yelled Matt as he reached her. Emir had jumped into the driver's seat.

Katie backed up and let Matt take over. He struggled too, but eventually the first lock dropped to the ground. It only took a few moments for the second lock to free the heavy chain. Both Katie and Matt wrestled with the gate until they opened it wide enough for the vehicles to enter.

"Get back into your Jeep!" he yelled over the storm, holding one side of the entrance open. "I'll get the garage open."

Katie nodded and fought the wind and rain to get behind the wheel again, breathing hard.

"You alright?" asked Ty.

"Yeah, I'm okay," she said, though she wasn't so sure as the soft, snow-like pelts that hit her windshield got larger and larger, until they were the size of golf balls.

Katie shoved the SUV into first gear and edged her way through the tight entrance that was made for quad vehicles. She kept moving, keeping an eye on the terrain and watching Matt grapple with the garage door. Battling to stay centered, he didn't let the storm knock him off his feet. To her relief, he was able to get the large door open and she drove in as quickly as she dared, followed closely by the SUV.

Inside the shelter Katie cut the engine and jumped out. The sound of the hail hitting the metal roof was deafening—no one could talk. Out of the vehicles, the group wanted to see first-hand the storm and stood awkwardly amidst the ear-shattering sound.

Katie rubbed her hands together in an effort to warm them, and to give herself something to do as they waited the hail storm out. Emir had one of the smaller cameras in his hand and was recording. He appeared to be enjoying the opportunity to film something so wild and unexpected—even if it was a close call that saw them nearly stranded.

After fifteen minutes the hail subsided, to Katie's relief, but the rain continued. She could hear it rushing outside and draining into specially designed channels for water shedding—for just this type of event.

"Everybody doing okay?" she said.

The film crew nodded. Most appeared relieved, except Butch who openly glared at Katie.

"Is there a problem?" asked Katie, taking a step toward Butch.

"If you're such an experienced hiker and have lived here all your life, why did you nearly get us stranded up here in this insane weather?" he seethed, his hands clenched in tight fists.

"I'm sorry. The weather can be unpredictable at this time of year. But a storm like this is *very* unusual for Pine Valley. And the weather channels didn't see it coming. I checked just before we set out."

"We could've been killed," he pushed.

Sensing the tension, Cisco jumped from the Jeep, his eyes alert to any change in tone and body language from everyone in the crew—especially Butch.

"C'mon, Butch, lighten up. Everything turned out fine," said Matt, shedding his jacket and hanging it on the SUV to dry.

"*Fine?* Does this look fine to you?" he complained, gesturing to the rain beyond and the trail they had entered from.

Ty spoke up. "We wouldn't be okay if Katie hadn't acted as quickly as she did."

"I think you just made Butch's point, because we wouldn't *be here* if it wasn't for Katie," said Keith, chuckling. It was unclear if he was also annoyed or just liked being the devil's advocate.

"Let's just calm down," said Katie. "The storm should be out of our way in about another half hour. That is… if you still want to continue." She didn't make any effort to hide her sarcasm.

The group remained quiet.

"We can easily go back the way we came."

Cisco padded over to her and sat obediently at her side—calm, alert, and focused.

"I think we should wait this out and then move forward. There's still plenty of time left today. It's up for a vote," said Matt looking to his crew.

Taking a break from his camera, Emir said enthusiastically, "I'm in."

"Why not," said Keith. "I'm in."

"I'm in," said Ty.

Matt looked at Butch—waiting.

"What do you think? Of course, I'm in," said Butch with some reluctance.

"Okay," said Matt, turning to Katie, "looks like we're all in."

"Good," said Katie. "Just relax. Have some water and a snack. And… we wait." She moved to the other side of the garage where there were several folding chairs. Grabbing one, she opened it and sat down. Cisco took his position at her side and lay down. Katie pulled her cell phone out and saw that she had a couple of voicemails and one text from McGaven.

The text read: *Hey, did you get stuck in that storm? Everything okay? Do we need to send out search and rescue?*

Katie decided to call McGaven as she watched the film crew settle down and eat.

McGaven answered on one ring. "You okay?"

"Yeah, we're all fine. We're at the ranger sub-station off Rifle Ridge waiting it out."

"Oh yeah, that sounds like fun. Tough road."

"It was, but we'll be just fine," she said.

"I feel bad for you," he said. "That was crazy. But it does get you out of the office." He laughed.

Katie watched the men mumbling quietly to one another—and looking over at her. Matt took out two folding chairs and gave her a smile. She wished she was anywhere but here—even testifying in court seemed like a better option.

She sighed. "It is what it is…"

"Okay, look, if you need anything or if something goes sideways—you know who to call, right?"

"Yeah, my uncle." She smiled.

"Funny… talk later." The connection went dead.

Katie slowly returned her cell phone to her pocket as Ty walked up to her. "Would you like some power brownies?" he said, munching on one.

"Oh, no, thank you," she said.

"They're really good. All organic with seeds, cacao, chopped-up fruit."

"Sounds great, but I'll pass."

Ty pulled up a chair. "Well, now is as good a time as any."

"For?"

"I wanted to get some background info about the town of Silo."

"I really don't know much, just what I've heard around town, from friends and family. I'm not sure what's fact from fiction."

He smiled. "That's okay. I've looked up some things, but you're right, there's not much out there. That's what makes it so intriguing… We want to give more facts than fiction. We're trying to find the angle on what made these places—now ghost towns—so prominent that they shaped towns like Pine Valley today."

"That sounds interesting," she said.

"See," he said. "Controversy. Economy. Land. Growth. That's what makes it so intriguing, and some ghost stories sprinkled in for good measure."

Katie laughed. She was beginning to like Ty. He was quiet, but it was clear that he really enjoyed history and storytelling. His eyes brightened and he became animated when he talked.

"Some people try to connect the Gold Rush to this area, the town of Silo, but the rush was from 1848–1855 and there is no record of Silo until the 1860s. I think they were mining for other minerals and even stones in this area."

"Really? You mean like silver or garnets?" she said.

"Possibly. The Gold Rush was over by 1855, and the only people who got rich were the merchants. Not the men panning for gold. Let's face it; Native Americans have been finding stones for a lot longer. I know that there are many mine shafts around Sequoia County."

"True."

"I just think that stones are more likely, or even silver, iron, lead, zinc, and manganese. Your town of Pine Valley is rich with these minerals."

"That's a good point. But really the only thing I know about Silo is that it was a small mining town of about a hundred people. And yes, there are many mine shafts around the area, but there's no other evidence of the town except some piles of brick, old square nails, and the occasional abandoned tool, like from a blacksmith or farmer."

"Well, maybe we'll get lucky," he said.

"Maybe."

"That's what we're here to see. We want to find facts, or artifacts, showing what made this area what it is today. We want to explore the sink holes, whether mines or geographical anomalies. Thanks for your time, Katie—whether you know it or not, they appreciate it too." He got up and joined the other crew members.

The mention of the sink hole made Katie shiver and her mouth go dry. The memory of the dark abyss below and the dirt caving in on her was terrifying beyond comprehension. The state geological association and the local colleges had studied them, but could never agree on how or why they existed… whether because of the movement of the mountains, impact of mining, earthquake shifts, or some freak of nature.

"Hey," said Emir. "Look. It's clearing up." He gestured outside, still filming to capture the beautiful sky as the last of the black clouds parted. "Wow, it's amazing," he continued, panning his camera. "One minute the storm from hell, and the next—sunshine."

Soon, bright light blanketed the area and lit up the regular fall day again. It felt to Katie that a weight had lifted off her shoulders.

The rain had ceased. The hail chunks were merging with the flood water, which was still draining off at a high rate. In another hour or so, there wouldn't be much trace of what had happened.

"What do you think?" asked Matt.

"Let me hike out to Rifle Ridge before we drive—in case there are any hazards we need to be aware of."

"I'll go with you," he said.

"You don't need to."

"I don't think you should be alone." He glanced back at his team.

Katie thought that was a strange thing to say, but she didn't mind the company.

"Hey!" Matt said, getting everyone's attention. "We'll be right back. DO NOT leave this area. Understood?"

"Yeah," everyone mumbled, going straight back to eating.

"Keep an eye on them," he said to Emir.

"They're not going anywhere," Emir replied, as he reviewed his footage. "Although," he laughed, as Katie and Matt headed off followed by Cisco, "I'm not really the babysitter type."

CHAPTER SIX

Thursday 1215 hours

After repacking the off-road vehicles and moving everyone out of the temporary garage at the Parks Patrol sub-station, Katie and the film crew were on their way again to the area where the town of Silo was rumored to be. Katie had put in a call to the park facilities to explain their situation and apologize for the broken locks.

Katie felt herself beginning to relax as the weather returned to normal. She and Ty rode mostly in a comfortable silence as before.

She rounded another sharp turn in the bumpy road and finally drove into a flat area.

"We're here," she said.

Ty looked up and surveyed the area. "So we walk from here?"

"Unless you want to get stuck in the Jeep along the way."

"Walking it is then." He pulled some things out of his pack and clipped a mini sports camera on a harness, before strapping it to his body. "Just my way of documenting things."

Katie parked and jumped out of the car, followed closely by Cisco. Opening the back hatch, she grabbed her backpack and hoisted it over her shoulders. Then she strapped Cisco into his hiking harness.

A cool breeze blew across the parking area. The chill stopped them for a moment, then as quickly as it came it was gone. It appeared that everyone was still on edge as they prepared the limited equipment they needed to carry to the location.

"Okay, listen up," she said. "The hike isn't difficult, but the rain will have made it harder to traverse, with some deep mud. So keep your eyes on the trail and your footings. We go in single file. Okay?"

"We're not children," said Keith, laughing alone at his stupid comment.

"Speak for yourself," replied Butch.

"Hey, watch your footing like she says, guys," warned Matt. "We don't want any equipment damaged."

Katie took the lead. Cisco seemed content and trotted uphill with the agility of a much younger dog. Every now and again Katie turned to check on the group, and as instructed, they were following in single file with about six feet between each of them. Matt took up the rear with Emir in front with his small digital camera.

"Everyone okay? No one needs a rest or to adjust their pack?"

No one responded.

"Okay then!" she said, and picked up her pace a little. Her mind relaxed.

Noticing that the trail was becoming extremely muddy, she slowed her pace a little and shifted to the right-hand side of the path where her hiking boots had better traction. Glancing behind, she saw the group followed her example. Their packs were heavier than hers, and she knew all too well from her army days how hard it was trekking through tricky conditions with a heavy pack on her back.

A sudden rustling sounded next to her. Katie instinctively stopped and made the motion for everyone to stop and stay still—which they obeyed. The noise was louder than a squirrel or nesting bird. She listened intently before moving on.

She whispered for Cisco to stay in his location in a German command that she had been originally trained in the army to do:

"*Bleib.*" The dog obeyed her command, but his body became rigid, his head slightly cocked. Hearing nothing more, Katie decided to trudge on. They were almost at the accessible area of Silo.

Soon they reached an open area where there were clusters of pine trees, some extremely tall, as well as some old fruit trees and foliage. Katie waited for the group to catch up and congregate.

"Is this it?" asked Matt, looking around.

"This is it," Katie said. "Don't be so quick to dismiss. There's a lot of history here and around the mountain areas. It's up to you to figure out what, where, and why."

"She's right," said Ty. "There were Native Americans here once—there are some caves with prehistoric writings. And obviously, there were some leftover Gold Rush enthusiasts still hunting down gold, wanting to strike it rich. Definitely more than meets the eye here."

"From what I've heard, it was a small town made up of farmers and ranchers who wanted to set down roots and build a community. They were, of course, attracted to the prospect of gold and silver," said Katie. "There are several areas where the mines have been sealed. Some believe they were instrumental in creating today's sink holes, rather than them being a geological phenomenon."

"I already contacted a town historian… Tony Beard… and he was full of information. Whether there is any validity or not remains to be seen," said Ty.

Glancing at her watch, Katie said, "In order to make it back at a reasonable time, you have an hour and forty-five minutes before we leave."

Matt made a salute and left to consult with Emir about some overall shots.

Katie smiled and decided to take a short walk to a dense area and sit down for some water and a snack. Cisco followed.

The rest of the team sat quietly as Katie watched Matt break down the area into individual shots, explaining with enthusiasm to Emir who nodded in agreement. Matt went to great lengths to demonstrate the flow of the story and how it would translate to film, which would have narration laid over the top. There were wonderful areas to film, with remnants of the stormy sky, billowy clouds, and distinct shades of the hillside and trees.

Butch was setting up some reflectors and small lighting systems.

Keith took a quick cigarette break before he organized his sound hardware. He seemed to watch Matt and Emir almost with disdain, his jaw clenched. Katie couldn't quite read him but there was something about him that bothered her—call it instinct, an unsettled feeling. But in the end, it didn't really matter if she liked him or not. Her duties were going to end when the day was over.

Ty sat with his iPad on his lap and read notes from his talks with the historian that would help with the areas they wanted to film. He glanced around and took a couple of photos for reference.

"Hey!" yelled Keith.

Everyone turned in his direction.

"Look, there's some remnants of what looks like a foundation to a house or building," he said.

The crew and Katie joined Keith to see what he was talking about. Two of the guys moved some of the brush away from the area and revealed what was left of an old wood and stone foundation.

"Wow," said Matt. He knelt closer, brushing his hand over the stones. "These were set to fit together like a jigsaw puzzle."

Ty pushed his way inside the circle and quickly knelt beside Matt. "How do you know they're old?"

"Look at the wood and the way the stones have been carved to fit," the director said.

Ty didn't look convinced and frowned. "What else is there?"

"You can find remnants of structures all over this area," said Katie. "When I was a kid, we used to hike around this canyon and would find things from houses like old belt buckles, dishes, and bottles."

"Cool," said Emir as he began to get some close-up shots.

"Yeah, well, we need some factual information that coincides with these so-called artifacts," said Ty. "Let me see if the historian might have some archived photos of old structures."

"Wait," said Matt as he scratched around the crumbling foundation. "I think I found some bones."

"What?" said the group.

Katie slipped in next to Matt and looked at the bones he was referring to. "Those are bones from a small animal," she said.

"You sure?" he asked.

"Yeah, small dog or farm animal. Was probably buried. Maybe a child's pet?" she said.

Matt shrugged his shoulders and stood up.

Keith pushed his way past them to take a look at the bones. "Cool," he said, which was inappropriate, thought Katie, as she walked back to where she had been sitting with Cisco.

Matt approached her. "Katie, can you draw us a map for the three locations that we've talked about?"

"Of course. I'll do you one better. I'll send maps with GPS coordinates to your phone. Will that do?"

"Great. Thank you," he said and hurried to take some last minute photos.

Katie waited patiently while watching the sky for any changes. She couldn't help but notice that Keith hovered near the animal's bones. He glanced around and then bent down to retrieve the small animal skull, placing it carefully in his backpack.

The group separated and began exploring the area more carefully.

Katie and Cisco walked near the canyon. The cool air filled her lungs as she took several deep breaths. The jagged sections of rock, before it completely plunged down the mountain, were both breathtaking and mesmerizing. The sky alternated between darkening and sunlight peeking through the artistic clouds—the crevices and jagged regions below Katie's feet brightening and fading almost on cue.

Something flashed.

Katie stopped and looked around her, daring to get close to the edge. There had been a bright sparkle of light—she was sure of it.

She kneeled down carefully. Cisco got on his belly and stayed by her side, picking up on her unease. Straining her eyes and waiting for another burst of light, she saw what looked like feet with socks covering them.

Katie quickly stood up swiftly inching closer to the edge and realizing that she left her binoculars in the SUV. "Anyone have binoculars?" she asked.

"Yeah." Matt walked up to her carrying a small pair. "What's up?"

Katie took a moment, focusing the lenses. Then she gasped, her heart pounding. Turning to Matt she said quickly, "I want everyone to stay at the clearing where we came in."

"What's the—" he started.

"Now!" she cut in. "Please, get everyone and their packs together at one location. Stay there. Do not move about, okay?"

"What's wrong?"

"This is officially a crime scene," she said.

Matt stared past her down the ravine, then immediately rushed to gather the others.

Katie looked through the binoculars again. It hadn't been a figment of her imagination. A small gold barrette holding a handful of blonde hair, which had flashed in the sunlight. She could see two small bodies wedged in a crevice.

CHAPTER SEVEN
Thursday 1445 hours

Katie spent the next half hour giving the exact information of the roads leading to Hidden Trail to the sheriff, and the best way to navigate the vehicles after the sudden storm to the detective in charge. She coordinated search and rescue, the fire department, morgue, and forensics to the crime scene. The area would soon be crowded with first-responder vehicles, police cars, and the forensic team.

Take a deep breath...

Taking another look through the binoculars, from what Katie could see there were two girls, approximately ten to twelve years old. The clothing appeared to be shorts and T-shirts. One girl had blonde hair, while the other had brown hair. From her vantage point, Katie couldn't see much else.

She was deeply saddened by the discovery, but there would be a family or two that would at least now have closure of what had happened to their children.

After the logistical whirlwind was over, there was nothing to do but wait at least an hour before anyone would reach the location. She dialed McGaven to give him the news and instructions to reach the location. She would feel more comfortable having him take statements from the crew, as since she was part of the group it would be a conflict of interest for her to conduct the statements.

She knew Detective Hamilton would have enough on his plate working with the rescue unit to retrieve the bodies.

She explained to him what was going on.

"I can't believe it," McGaven said. "Do you know who the girls are?"

"No, I don't have much to go on. Hopefully we'll know more soon."

"You alright?" he asked.

"I'm fine," she said, trying to sound like she usually did. "Call me when you get close to the area where my Jeep and the film crew's SUV are located. Cisco and I will meet you there and ride up with you."

"Sounds good. Talk later."

Within the hour, Katie escorted the first responders of search and rescue and forensic services to the area. They waited for Detective Hamilton and Sheriff Scott to arrive before moving forward.

Katie rode shotgun, staring out the passenger window, as McGaven raced as fast as he dared until they reached the mountain road leading to Hidden Trail.

Cisco sat quiet and alert in the back seat.

Katie felt calmer with her partner. Whatever was necessary for them to perform, it was easier with him.

McGaven, always steady, drove in silence as the road turned bumpy and had to reduce his speed to avoid large potholes caused by the extreme rainfall. Katie closed her eyes to maintain her calm. The last time she had been to the Hidden Trail she had almost lost her life, and thought she would die alone. Flashbacks flooded her mind—things she never wanted to remember. Just when she was getting a grip on her PTSD, it felt like her world was coming full circle with the discovery of the girls.

"Damn!" exclaimed McGaven. "This road is brutal in a sedan."

Katie fluttered her eyes open and saw that the trees were closing in on the roadway. She knew how hazardous these roads leading up the mountain were, even when the weather wasn't an issue. "There has been more than twelve inches of rain in a couple of days up here."

"Well, hang on," he said grimacing.

Katie noticed that the road had deep grooves plowed along the sides, leaving distinct tire marks from the regular and oversized vehicles of the first responders.

"Isn't this fun…" complained McGaven, as he shifted his weight and repositioned his hands on the steering wheel to keep the car on the road. "So I take it we're going to crash some kind of party?" he said with sarcasm.

"I wonder if they've been able to identify the two bodies yet?" she said, more to herself than McGaven.

The road was beginning to smooth out. McGaven steadied the police car and was able to increase speed. What felt like an hour had only been about fifteen minutes.

Katie had the start of a tension headache after all the bouncing along the road, in addition to the worry of what she was about to experience at the site.

As McGaven made a sharp right turn, he slammed on the brakes to avoid hitting the responder vehicles, forensic truck, fire truck, search and rescue SUVs, and a variety of sheriff's department cars parked in formation along the road.

"Wow," said McGaven. "It looks like the beginning of some kind of event."

"More like a very serious crime scene," said Katie. "I coordinated with the sheriff and then there were more vehicles that came up as well. I guess he wanted to make sure that the area was handled correctly."

McGaven managed to park along the left side, tucked in between two large pine trees.

Katie exited the car, taking a few moments to steady her nerves and focus on what her job was going to entail.

Take a deep breath…

Leaving Cisco behind, Katie quickly moved toward the crowd looking for Detective Hamilton or her uncle to report to. She didn't have to search long. Sheriff Scott pushed through the crowd at the sight of her.

"You made good time," the sheriff said to McGaven, with his characteristic gruffness.

"It wasn't easy on that road," replied Katie.

"Sir," McGaven nodded in greeting.

"As Katie has suggested, go ahead and take the film crew's statements," the sheriff ordered McGaven.

"On it," he said, and moved toward the group of filmmakers who appeared somber.

"Has there been any identification?" she asked, trying to keep her pulse steady.

"We think they might be the two little girls who went missing from Rock Creek two years ago."

"Rock Creek," she said, trying to remember if she had read the cold case recently. It was vague to her, but she did remember something about the sisters.

"Yes, Tessa Mayfield, ten years old, and her eleven-year-old sister Megan. The girls walked to a play area near where they lived. And disappeared without a trace. The general description of the girls and the clothing matches the initial report."

Katie's heart sank as the image of the little girls she had found buried in specially made coffins after she returned home from her tours came back to her. The thought of another two little girls tossed into a ravine made Katie tremble so much she had to put her hands in her pockets to hide her unsteadiness.

"What do you need me to do?" she asked.

"I need you to search the crime scene," the sheriff said.

"Why me? I assume Detective Hamilton is here and this is his case, right?" Just as she spoke, she saw John walking up, dressed in mountain-climbing attire. He had been a Navy Seal for almost ten years and the Pine Valley Sheriff's Department was lucky to get someone like him to run the forensic division.

John said, "Did you tell her yet?" His expression was subdued, but there was something about his eyes that told Katie that he was excited.

"Tell me what?"

"You and I are going to have to rappel down to the crime scene," he said.

"What?" she said, as her stomach dropped. "Why don't you have one of the search and rescue guys assist you? They are more qualified for a tricky climb."

"You were trained in rappelling from helicopters in the army, right? You've done this before, correct?"

"Well, yes, but…"

"And we don't want to compromise or contaminate the crime scene."

"Well… of course not, but…"

"You and I are the most qualified for this venture and we search crime scenes."

"He's absolutely right," stated the sheriff. "That's why I wanted you to be here. We have to preserve any remaining evidence—if it's even possible. So you and John are going down there to search and document the crime scene."

Katie understood why they thought this was the best idea, but what everyone *didn't* understand was that that part of her army training was the worst by far—until now. To put it mildly, she'd hated every moment of the drill that day. The height. The falling. It was absolutely terrifying. She had never told anyone about her fears. She never thought it would come up in her work.

"You're going to need to change," said the sheriff.

"I…" Katie said weakly.

"C'mon, Katie," said John. "This is the kind of stuff you and I live for—what we were trained for." He looked at her shoes. "Do you have any other shoes with you?"

"Yes, I have my hiking shoes and running shoes in my duffel in the police sedan." Her mouth went dry, and what she really wanted to do was turn and run away. Her heart pounded so loudly in her ears she wondered if it was possible for others to hear it too.

"Okay, get changed. We have the rest of the gear for you," said John. He gave a quick smile and walked away, followed by the sheriff.

Katie didn't say anything and turned back to the sedan. She concentrated on her footsteps, one in front of the other, as she felt a bit lightheaded. It would soon pass—at least until she was dangling in a ravine. How did she get herself into this?

"Hey, Katie, wait up," said McGaven as he jogged up to her. "You okay?"

"Sure," she mumbled. "You done with the statements?"

"Yeah, they are writing out everything they saw in addition to my notes," he said. "What's wrong? I heard how you're going to search the crime scene. I thought all you soldiers dig this stuff? At least that's what it shows on TV!" He tried to make light of the situation in order to make Katie laugh.

"No, Gav. It sucks. It's the worst possible scenario—at least for me. I hate heights, and dangling over an abyss. Oh, and having a huge audience to watch me in the process. So no, I hate this. But… I'll get through it because there's an important case that needs closure and a killer to find."

"Say something then."

"I can't do that," she said as she opened the trunk of the vehicle and grabbed her gym bag. "It's just like the army, you don't do it because you have to, you do it because it's the right thing to do."

"What can I do to help?"

Katie glanced around the area as people were moving about. "Just make sure I have some privacy as I change my clothes." She forced a smile, trying to get past her nervous tension and focus on what she had to do.

"You got it, partner," he said and turned, leaning against the car watching for anyone approaching—talking to Cisco through a partially open window.

Katie quickly took a few steps into the trees, shed her hiking clothes and pulled on a pair of black running pants, sports bra, and long-sleeve T-shirt.

"This is going to be one of the most unusual crime scene searches in department history," McGaven said, still keeping watch.

"True."

"At least you won't be alone."

"True."

"And it's not in a dark cave."

"Okay, I get it, Gav. It could always be worse," she said, knowing that he was trying to be a supportive partner and help her relax.

Once she was dressed and had stretched her muscles, she walked back to be fitted with the climbing gear. She tried to ignore the stares of everyone at the scene, pushing bad memories from her mind. It was clear that having both her and John pursue, search, and document the crime scene was the best-case scenario. Her mind wandered to what, if anything, they might discover.

"How are you feeling?" asked John.

"Good," she lied, forcing a smile.

"This is Tim Ludlum and he's one of the sheriff department's search and rescue guys."

Katie nodded. "Nice to meet you."

"Okay," Tim said. "You're going to be in a full body harness instead of just a chest or seat harness, which was probably what you used in the army."

"Yeah, that's right," she said, stepping into the lower part of the harness and pulling upward.

"This will better distribute the impact of the force throughout your body. Basically make it an easy ride so you can do your job," he said, smiling. He adjusted the leg straps snug to fit Katie's thighs. "How's that? Comfortable?"

"It's fine," she said, as he slipped her arms through the chest harness. It was comfortable, but confining. She tried not to think about anything but finding the evidence that would lead to the killer. Nothing was more important at the moment than the two little victims.

John handed Katie some gloves, which she pulled over her fingers, making sure she could move her hands easily.

Tim double-checked Katie's harness and seemed satisfied. "You're good to go."

"One last thing," said John. He retrieved a helmet with a camera affixed to the top to help document the scene. He would take photographs, but the video camera would act as an additional overview.

Katie slowly pulled on her helmet. It was surprisingly light-weight, and not so cumbersome it would obstruct her movements or views. Everything around her felt surreal, as if it was running in slow motion, but she kept moving forward.

"How does that feel?" asked John, as he tightened his own harness and got ready to attach the ropes and carabiners which would secure Katie.

"It's fine," she managed to say.

The daylight was wavering, flickering in between the branches of tall trees as the afternoon dragged on.

Detective Hamilton finally approached Katie as she checked and rechecked her restraints, running through the motions.

"Scott," the detective said. "You must live for this kind of stuff."

"I don't know what you've been told," she said, forcing a smile.

"We'll be able to see and hear everything you do through the cameras. So it's like we'll be with you every step of the way."

"Thanks. I appreciate that," she said, looking around at the crowd grouping together towards the cliff.

"You okay?" asked John again as he came in close to check her gear one last time. He had a way of looking right through her with his intense gaze that made her nervous.

"Let's get the show on the road," she said, as Matt from Wild Oats Productions approached.

"Do you think I could have some of the footage?" he said.

"It's a current open investigation, so no, but I'm sure you can watch the live feed with Detective Hamilton. Otherwise, you'll have to go through legal channels and the video will be edited for obvious reasons," she said.

"Thanks. All I can do is ask," he said. "Good luck." Matt eyed her and then walked away. Katie couldn't help but detect a bit of cynicism, which seemed strange.

John came back with their ropes, looking eager to get to the site while daylight permitted. The wind was already picking up and the temperature had dropped, which would make the downward climb a little uncomfortable.

"You ready?"

"As I'll ever be."

Katie silently prepared herself to get to the scene. A large predatory bird glided over the area as she looked overhead. It was like an omen to Katie, but she kept her wits and followed John.

At least she wasn't alone.

At the edge of the precipice, the crevice turned into a deep cavern that appeared to go on forever—and reminded her of the sink hole she had located in her first case as she searched for Chelsea Compton. But this was no time for thinking about the past.

Katie made herself look about fifty feet into the ravine they would rappel down. She could see what looked like two rag dolls facing one another, one seemed stuck to one side and the other tiny body wedged into a crevice in the rocks below. Both girls were wearing what looked to be matching jean shorts and T-shirts—yellow and pink.

She gasped as a deep sadness overwhelmed her—weighing down her soul for the lives of the two little girls that had been brutally ended too soon.

"Okay, I'll go first and you follow," said John. "You know how to attach safety anchors to secure the ropes as you go?"

Katie nodded. She knew how to climb and rappel, but wished she didn't. She thought of Dr. Carver.

Take a deep breath...

Without another word, John effortlessly swung out over the edge and caught himself with his feet against the rock. He held to the ropes, pushed backward with his feet with the right pressure, and rappelled about three and half feet downward. Then he stopped and looked up at Katie. "Your turn," he said.

It's now or never...

Katie's pulse was at an all-time high, throbbing in her head, making her vision blurry. The rock looked as if it were moving—undulating —like it was breathing and alive. Concentrating and remembering all her skills for the task at hand, she readied herself.

She stood at the precipice of the cliff, before bracing her body and swinging outward, making her descent. The flat part of her shoes made contact with the rock in front of her. It was solid and for a brief moment gave her some comfort as she exhaled. Sitting back in her harness with her legs slightly bent she kept her eyes forward, not wanting to look down. But the memories flooded back at warp speed.

The chopper blades circled above with a loud whooshing noise and blasts of a wind like a category three hurricane. First she felt weightless and free, but then it was like being a doll dangling with nothing to cling to and nothing to save her. With one hand in front holding onto a rope and the other behind, there was a delicate balance that kept her body upright and sent it downward. Jerking and moving in disharmony, Katie made several attempts to keep herself steady and to get to the ground as quickly as possible. She also made a fatal, rookie mistake—she looked down. Even though it was a training area, it looked like she was atop a city skyscraper and would soon be crushed at the bottom…

Hearing the pace of her own breathing, she tried to conceal the sound, anxious that everyone above would hear her distress. She needed to focus. Those two sweet girls below needed her right now, and she was the only one that could help them. All her military training rushed back and gave her a punch of strength she desperately needed. She felt the ropes in her gloved hands, settled into her harness, and rappelled, descending until she caught up with John.

As she neared the area where the bodies were located, a strong gust blew around both of them, pushing them against the rock. She kept her mind focused on the assignment that awaited her and let her body go into autopilot.

"You okay?" asked John, having to yell over the sudden burst of wind.

Katie nodded.

"We're almost there. Be careful. There's some loose rocks," he said. "Once we're there, I'll make sure that we're tied in securely. Okay?"

Katie gave a thumbs up.

She looked slightly from left to right before rappelling again. Her footing felt loose and slippery in contrast to where they had started. She tried to gain a better foothold, keeping her balance in check by moving slightly to the side, but it didn't rectify the problem. Instead, she began to slide, slowly at first, then unable to stop. Her shoes didn't have enough traction to hold the position.

Feeling a strong tug on her harness and without securing her feet, she was soon in a free-hanging dive. She spun around in a complete circle twice—as her back bumped the rocky mountain terrain several times.

Stopping abruptly about twenty feet past the crime scene area, Katie tried to straighten her posture and position her body to get ready to climb but instead slammed into the mountain, knocking the wind from her lungs. Refusing to give in to the fear that was racing inside her, she focused on steadying her breath—as everything slowly went dark around her.

CHAPTER EIGHT
Thursday 1715 hours

A strange incessant droning overcame Katie's ears, resembling a large crowd yelling and clapping in unison. Through it, she heard her name, softly at first, like someone calling out in the wind, but then it became louder and more insistent.

"Katie! Katie!"

The roaring sounds began to fade as her name sharpened. Her eyes fluttered open and her body jerked in a sudden startle as she realized where she was; hanging from a rope in a ravine in the dying light.

"Katie, are you okay? You blacked out." John held her body against his, checking her ropes and carabiners.

"Yeah," she managed to whisper. Her throat felt dry and constricted. "I'm okay," she whispered. "Lost my footing."

"You want to continue?"

She nodded. She was shaking, but John's strong embrace and calm voice brought her the stability she needed.

"You're sure?" he said as his eyes showed deep concern. Something Katie had never witnessed in him before.

"Yes. We need to do this—who knows what damage to the scene more weather could bring. We can't wait any longer if we want to find any remaining evidence today."

He hesitantly released his hold, allowing her to swing back into formation. Nodding, he began to climb. As Katie followed she felt her body relax, enjoying the sensation of working up toward something instead of falling into the unknown. She didn't look down, but kept her eyes on the ledge where she knew the two girls were.

John moved as close as possible to the crevice and secured the ropes. She allowed herself to take in the horror of the scene before her as he fitted lightweight earphones into his ears.

"Blackburn," John said, looking at Katie with a sly smile. "Yes, she's fine, just some loose footing down here. We're beginning the search now." He turned to Katie and nodded.

Katie dragged her eyes from the rock formation in front of her and took in the faded blue sneaker on the foot of the girl closest to her. Then her eyes moved across to the girl's other foot, which was bare, and several toes were missing nails—as if they had simply melted away. Was this part of the natural decomposition? she wondered. The sickly bluish-purple skin looked weathered and shriveled from exposure to the elements, and even though the bodies were somewhat shielded in the crevice there was still a significant amount of skeletonized decomposition—Katie estimated a third to half of the bodies. Part of the skin on the exposed area had completed dried up, leaving areas of bone visible. If it weren't for their small size and the remains of childlike clothes, you'd assume them to be elderly.

Looking up the petite legs, there were several areas of missing flesh and deep dark marks that most likely were the result of tumbling down the gully. The blackened areas coincided with compound fractures with a bone poking up through the dead skin.

Katie moved slightly to the side so that John could digitally document the bodies—both up close and overall. He, too, studied the bodies.

Since the bodies faced inward to one another, the girls' arms and hands weren't immediately visible, but it was as if they were hugging each other as they said goodbye. This thought caused a lump in Katie's throat as she imagined the terror they had endured up to their brutal deaths.

Katie leaned in closer, trying to get a better view of their heads and necks. One girl, with blonde curled hair still fastened with a barrette, had what appeared to be a pink T-shirt, now deteriorating and shredded in places, and the other wore a yellow T-shirt with some type of iron-on picture that had long faded from the outdoor exposure.

The first girl had a deep indentation around her neck in a distinct pattern—what appeared to be some type of chain or rope. The other girl had an impact wound to the back of her exposed skull. Questions began to form in Katie's mind that only the medical examiner could answer.

"Her hand," said John, motioning to the hand of one of the girls which was curled into a tight fist around what looked like a strip of fabric of some kind. He leaned in and photographed it in its current position. "Let's not pull the fabric, but protect their hands in case there's anything else," he said, as he cautiously took out an evidence bag and began covering her hand and securing it with tape, carefully pulling it from its position. Katie did the same for the hands of the other girl. She saw that both girls had the remnants of friendship bracelets with faded pink and yellow threads. Best friends? Sisters?

Next, Katie looked around the surrounding rocks and inside the crevice to see if they'd missed anything—but there was nothing she could see.

The air temperature was dropping quickly as clouds gathered overhead and the daylight ebbed away—it was nearly dusk. Katie knew they would have to be out of here soon, but something caught her eye.

"What is that?" asked John, following Katie for a closer look as she gently turned the girl's torso a little to reveal the back of her head. With a gloved hand, she brushed away the blonde locks to reveal a set of numbers. "Does that look like a tattoo of 372 to you?" she asked, fear flooding her body as she ran through different scenarios; GPS, tracking, tracing, trafficking, and worse.

John used his camera lens to get a closer look and clicked several images. "I think you're right," he said, nodding.

"What would those numbers mean?"

"I don't know. I've never heard of a child's scalp being tattooed with a number."

Katie ran her eyes over the girls' broken bodies to take everything in one last time.

"I think we need to have the rescuers pull them out. We're running out of daylight and we need to preserve what we have," John said.

Katie knew that this was the only chance they might catch some evidence before the rescuers got them out. They would need to pull them, and risked losing any evidence that was on the bodies or caught in their clothes or hands.

"Okay, our job is done," he said.

Katie nodded—then hesitated. It was a long shot, but she had to try. "Wait," she said. "Let's extract and bag their clothes and the remaining shoe ourselves. The rescue team will do their best, but they're not trained for retrieving evidence from crime scenes in the way that we are."

"Okay."

Working as fast as they dared, Katie and John gently cut the clothing from the bodies with a small pair of scissors and a pocket knife that John had. After packaging the clothing and shoe as carefully as possible, they were done.

Katie readied herself to climb back up. As she checked everything in her gear, she looked over the bodies one last time. It was difficult not to cry at the sight of the two little girls, now stripped of their clothes, dead, and broken. She wanted to cover them with a blanket, to keep them warm and give them their decency, but the circumstances didn't allow for that and there was nothing more she could do for now.

John updated the sheriff from his cell phone and told him that they were on their way up, ascending without any problems.

They both used a bit of extra strength to pull their body weight upward. Katie huffed more than usual as she thought about the two little girls and their final resting place. Her pulse pounding with adrenalin as she reached the top.

As Katie stood on the sidelines, glad to be free from the climbing gear and wrapped in a warm coat, she watched as the rescue stretcher was hoisted to the top to a waiting gurney. Both bodies were so small they were able to fit on one stretcher. Again Katie felt a deep sadness weighing on her soul as she witnessed how fragile the girls were, finally free from their rocky tomb.

This double homicide would likely be Detective Hamilton's case, but Katie swore then and there that she was going to do everything she could to find their killer.

CHAPTER NINE

Friday 0830 hours

Katie had spent most of the night tossing and turning in her bed, unable to rid her mind of the images of the two little girls clinging to one another in their final moments. Katie often had dreams where the dead reached out to her, begging her to find their killer. And with two such vulnerable victims, never had those voices been louder or more real.

As she drove to the station, it became clear to her that she and McGaven were far better placed than Detective Hamilton to work this case. The bodies of those poor girls may only have been found yesterday, but the fact that they had been down there for so long meant that the trail would be about as cold as could be. She and McGaven had the experience needed to crack such an unusual case, and Katie was determined to plead her cause to the sheriff.

She sped into the parking lot, found her usual spot and cut the engine. Once inside, she made a quick dash to her uncle's office. Sheriff Scott's assistant wasn't at her desk, so Katie walked straight to her uncle's door and knocked. There was a moment's pause, before she heard him say, "Come in."

The sheriff looked up from his paperwork and smiled. "Hi, Katie. What brings you here?"

She quietly closed the door and moved to one of the chairs. He put his pen down and leaned back. "You look serious. Everything okay?"

"Yes, I'm fine. And well, no, everything isn't okay."

"McGaven okay?" he said.

"No, we're great. Nothing like that."

"Okay then, spit it out."

Katie took a deep breath. "I think the two little girls we found yesterday should be my case—mine and McGaven's."

"You do," he said.

"Yes, I do," she fired back, with as much conviction as she could muster.

"And why is that? You can't solve every homicide that comes in," he said, raising his brows and studying her even closer.

"No, not every homicide. But this is technically a cold-case homicide, so it should be ours." She bit her lip, hoping he could see her reasoning before adding, "We've got a solid record."

"No one is doubting that, but you also haven't been in the game that long."

Katie's eyes wandered around the room and she stopped on a photograph of her uncle with her aunt Claire smiling brightly. They looked so happy and content with one another. Her aunt's recent murder made it that much more heartbreaking. Her thoughts went to the family of the two little girls, and their heartbreak.

She lowered her voice. "Uncle Wayne, I know that Gav and I are the best team to work this case. Detective Hamilton is good, but it's just him; he doesn't have a partner or team. And the trail will be so cold by now that it's going to take an awful lot of painstaking work to even get a hint of a lead. Work that Gav and I are used to doing."

He leaned forward. "You make a good point."

"I also heard that they are short-handed in the detective division. Actually, everybody knows that. So, until another officer is promoted or another detective hired, I'm here to help to pick up a case like this."

When the sheriff didn't immediately respond she added, "You know, having two little girls murdered in the small neighboring town is a very big deal, people are going to be watching our every move. Having a large team on the case looks good for the department—and that will make Undersheriff Sullivan happy, won't it?"

"Now, let's just stay on point here," he said. It was unclear if Katie was making her case or if things had already been decided. "I appreciate your dedication and I know yesterday was difficult for you. But do you really think that you're the best person for the case?"

"What homicide case is ever easy—for anyone? And yes, it was difficult yesterday but not for the reason you think. I hate rock climbing and rappelling."

"That's surprising," he said with a slight smile.

"I'd rather take on gunfire than rappel down into a dark canyon," Katie said, still shuddering internally about her fall.

He paused a moment to ponder. "Detective Scott, what do you want me to do? You know that I can't just kick people off cases because you want to work them."

"That's not what I'm asking. I'm asking to work the case because me and Gav are the right team to work a cold homicide."

"It was initially a missing persons."

Katie didn't know what else to say.

"Look, there are some things we are reorganizing in the detective division that I cannot comment on right now…" he said, pausing. "The medical examiner is establishing the girls' identities as we speak—so there's nothing we can do for the moment. I know you wouldn't ask to work this case if it wasn't important to you, so I'll take that under advisement and see what we can do."

"Thank you. That's all I can ask for," she forced herself to say, quietly cursing the complications of working with family members.

"I'll let you know by Monday. Continue working your current case. I look forward to your report."

Katie nodded and then turned to leave the office.

"Lunch soon?" he said, with his usual Uncle Wayne smile.

She smiled. "Any time."

Katie had felt defeated and outnumbered at times in her work, but she was a strong believer that it would all work out for the best. Right now, it just had to be enough.

CHAPTER TEN

Monday 0930 hours

The cold-case investigation needed a new lead or punch to move forward. As Katie reread what they had so far the internal phone rang.

She snatched up the receiver. "Scott." She was expecting something from John or Denise.

"Katie," said Sheriff Scott. His voice was official, causing her to sit up straighter waiting for the answer to her earlier request about taking over the investigation.

"Yes," she said slowly.

"After careful thought and consideration of what's best for the double homicide, it's been decided…"

Katie closed her eyes.

"…that it would be the most efficient course of action to have you and McGaven run the case."

She let out a breath quietly. "Thank you."

"That still doesn't change that I want daily reports."

"Of course."

"I believe that Dr. Dean has some information for you at the morgue."

"Thank you."

The phone clicked and her uncle was gone.

McGaven swiveled in his chair, staring at her.

"It's ours."

*

Katie and McGaven hurried to meet with Dr. Dean at the morgue. It was up to them to find justice for those two sweet souls left broken and forgotten. They would hopefully soon know for certain if the girls were related or friends, and if they had been identified from missing persons' reports.

As Katie passed the usual examination rooms, she didn't see Dr. Dean or the two little girls. There were morgue technicians going about their duties, documenting and weighing organs for two middle-aged men and one elderly woman. Katie slowed her walk and kept moving deeper into the building—she had never been in this far before.

The hallway's fluorescent lights flickered above their heads, making a weird crackling noise as Katie peered inside a large double examination room holding the girls' two frail broken bodies—one on each table, mostly covered with a white sheet.

She turned slightly and looked at McGaven whose face was emotionless, but slightly pale. He usually had difficulty viewing autopsies, but was overcoming much of his discomfort with every case. However, this case seemed to dig deep with them both.

"Detective Scott," said a familiar voice behind them. "So glad you found the exam room. We don't use this area on a regular basis, but this case seemed to require a room to itself. I spoke with the sheriff. I guess you've been assigned?"

"Yes. It's nice to see you, Doctor," Katie said as she entered.

McGaven nodded his greeting through gritted teeth.

"Well," began Dr. Dean. "I'll clue you in on what I have so far, but the full report will follow by email." As he spoke he pulled on his white lab coat over his trademark khaki shorts and Hawaiian shirt.

"Are the girls related?" Katie asked.

"Yes, and no," was his reply.

Katie didn't understand. Stepsisters, perhaps?

"The two girls match a missing persons' report from Rock Creek from about two years ago," he said, reading from his file. "They are Tessa Mayfield, ten years old, and Megan Mayfield, eleven years old. Their mother, Mrs. Robin Mayfield, came in yesterday and identified them. But we still run a DNA as protocol due to the state of decomposition."

"Oh," Katie said aloud and didn't realize she had uttered a sound. She thought of how terrible it must've been for a mother to ID her two children. Clearing her throat, she said, "You said yes and no when I asked about them being sisters. What do you mean?"

"This is where it gets complicated, and that's why I waited for the investigator to be assigned to the case." Katie was momentarily confused. "Mrs. Mayfield swore that she had given birth to both girls and had their birth certificates to prove it. But the DNA of both girls didn't match as her children. Megan, the older one, is her biological daughter, but Tessa is not," said Dr. Dean.

"How is that possible?" she asked.

"The hospital," said McGaven. "Maybe a mix-up?"

"That's terrible," Katie said, thinking of the numbers 3 7 2 on the one girl's scalp and wondering what that meant.

"A mix-up is one possibility, but it goes a step further. The DNA from Tessa came back as a match to another girl who had been kidnapped nine and half years ago, according to a report from the state of Texas."

Just when Katie didn't think anything else could shock her, the news that one of the girls may have been kidnapped left her reeling. She took out her small notebook and made notes in her personal shorthand to buy herself a moment to think.

"I know this is a lot to grasp," said the examiner.

"To say the least," said Katie as she finished scribbling. She took a deep breath and followed Dr. Dean over to the closest table to begin going through his findings.

Dr. Dean turned back the sheet halfway to reveal the first small body. She looked so small, even for her age of almost eleven. Almost frozen in a fetal position from being attached to her sister, her curved body made Katie think of an ancient hieroglyph, a symbol that she had to decode. Advanced skeletonized decomposition meant there were missing patches of skin, but most of the girl's blonde hair was intact, except near the area of the branding.

"This is Tessa Mayfield," the doctor confirmed. "She had various injuries, broken bones, fractures and such post mortem, most likely due to the fall from the canyon." He indicated with his fingers towards her head. "But the marks on her neck indicate her cause of death was strangulation and I'm deeming it homicide. The strangulation and death was before she sustained injuries consistent with the fall into the canyon."

Katie studied the neck area which had darkened, making the pattern visible. "It looks like the damage was caused by some kind of chain," she said.

"Could be," he said.

"And it's definitely the cause of death?"

"No doubt—the proof is in the extended damage to her vertebrae and broken hyoid bone."

"It's a bit overkill, wouldn't you say? She's so small and delicate. Isn't this much more than would be necessary to kill her?" asked Katie. Her mind moved through killers who used brute force to subdue or kill their victims. Why did he do this?

"Most definitely. Brute strength was used, excessively, to break this child's neck."

Katie thought about that. "Anything under her nails?" She was hopeful, but it was unlikely after so long.

"No DNA, just dirt and debris. The samples have been sent to John along with the remnants of their clothing and a small piece of fabric found in her hand."

Katie nodded as she noted those pieces of evidence. "Is there anything else that stands out about Tessa Mayfield's body?"

The medical examiner pulled the rest of the sheet away. It was clear that there were numerous broken bones and crushed areas. Large patches of her arms, stomach, and the top of her thighs were a strange purplish-orange color, unlike rigor mortis but more like the result of severe first-degree burns.

"Is that an injury?" she asked.

"These were the areas that were in contact with her sister's body. It wasn't clear if they clung to one another after they were thrown down the ravine—or even *as* they were thrown—and remained entwined, or if it was where they had landed. And after time, skeletonized decomposition in the open air fused them together."

Katie thought she heard McGaven suck in a breath. He asked, "Would you put the time of death close to the time they were reported missing?"

"Yes, being outdoors, with cooler temperatures mostly, and protected by the crevice they had landed in, I would estimate their time of death within days of their abduction."

Katie couldn't tear her eyes away from Tessa's body and the obvious question that Dr. Dean hadn't answered yet. "And the tattoo on her scalp?"

"I had to ask one of my colleagues because it's not like traditional tattoos I'm used to seeing. The numbers 3 7 2 were actually stamped, like a brand."

"You mean like something that would be used to brand cattle?" she asked.

"It's actually exactly like a brand for cattle," he said. "It was confirmed by my colleague who grew up on a cattle ranch and is familiar with branding." He moved the small bit of blonde curly hair remaining with his hand to reveal the numbers more clearly.

"Can you tell how old it is?"

"It's difficult to tell, but it's been there a long time by the way it's stretched its imprint with the growth. My estimation, and it's only a guess, was that it was branded before she was two years old."

"Okay," she said, her mind reeling as the case became more complex and sinister by the minute.

Dr. Dean waited good-naturedly for Katie and McGaven to make their notes before he moved to the other exam table. Katie hesitated over leaving poor Tessa so exposed, but realized Dr. Dean wanted to compare the two victims, so she turned her attention to the girl's older sister, Megan, who was more severely decomposed.

Katie moved her body a bit so McGaven didn't have to take the entire view as Dr. Dean unveiled Megan's body. "This is Megan Mayfield. She died from a blunt force trauma to the head, quite severe. It would have caused death instantaneously."

"Is there any indication what caused the injury: the impact of the fall or an attack beforehand?" said Katie.

"It's almost impossible to tell as there are so many skull fragments missing, probably due to the impact of the canyon. It's impossible to match any type of weapon to her injuries."

"A bat, hammer, or any type of heavy tool could have caused it?" she pressed.

"Just about any object that could crush bone."

"Anything else?" Katie asked, really wanting to leave the morgue to gather her thoughts and get some space from the horror of what these girls went through in their final hours.

"Unfortunately, with Megan Mayfield there's nothing else to report. You'll have to see what John comes up with from the forensics."

"Okay then…"

"Detective Scott, Deputy McGaven, if you have any questions, please don't hesitate to call. I'll try to do everything I can to help. Expect my full report in a couple of hours." He smiled and it seemed clear that he understood how difficult and upsetting this case would be for them.

"Thank you, Dr. Dean," Katie said.

"It's always a pleasure working with you both."

Katie and McGaven hurried out of the room. Katie's legs felt strangely rubbery as she stopped dead when she turned a corner and spotted a body on one of the exam tables. It was covered in something sticky, with the skin blackened and slipping in places. She knew from experience that this meant the body must have been retrieved from water after a long period of time. She had seen this kind of exposure before when she was a beat cop in Sacramento. It made her wonder how the girls remained fused together—since it wasn't entirely clear at this point.

Her mind full of horrors she had experienced from the army and from her previous investigations, she hurried after McGaven to get started on the case.

CHAPTER ELEVEN
Tuesday 0730 hours

"I didn't think you were going to be here this early," said McGaven as he entered their small office. He shed his jacket and took his seat, ready to get to work again.

"Yesterday was a long day and it's put us slightly behind," she said, not looking up from the computer screen.

"Katie."

She didn't respond right away, knowing where this was going and hoping her silence might put McGaven off.

"Katie?" McGaven said again. He moved closer to her and put his hand on her shoulder so that she would stop typing. "Katie, you okay?"

She sighed and then slowly turned to him. This was one of the downsides of getting close to your partner; sometimes she just wanted to let things ride and not get into a deep conversation. It was enough to know that he cared, but she didn't want to talk about it.

"Hey…" he said gently and then moved back out of her immediate space.

"Look, I appreciate the concern. The last few days have been long and filled with stresses and details."

"That's the job. *Our* job."

"Of course I know that, but it's just difficult… Those two sisters. It's a lot to deal with… and I know you're supposed to maintain an emotional distance and look at the investigation more scientifically."

"I guarantee everyone up at the crime scene felt the same way you do."

Katie nodded in agreement. "I know. It was just a tough day for me, that's all."

"Okay. You can talk to me anytime you like. We're partners, remember?" he said, accompanied by his huge infectious smile.

"I know…" she said, and couldn't help but smile back.

"Okay, now that we have that business out of the way." He glanced at the lists and the maps posted on the wall. "What are you working on?"

"I called the girls' mother, Mrs. Mayfield, and set up a time to speak with her today in Rock Creek. I've been reading over the case files from the Rock Creek PD from the time they went missing. There isn't much information, unfortunately."

"What about Mr. Mayfield?"

"Don't know. He moved out before the girls disappeared and there's no forwarding address for him. I checked a few phone numbers in the old statements, but they are all disconnected."

"Hmmm…"

"And he has had no contact with his family since," she said.

McGaven turned to his laptop. "Okay, what's his full name?"

"Whitney Allen Mayfield."

"Whitney?" he repeated.

Katie shrugged. "His monikers are Whit, Whitey, and Wit if that helps. He was arrested twice for trespassing and minor assault about five years ago, then released. From there, no one knows."

"I'll see what I can find out," he said as his fingers glided over the keyboard with speed.

"And," said Katie, "after we check out the area where the girls were last seen, we are going to talk to Rock Creek's police chief—by the name of Osborne. Police Chief Richard Osborne. There are only two police officers on the force. Have you ever met him or the officers?"

"Nope. This will be my first time meeting any of them," he said, watching Katie. "What's wrong?"

"It's just that from my experience, which may not be a lot, these small-town folk don't trust outsiders too easily. Know what I mean?"

"I know completely what you mean. But…"

"But what?"

"I'm sure you'll find a way to charm them."

She laughed. "You sure *you* don't want to do it?"

"Nope, I'm just the muscle." He winked.

CHAPTER TWELVE
Tuesday 0930 hours

The drive to Rock Creek was slow, along country roads lined with trees, trunk to trunk. The speckled sunlight that managed to push through the branches danced across the windshield, reminding Katie that it was still morning even though she had been up for hours. Through the cracked open windows of the car, the deep smell of the forest infiltrated the vehicle's interior. There was nothing like it—it brought back pleasant times for her.

The small town was located northeast of Pine Valley and was in one of the most rural parts of the county. Some of the turns in the road were only wide enough for one car making it, at times, hazardous. The population was barely five hundred people; mostly generation farmers who didn't like outsiders or city people coming to their town asking questions and telling them what to do.

Katie tried to relax, keeping her shoulders down, neck eased, and eyes on the road. But the two young girls were always on her mind whether she was at work or at home. Their case had already gone unnoticed and unsolved for far too long; every hour that passed now was like a needle in her heart.

"… I can't imagine how Mrs. Mayfield is handling her loss," said McGaven.

Katie had been so involved in her own thoughts, she barely heard what her partner said. "It's unimaginable," she said. "But…"

"Here it comes."

"Didn't you find it strange that Dr. Dean said that Mrs. Mayfield had the two girls' birth certificates with her when she identified the bodies? Doesn't that seem *odd*? It's not like anyone would have asked for them."

"I don't know. Maybe because it had all the information that the investigation needed with names, parents, and DOB? That kind of stuff. I wonder if Mr. Mayfield knew that Tessa wasn't his biological daughter?"

"Good question. Still… And those numbers on Tessa's scalp… 3 7 2. What could that possibly mean?" Katie couldn't get that image of those numbers underneath the blonde curls out of her head. "Why was she branded?" she said. "The only thing that comes to my mind is trafficking."

McGaven was quiet for a moment as he gazed outside, watching the landscape change from forest to open farming land to the small town. "Mrs. Mayfield had to know about it. We'll have to see what she has to say."

"This interview is going to be difficult," Katie said—more an observation than a prediction—as she made a sweeping three-hundred-degree turn to take the steep incline into the small town of Rock Creek.

Slowing her speed, Katie checked her cell phone for the address, 1402 Sandstone Way. It was located at the far end of town. She continued to drive down the main streets, passing a gas station with full service, small grocery store, auto shop, and a small building where you could pay your phone, Internet, utility, and gas bills.

"Wow, it's pretty basic here," said McGaven marveling at the simple signs. "I've been here a couple of times, but it seems different. So isolated."

"There's something to be said for simple."

They drove past a weathered old man with a walking stick, out for his daily exercise, and a middle-aged woman sitting on a bench.

"I bet everyone knows everyone in this town," McGaven said, studying the area. "It should be easy to notice someone that doesn't belong—like whoever took the Mayfield girls. Or it was someone that everyone knows."

Katie stopped at the only traffic light in town, waiting for the green light before continuing. They were the only car on the road. She drove down another block intersecting Sandstone Way and kept going to the end of the street, which faced a wooded area with what appeared to be a creek below.

She parked at the end of the street so they could get a better view of their surroundings. The small dark blue house with white trim was a one-story stucco residence with no garage, but a small storage building in the backyard. The front yard had a well-manicured lawn with a trampoline in the far corner and a low white fence. An older model white car was parked in front of the house.

Katie took everything in. The slight breeze rustled the leaves on the ground. The smell of damp earth and pine needles permeated her senses. The lack of traffic noise was noticeable—just the faint sound of running water from the creek across the street. She imagined the girls playing in the front yard and jumping on the trampoline, then pushed the image aside as she walked across the street.

It struck Katie that this would be an optimal place to grow up or to raise a family. Simple living. Quiet. Secluded. Everyone knowing one another. How would someone slip in and snatch not one, but two girls?

"You ready?" asked McGaven.

Turning back to look across the street, she said, "I want to check out the area the girls were supposed to visit—with the swing."

McGaven hesitated. "Okay, let's go."

"It's just a short walk."

Katie looked at the dense trees and took in the overwhelming pine scent. It would be difficult to see anything, or anyone, if they were hiding and watching. And if the girls were excited as they raced to the trail and swing area they might not notice anyone following them.

They reached the top of a well-worn trail.

"Is this it?" asked McGaven.

"I think so from the description of the statements." Katie stopped and looked around slowly. "No one has a direct view to the trail. There's one house over there, but it's blocked by trees and those tall shrubs." She frowned and pondered before moving on.

"I bet the trees could act as a sound buffer too," said McGaven, taking in the area. "Maybe that's why no one heard a car or voices."

Katie nodded.

She stepped to the top of the path and looked down. The trail was wide and easily navigated, but there were the same heavily dense areas on the sides—again, most wouldn't notice someone lying in wait.

Expecting to pass someone that was coming back up or a couple of kids running down, Katie was surprised at how quiet and deserted it was.

McGaven kept a distance of about seven feet behind her as he too looked around.

Finally they reached the area of interest; there was a swing but not the average kind. This was a long rope that had been securely tied around a tire allowing for kids to either sit or stand before jetting out over the running creek below.

"Wow," said Katie, observing how far the rope would send you out between the trees and above the water. She touched the rope which appeared thick and secure. "What do you think, Gav? Give it a try?"

"That's a firm no."

She laughed. "These kids have more confidence than I would." She pulled back the tire and let it soar across away from her.

Katie peered down toward the creek. She could see the water running over the rocks along the side. It was obviously higher now that it was fall going into winter. She stared at the movement and tried to imagine someone sneaking up to the swing area, but it didn't seem likely.

"Hey, look at this," said McGaven.

Katie turned in his direction and saw his focus was on a faint trail heading into the forest area leading up to the Mayfields' house. It was overgrown with weeds, but the foliage was flattened as if someone had moved through recently. She decided to follow it to see if it was actually passable. There were outlines of footprints from heavy boots, but nothing recent.

McGaven followed.

"It's probably a shortcut for wildlife—like deer," she said.

The faint trail suddenly stopped and on one of the trees was a camera fitted with outdoor and weather protection, the kind commonly used by hunters or wildlife enthusiasts.

"Gav, here's a camera and I bet there's another one facing the other direction." She followed her instincts, moving deeper into the trees, and found another video camera. "Another one," she said. "It wouldn't show who was on the swing, but it might show someone moving around."

"I'm sure it's motion-sensored too," said McGaven.

Katie studied the cameras without touching them. Craning her neck and standing on her tiptoes, she said, "There's a company name... looks like ACE Visions Incorporated and a very faded contact phone number." She put the number in her cell phone. "Well, let's give them a call, shall we?"

She dialed the number and waited. "It's an answerphone." Katie left her name, and that she was from the sheriff's department, contact number, and what cameras she was inquiring about.

She walked back out to the swing area. "Let's see. We might just get lucky." Still looking around, she studied every possible way someone could approach to grab the girls. With all things considered, it seemed the only logical way they would not be seen would be to hide in one of the wooded areas—and wait.

"What do you think?" asked McGaven.

"It's still wide open here and a person could hide anywhere for as long as it took."

Just as she finished her sentence, there were two snaps from the underbrush to the right of the swing. Then what sounded like rapid footsteps.

Katie gestured to McGaven to take the faint trail and she would run back to the street and try to cut them off.

Running back, Katie pushed her steps hard until she reached the top. She glanced from left to right and back to the left again before heading toward the Mayfield residence. She hurried, feeling the cool air fill her lungs as she breathed heavily. Looking around, she heard only the quiet of the forest until the heavy footsteps of McGaven approached.

"Anything?" he said, a bit breathless.

"No, nothing."

"Could've been an animal—deer or dog maybe."

"Not likely, with those heavy steps."

"I'm sure there are other ways to cut through this thicket."

Slowly scanning the area, Katie said, "You're probably right. But something seems off." She didn't tell McGaven, but she felt like they were being watched. Deciding to blow off the shivers for now, they headed to the little house to speak with Mrs. Mayfield.

CHAPTER THIRTEEN

Tuesday 1145 hours

Katie flipped the latch to the little gate and entered. McGaven paused, looking around at the yard, and then followed his partner to the front door.

Pulling the squeaky screen open and then knocking on the door, Katie waited. At first, she thought no one was home but after several minutes the door unlocked and slowly opened. A thin woman with blonde hair pulled tightly back peered out. "Yes?" she said.

"Mrs. Mayfield?" asked Katie.

"Yes," the woman said.

"I'm Detective Katie Scott and this is my partner Deputy Sean McGaven."

Her eyes, red and swollen, widened with acknowledgment. "Of course. Please come in," she said and pulled the door open to welcome them.

"Thank you," Katie said as she entered.

The house was tidy and organized, but very small. The living room was used as the dining, laundry, and gathering area all rolled into one. The large couch looked like it might have been bought from a thrift store. Throw pillows in bright colors were neatly placed at the back. A small table with four simple wooden chairs sat in one corner of the room.

Katie saw the kitchen through a doorway and it too was basic but clean and orderly. She walked to the couch and sat down, McGaven opting for a chair at the dining table. Two large paintings of mountain views hung on the wall, along with several framed photos of the girls growing up through the years.

Mrs. Mayfield sat on the couch facing Katie and wouldn't immediately give eye contact as she seemed to prepare herself for more bad news.

"Mrs. Mayfield, first I would like to express our deepest condolences to you and your family," said Katie. "We are here to gather any information that might be helpful to the investigation. Are you up to it? Do you need to call anyone for support?" Katie watched the woman and she exhibited all the usual signs of stress, trauma, and grief.

"No. I'm fine. And there isn't anyone to call." She finally looked up and made eye contact with Katie. "Please, I'll help in any way I can."

"Can you take us briefly through the day Tessa and Megan went missing?"

Mrs. Mayfield took a deep breath, wringing her hands on her lap before she answered. "It was a typical day like any other Saturday. The girls had been playing croquet in the front. Tessa came in and begged me to let them go to the swing."

"The swing down the street?"

"Yes, it's a place not far where the kids go to play on this long swing that sweeps them into the trees and over a small creek."

"And had they been there before?"

"Yes, many times, but always with a group—older kids, or one of the parents."

"What was different that day?" Katie gently probed.

Mrs. Mayfield jumped up and said, "I'm sorry, where are my manners? Would you like a cup of coffee, or maybe a soda?"

"Oh, no, thank you. We're fine." Katie watched the woman's distress escalate as she was forced to answer questions about what happened that day.

Mrs. Mayfield sat back down slowly, looking like she felt cornered and ready to bolt given half a chance. "Tessa was so insistent, more than normal. She was a very strong-willed child; much more so than her sister."

"Was there a particular reason why she wanted to go that day? A friend maybe?"

"No… she seemed pretty eager though. I guess everything here was boring her. Oh yes, she said that her friends, Janey and her brother, would probably be there. But they weren't."

"I see. Were there any other kids there?"

"No. I called everyone I could think of. No one was down at the swing that day."

"Had the girls done anything different recently, or made new friends in the days leading up to their disappearance? Anything notable that was new in their lives?"

"No. There's honestly nothing that I can think of… they just *vanished…*"

"You mentioned Janey and her brother. Had they seen the girls?"

"No, they hadn't and didn't go to the swing that day. And about a year ago, their family moved away—like so many…" Her voice trailed off.

"Did you notice any change in the girls' moods?"

"Like what?" she asked.

"Well, like moodiness, anger, isolation, secretiveness, anything."

"No. Everything was normal, just like any other day."

Katie shifted her weight and asked, "Had you seen anyone that you'd never seen before hanging around, an unknown car, perhaps, or anyone watching you or the girls?"

"No, no. Nothing like that. *Nothing.*"

"Mrs. Mayfield, I'm sorry but I have to ask this. Have you heard from Mr. Mayfield recently?"

She stopped crying to stare directly at Katie. "No. I would call the police if I did. I would never let him in my house again."

"When was the last time you talked to him?"

"It was on Tessa's sixth birthday and that was the last time. He left us for good after that. That was fine with me—he was overbearing, controlling of everything, and I thought… well, I thought it was only a matter of time before he hurt us…"

"What makes you say that?"

"He was… he threatened us. I think it was because of his home life. He lost his parents and his sister died later in an accident. He was always… whenever he thought about his sister, he would go to another place in his mind."

"Would you know where he is?"

"Not a clue. And I don't care."

Katie glanced at McGaven before she said, "I know this is difficult, but I have a couple more questions. Is that okay?"

"Of course."

"How long have you lived here?"

"About ten years."

"So this is the only house that your girls had ever known?"

"Yes."

Katie trod lightly, not wanting to make the woman retreat and not cooperate in the investigation. "When we spoke with the medical examiner yesterday, he mentioned that you had the girls' birth certificates with you. Why is that?"

Without hesitating, she said, "I always have copies in my purse—in case something happens to me or I'm in a car accident. They would know about the girls and their personal information."

"Okay," said Katie making notes. She still thought it was strange, but Mrs. Mayfield answered easily. "Also, at the medical examiner's office, I noticed that Tessa had numbers printed on her scalp. What was the reason for that?"

This was the first time Mrs. Mayfield's emotions changed from grieving mother. "What are you talking about?" she said strongly. "She had some birthmarks, but no numbers. Maybe it looks like numbers to you."

Katie didn't want to push until she became combative, so she decided to change her approach. "Those are all the questions we have for now, but I'm sure we'll have more. If it's okay with you, may we see the girls' rooms?"

Standing up and smoothing her top, she said, "Of course. They shared the small back bedroom." She motioned for them to follow her. "It's just the way they left it. I've tried and tried to clean it up, but I... just... couldn't..."

"That's okay," said Katie.

"I have something to do in the kitchen," she said, not looking at the room.

McGaven stood close to Katie and whispered, "What's she hiding?"

She shrugged. "She may not be hiding anything—maybe it's just denial." Looking around, she said, "Let's see if we can find anything that they didn't want their mom to know about."

The overall size of the room was about ten by ten feet. It had been painted white, but was adorned with colorful pictures, drawings, cartoons and posters of young actors. There were twin beds, each against a wall; both were unmade with white sheets, pillowcases, and matching pink-and-yellow flowered comforters. Two small dressers stood across the room on the opposite wall.

Katie started her search with the dressers. She opened the drawers of both with care, methodically looking through the contents of unfolded clothes and various school supplies. She started at the top of each dresser, working her way down to the bottom, making sure she wasn't making a mess.

McGaven worked more slowly, carefully picking up and opening a jewelry box and looking inside and outside, even underneath, for any secrets that might help them find out what happened that day.

Katie stood up and stared down at one of the dressers. Instinctively, she tried to pull the bottom drawer completely out. It made a scraping noise and hung. Katie wiggled and shifted the drawer from side to side, until finally, with a dry screech, the drawer freed.

McGaven glanced at the door and then to Katie. "Anything?" His voice was hopeful.

"I'm not sure," she said. "When I was a teenager and didn't want my uncle to find something, I would tape it underneath a drawer—usually a desk drawer."

"What kind of stuff?"

Katie chuckled. "Just girl stuff. A photo of a boy I liked. A note someone passed me. Stuff like that. We might find something that the girls were hiding… a new friend… something."

"Was that boy Chad?"

"I'm not telling," she said. Carefully removing some clothes and flipping over the bureau drawer, she found a small book taped with masking tape. "Got something." She peeled the tape and it revealed a thin photo album.

"Whose dresser is that?" McGaven asked.

"I think it's… Tessa's."

Opening the five inch by seven inch booklet, Katie found a collection of old family photos. One showed a man and woman, Katie guessed it was a picture of Mr. and Mrs. Mayfield before they were married and much younger. As she flipped through photos, she saw they were all family related. Pulling out two of the photos, there was handwriting on the back: *Mack and Cyndi Mayfield 1992.* Another photo said: *Housewarming Party Guests.* She looked at all the faces closely but it was taken about ten years ago.

McGaven peered over Katie's shoulder. "What do you think?"

"I'm going to have Mrs. Mayfield identify everyone for us," she said, taking photos with her phone as backup.

"Good idea."

A white frame with two smiling girls caught Katie's eye— she immediately recognized them as Tessa and Megan. The girls were happy and excited about something. Maybe it was a birthday? Or a trip somewhere? They each had their arm around the other's waist. Someone must've said something funny because Tessa was laughing out loud. It was a recent photo, taken six months before they disappeared. Tessa had a necklace around her neck—a long, intricate chain with a turquoise pendant.

Katie went to the jewelry box, a soft tune that she couldn't place playing when she flipped up the lid. But there was no turquoise pendant.

A small closet was on the other side of the room. It was the last place that they had left to search. Katie put her hand on the doorknob but it spun strangely in her grasp. She tried to pull but the door wouldn't budge.

"Strange," she said.

"What?" said McGaven, turning to her.

"This closet."

McGaven checked it out. "There's something holding it in place." He bent down and saw that there was a small chunk of wood wedged underneath. It was difficult to see unless you were on the floor. He pulled it out and the door swung open with a high-pitched squeak.

Katie was relieved to see nothing but clothes on hangers when the door fell open—her curious cop mind reeling with possible scenarios. On the surface beneath the clothes was a cleared area, with a folded blanket and pillow as if someone was sleeping in the closet. "What do you make of this?" she asked her partner.

"One of them sleeping in the closet?" he said. "Makes me wonder what she, or maybe both of them were afraid of."

Katie looked at McGaven. "Good question."

They took another look around but didn't find anything else. As they walked back through the house, they found Mrs. Mayfield washing dishes.

"Mrs. Mayfield?" said Katie.

"Yes."

"I need to take this photo of the girls. I'll have it returned to you after I've made a copy."

"Oh," she said. "Of course."

"And," Katie said, "I found this small photo album hidden in one of the drawers."

Mrs. Mayfield looked at it and didn't respond for a moment. Katie wasn't sure if she knew about it or not.

"I was wondering if you would identify everyone for us. Here's my card. You can email it to me if you like." Katie didn't want to put Mrs. Mayfield through any more trauma for the day.

"Of course. It's been a while, I'm not sure if I know everyone from the party."

"Anything you can do would be great," said Katie. "Thank you for your time. And please, if there's anything you remember or would like to talk about, don't hesitate to call me."

Mrs. Mayfield escorted them to the door.

"Oh, where is Tessa's necklace? The one with the turquoise pendant?" Katie asked.

With a trembling lip, Mrs. Mayfield looked to the side as she spoke. "She always wore it. Never took it off. She was wearing it when I last saw her…"

Katie felt bad for asking. "Thank you. We'll be in touch."

"We went on a trip through New Mexico and Tessa was mesmerized by all the turquoise jewelry. She picked out that necklace. Megan didn't care much about jewelry… but…"

Katie touched her arm. "Thank you. If you need anything, please don't hesitate to call me. Okay?"

The woman nodded.

After Katie latched the gate, she turned to McGaven. "There was something else going on here."

"What are you thinking?"

"I don't know, but maybe the chief will be able to fill us in."

"Oh crap," interrupted McGaven, gesturing to the left rear tire.

"What?"

"We have a flat."

Katie turned and scrutinized the neighborhood—looking up and down the street. She slowly scanned the wooded area, but there wasn't anyone around and no cars. Something unsettled her again—awakened her instinct. She knelt down and examined the tire, running her hand over the reinforced rubber. There was a large slash through the tread about four inches in length.

"It was intentional. Someone slashed our tire."

"What?"

"Someone is sending us a clear message… they don't want us here."

CHAPTER FOURTEEN

Tuesday 1715 hours

After roadside assistance changed the tire and left, Katie and McGaven were back on the road heading to the Rock Creek Police Department. Katie had spoken with the chief and luckily he was happy to wait for them.

Katie thought about the Mayfield house and the little girls. A strong feeling in her gut told her something was off about the story of where the girls went that day, the home, and even the town.

"Is that the police department?" said McGaven, pointing to a small building that looked like it had once been a grocery store or vegetable stand. There was a community bulletin board on one side filled with flyers and business cards.

"This is it," she said.

The building was on the corner of Second Street and Persimmon Street, with two police cars parked on the side street in areas that had once been handicapped spaces. A small sign was nailed to the middle of the wooden door, which read: *Rock Creek Police Department.*

Katie parked and cut the engine. She turned to McGaven and said, "Now, be nice. We cannot afford to alienate them, okay?"

"Got it."

"I mean it, Gav," she stressed.

"Don't worry, I understand."

Katie stepped from the sedan and took a couple of breaths for good measure. She instinctively turned and scanned the streets before going in, but only saw emptiness and quiet.

Entering, she called out. "Hello? Chief Osborne?"

There was an old wooden desk, reminiscent of a teacher's desk in the 1960s, pushed across the far corner facing the door, with a laptop, cell phone, and a large set of keys on a round holder. There were two long folding tables with papers, miscellaneous manila files with handwritten tabs, and various handouts. On a small metal TV tray, there was a coffee maker, two Styrofoam cups, and a small pile of plastic stirrers.

"Hello?" she said again.

There was a rustling noise from a room behind a closed door. Katie and McGaven took a step back and waited. The small door opened and a tall man wearing a police uniform emerged readjusting his belt buckle. He wasn't startled by their presence, or embarrassed.

"You must be Detectives Scott and McGaven," he said and smiled. Chief Osborne was a middle-aged man with dark hair, dark eyes, and an average build. Aside from his height he didn't stand out in any way. There was a slight southern twang to his speech—most likely after years of being away from his home town.

Katie nodded and shook his hand. "Yes, nice to meet you, sir."

"No need for formalities here. We're all law enforcement. You can call me Chief, that's just fine. Have a seat."

"Okay, Chief," she said, feeling awkward and sitting on an uncomfortable metal chair while McGaven kept his usual standing position. "Thank you for waiting to see us. We had a flat and it took longer to get roadside service than we expected."

"Sorry to hear that. I'm surprised you were able to find anyone to fix it today." He sat down behind the corner desk and rested his hands on the top.

"I wanted to ask you a few questions about the Mayfield girls."

The chief hung his head slightly. "Terrible. Just terrible."

"Yes, sir," she said and corrected herself. "Chief."

"What did you want to know?" he asked.

"What can you tell us about the Mayfield family?"

He unwrapped a stick of gum and shoved it into his mouth. "Well, they were a nice family and those girls were just the cutest," he said, noisily chewing down the gum.

Katie was about to push for more when the chief asked her a question.

"Detective Scott, with this case and the fact you found the Mayfield girls' bodies… We really need your help."

"What do you mean?" she said.

"We're so short-staffed, and without anyone with any real homicide investigative experience, we could do with someone like you."

"We're already working hard on this case. We just spoke to Mrs. Mayfield—although she didn't really offer anything that was very helpful," she said.

"I bet not," he said.

"What do you mean, Chief?"

"This is a very small town, and when something happens to one of its citizens, the entire town mourns—not just the immediate friends and family."

"So you're saying it works differently here?" said McGaven. "That maybe some people don't want to talk?"

"That's part of it. But a crime this heinous has everyone scared, looking at each other differently, not feeling safe. So we welcome help in any way. I know that the bodies were found in your jurisdiction, but I would like to think that we could help you too—with whatever we can."

Katie remembered the police files lying on a table when they entered. There were probably complaints as well as unfiled crime reports available for everyone to see. "We're just trying to get some background information. It appears that the two girls were taken from their own neighborhood and it's more than possible that someone here knows or saw something."

"That might be difficult," he said. "People are close-lipped here—but I'll do whatever I can."

"Even if it might help catch a murderer?" asked Katie, trying to keep her frustration under control.

The chief sighed and said, "I know exactly where you're coming from. I was born and raised in Missouri and things are different there. These people don't want to be bothered or reminded about anything unpleasant."

Unpleasant?

"Chief, can you tell us anything about the Mayfields? Like, what about Mr. Mayfield?" she said.

"He's got problems. Can't make up his mind… leaving his wife."

"How about the girls? What was the family like when they bought the house and moved here—was it ten years ago?"

The chief leaned back. "They were always a nice family, quiet, no problems, everyone seemed to like them."

"Did either of the girls have any medical issues or accidents that you know of?"

He took a moment to contemplate the question but finally said, "No, none that I can think of. Even when they were at the first house."

"First house?" Katie asked, surprised.

"The one over on Sycamore. But no one has lived there in years."

"Why did they move?"

"Well, they were just married, not much money, no kids yet, and that was all they could afford. Then when the girls were about one and two, they bought that house Mrs. Mayfield is living in now."

"Would you have any idea where Mr. Mayfield is now? Or is there anyone in town that might still be in contact with him?"

"I'll have to think about that, Detective."

"That's fine."

"So where is the Sycamore place?" asked McGaven.

"It's a couple of blocks away, the last house at the end of the road. You can't miss it. Don't know what you're going to find though…"

Katie stood up. "We run down every possible lead that might give more information about the case."

Police Chief Osborne stood up respectfully as Katie made to leave. "Is it true that you found the bodies?"

"Yes. I was with a film crew who were looking for sites for a documentary."

"Well, what do you think about that… those girls might never have been found if it weren't for you and the film crew. Does that seem strange to you?" he asked.

Those words struck Katie. She had never thought about the case from that perspective before, but it did seem strange. What were the odds? "You never know who's going to lead you to the truth," she said. "Well, thank you, Chief. We'll be in touch."

"Just a word of advice."

"Yes?" she said, looking directly at him.

"Be careful where you go poking around."

"Chief Osborne, we are going wherever the investigation takes us. I hope that we have your support."

"Of course, just giving you a heads up, that's all. Give me a call if you need anything."

There was more of a warning there than concern, Katie was sure of it. "Thanks again for seeing us," she said. "I'll be waiting for the names of anyone you think might still be in touch with Mr. Mayfield."

Katie and McGaven remained silent until they were inside the car and Katie had turned the engine over. The fan air blew into the Jeep as she eased the vehicle onto Second Street.

"Weird?" said McGaven.

"Weird, and I'll raise you a strange."

Unusual…

Unpleasant…

"Did you get the feeling that he was keeping something from us?" she said.

"Absolutely."

"But why? Is he protecting someone here?"

"Don't know, but I'll do a bit of a background on him and this town when we get back," he said."

"And I'll see what I dig up tomorrow." She wanted to do a deep dive into this mysterious town and any other abductions in the area.

"There it is," McGaven instructed.

Katie turned onto Sycamore and continued slowly. Willow trees hung down low, obscuring the views of the homes on the street. When they finally came to the end, there was a small two-story house tucked deep into overgrown trees, bushes, and weeds. It was obvious that no one had stepped foot on the property in years. In the dwindling daylight, the effect was ominous.

"Wow," said Katie.

"Disturbing."

"It's just an old house that no one has lived in for a while… a long while."

"It's creepy. I've seen old abandoned houses before but this is just plain scary."

Katie parked. Turning to McGaven, she said, "Scary? Really? I thought nothing scared you." She got out of the car and stood in front of the home, wishing she had worn jeans instead of her nice suit slacks. She grabbed a flashlight, deciding to shed her jacket and tossing it into the car.

"You're going in there?" he asked. "We're running out of daylight."

"I'm just going to quickly check it out."

"What do you expect to find?"

"You never know. The Mayfields lived there for a while before it was abandoned. There could be anything inside. Then again, nothing at all."

"I'll go around back and check the area," he said. "Watch your step," he ordered, and disappeared around the side of the house.

Katie looked for a front entrance, which was difficult to ascertain due to the overgrowth. The trees and bushes were so overrun that the small house had all but disappeared behind them. The deep odor of wet earth made everything seem dank and moldy.

Next to the house, she found a small side gate that was now only a couple of boards loosely nailed together. Pulling it open, her boots sank into the decomposed leaves, branches, and dirt that lined the path that used to lead to the porch and front door. Turning the rusty doorknob, the old wooden door stuck, so she used her shoulder to push it open and drag it across the threshold. Pausing a moment, Katie allowed her eyes to adjust to the darkness. Stepping slowly inside, it was now just an empty space, and she switched on the flashlight to find her way to the middle of what was the living room. It stank of mold, and possibly decomposing small animals.

Sweeping the light back and forth, she tried to imagine what it was like when the Mayfields lived here. Homey furnishings, a rug, family photographs, delicious aromas coming from the kitchen—a newlywed couple's first home. It would have been a warm place of love and sanctuary.

Or was it?

Looking around in its present condition, it was dark, with shadows morphing into shapes. The large window in the living room was gone, boarded with several pieces of wood. Katie could see windows in the back of house that were still intact but filthy from neglect. Streaks of heavy grime covered the only areas where light could shine through.

The staircase caught her attention. She had enough time for a quick trip upstairs before she ran out of daylight completely.

Her boots pressed the first stair with a creak that continued with each step upward. Intrigued, she found the upper part of the house in much better condition, although cramped. She stood a moment in silence and stillness before moving down the hallway, sweeping the flashlight beam across the walls and around the bedroom doorways.

It wasn't until she reached the middle of the hallway that she felt the floorboard beneath her shift and give way. A second later, the ground disappeared from underneath her and she fell straight down to the first floor, before immediately crashing through those rotten boards and landing in the basement. Debris from the house consumed her in a putrid dust cloud.

The flashlight she had been carrying miraculously landed near her, with the beam highlighting a stone wall as it slowly rolled back and forth. Katie lay on her back, looking straight up, as everything went black.

CHAPTER FIFTEEN

Tuesday 1915 hours

The loud buzzing in Katie's ears sounded as if someone was trying to fine tune a radio without much luck. Her heartbeat was loud in her ears.

Bump. Ba bump… Bump. Ba bump…

The cacophony of sounds morphed into overhead high-powered aircraft buzzing the skyline. Explosions. Voices yelling. Katie knew they were things that had already happened, but the vibration shook her insides as her memories came and went.

"*Katie!*"

Her senses slowly came into focus.

It was just a lapse. The fact that she had fallen through two floors, two stories of an old house, and landed on cool dirt, pushed its way into the present. There was almost a relief that she wasn't on a battlefield somewhere.

"Katie!" yelled a familiar voice.

She let out a groan, turning on her side. She pushed up into a sitting position, catching her breath and taking a moment to see if she had any obvious injuries. There was a rip in her pants and blouse but very little blood. She was bruised, but she'd live.

"Katie!"

McGaven. He must have heard the crash and come looking for her.

"I'm okay," she said, hoping he could hear her. Her voice sounded tinny and far away. "I'm okay!" she repeated, this time much louder.

With a heave of strength, Katie stood up. She took even breaths to steady the dizziness.

"Where are you?" yelled McGaven. He sounded alarmed.

"I'm in the…" She looked around. "Basement."

"Okay, I'll look for an entrance… Don't move."

"I'm okay," she said.

Feeling her senses come back as her head cleared, she picked up her flashlight, amazed that it was still working. She directed it all around her, three hundred sixty degrees. There were no windows except for two vents to the outside. Even with her limited view, she could see that she was below ground level. The weeds and land outside were at eye view. She saw a trapdoor opening beside the hole she fell through.

"Hey," said McGaven through the hole on the first floor. "You okay?"

"Yeah, I'm going to be sore though… and probably never live this incident down."

"I'm not going to say anything… at first," he said, obviously relieved.

"There's what looks like a trapdoor leading to the outside."

"Okay, got it," he said and backtracked carefully.

"Gav," she said. "Be careful."

As Katie waited she looked around her again, but the basement was just a dirt floor underneath the house. There were no shelves, cabinets, or anything that would indicate it had been put to use. One entire wall was made of stone. She studied it further and saw something that caught her eye. Was it an engraving?

Shining the flashlight directly on the area, Katie rubbed against the stone until a number appeared. It looked like a 3. Cleaning the area harder, underneath the dirt she uncovered two more numbers to reveal the sequence: 3 7 2. It had obviously been there for quite some time.

Katie stepped back in astonishment. "How can that be?" she whispered.

She looked more closely at the wall, but there was nothing else except the number. Questions flooded her. What were the odds? What did it mean? Why would those same numbers be stamped on Tessa Mayfield's scalp?

A crash interrupted her thoughts.

Katie turned and saw the square trapdoor move. Then another crash, as the door heaved open to reveal the entrance.

McGaven leaned in. "C'mon, let's get you out of here." He offered his hand.

"Wait," said Katie.

"For what?"

"I found something carved on the wall. Do you have your cell on you? Mine's in my jacket in the car." She cursed herself for not keeping her phone with her.

"Yeah," he said and gave it to her.

Katie quickly took a photo of the numbers.

"What is it?" he asked.

"The numbers 3 7 2 are carved on the wall."

"3 7 2?"

"Now there's your creepy," she said, and felt a shiver up her spine.

"What the hell does it mean?"

"Well, we know the Mayfields did live here before moving to Sandstone. But Mrs. Mayfield shrugged it off when we mentioned another house. Is she keeping it secret?"

"We need to find Mr. Mayfield—White or Wit or whatever he goes by."

"Hey, give me a hand," she said as she passed the cell phone back to McGaven.

McGaven grabbed Katie around the wrist and, with an easy hoist, pulled her to safety outside the house. It was now dark, and the surrounding trees were alive with insect noises.

"Thanks," she said.

"Are you sure you're okay?" he said, looking at her clothes and picking some flooring out of her hair.

"Yes, but I ruined another pair of pants." She laughed half-heartedly.

"Stay right where you are! Show me your hands!" yelled two men suddenly.

Bright lights blinded Katie and McGaven. Neither moved right away, not wanting to antagonize the two men or give up their authority.

"Show me your hands now!" yelled the shorter, stockier man.

McGaven slowly raised his hands slightly. "We're police officers."

"I don't care who you think you are," said the taller man.

Katie squinted at the light, keeping her hands in full view, and then realized that the two men were the Rock Creek police officers with their guns trained on her and McGaven. "I'm Detective Scott and this is Deputy McGaven from Pine Valley Sheriff's Department. We just spoke with your chief about an hour ago."

McGaven cautiously opened his jacket to reveal his badge and gun.

"Oh crap, Brad," one officer said to the other. "It's those cops from PVSD."

Lowering their guns, they apologized, as Katie let out a deep breath.

"What are you two doing here?" asked the taller patrol officer.

"The chief told us that the Mayfields lived here," said Katie. "We were just checking it out."

"Mayfields?"

"The parents of the two girls that were murdered," reminded Katie.

"Oh yeah," said the shorter one.

"Do you know them?" she asked.

"Yeah, of course, everyone does."

"We're trying to locate Mr. Mayfield right now, actually. Any idea where he could be?"

"Nah, Whitey could be anywhere."

"Haven't seen him in a long time," countered the tall cop.

Katie moved closer to the men. Close enough to see their identification tags: Mason and McKinney.

"Officer Mason, is it?" said Katie.

"Yes, ma'am."

Katie couldn't help but notice the sarcasm in his voice.

"Do you know anything about Mayfield that could help us track him down? Like what he likes, places he might go, his favorite thing to do, other family members. Anything?"

Mason shrugged. "He's just a guy."

"What about you?" she said to the other officer, who was trying to avoid eye contact.

Officer McKinney hesitated then stared directly at her. "We don't know nuthin' about him except he was a guy who lived here. He worked odd jobs whenever he could."

"Like?" Katie prodded.

"Handyman, bus driver, auto parts store, stuff like that."

"Was he ever in trouble?"

"Nothing serious. Bar fights mostly. But that was before my time on the force."

"We're working the double homicide case, so we're running down every lead to find their killer. You understand that, right?" she said.

"We understand," said Mason.

"Good. Because I think you're going to be seeing a lot of us in the future, so we would appreciate you not pointing your guns at us."

"Noted."

"How long you staying?" asked Officer Mason.

"We're leaving now. But we'll be back," said McGaven. He moved closer to the two men, towering over them. For such a gentle guy, he could turn on the intimidation when he wanted.

"We'll be in touch," Katie said as she walked by the two officers, followed by McGaven.

Only when they were heading back to Pine Valley, did they finally speak.

"I think you're right," said McGaven.

"About?"

"Trying not to alienate the locals."

"Well…"

"I don't think those cops liked us much."

"Maybe not."

"We need more information about that house."

"Yep."

"Why are you so calm? You feeling okay?"

"For the tenth time, I'm fine, nothing that a nice hot bath won't ease," she said. In truth, her neck was stiff and her right side ached—and she might've chipped a tooth.

"Then what?"

"I think our biggest clue is that number—3 7 2."

"You think it could connect the killer and Tessa Mayfield?"

"I think it's the key to unlock this entire investigation."

CHAPTER SIXTEEN

Tuesday 2120 hours

Katie was exhausted. As she drove home from the station, recalling the hours she had spent researching Whitney Mayfield, it caused her much frustration. Just when she thought she had some background, it proved to be a false lead.

Turning up her long driveway, she thought she saw a flash of light—but her house was dark. Strange. Her uncle had stopped by earlier to play with Cisco and let him outside, and usually he would leave a couple of interior lights on. She didn't want Cisco to be left alone in the dark.

Her body still ached from her fall, but slipping into a nice hot bath would be the answer. She had called Chad earlier to invite him over, thinking they could have a nice quiet evening alone, but he'd said that he had been called into work to cover a shift for one of the other firefighters.

Katie pulled her Jeep up close to the house and turned off the engine. She stepped out, feeling a throbbing ache from her neck down to her right leg.

Odd. Usually she would hear Cisco barking as his way of greeting her, but it was completely quiet as she stood on the driveway. Walking up to the front door, she inserted her key and stepped inside to disarm her security alarm. Still no Cisco.

"Cisco," she called. "Hey, boy, sorry I'm late."

Katie turned on the lamp in the living room. Everything appeared to be just as she had left it.

"Cisco?"

She walked into the kitchen and turned on the light. Her skin prickled in the silence. Something wasn't right. She rushed down the hallway to her room, but it was empty.

"Cisco!" she called, louder this time. Now she was worried, but maybe her uncle had taken him for some reason. She glanced at her phone, but there was no message. She was just about to call him when she noticed that the door to her guest room was closed. It was never closed. Something told her to move forward with caution.

She stood in front of the door and listened. Then, counting to three, she grasped the doorknob, turned it and pushed the door open with force.

The light flashed on instantly, followed by a large group yelling, "Happy Birthday!"

Katie stepped back in shock. It took her a moment to respond.

"What are you all doing here?"

"It's your birthday!" said Chad, as he greeted her with Cisco at his side.

"It's not my birthday until Friday."

"That doesn't stop us," said her uncle.

"Wow… you all hid in here waiting," she laughed, her heart racing.

"We had spies at the department that let us know when you left," said McGaven, standing next to his girlfriend Denise.

"Of course," Katie smiled. "John… that sneak."

"He's on his way," said McGaven.

Katie was pleased to see her sergeant from the army, Nick, and his brother James and girlfriend Nadine. Nick cut through the crowd as everyone moved to the kitchen with food to be barbecued outside. Even in fall, there was nothing quite as tasty as food tossed onto the barbecue and then enjoying it indoors.

"Hey, Scotty. Happy Birthday," he said, giving her a peck on the cheek.

"I'm so glad you could be here. I haven't seen you in a while."

"Well, things are going well," he said.

"So great to hear." Her sergeant had been honorably discharged after he lost his leg, and he had returned to the area looking for his estranged brother. Katie had helped to reunite them—they were a family now.

The rest of the guests funneled down the hallway with Katie following.

"Oh, wait," said her uncle.

"That's right," replied McGaven.

"There's one more surprise. Well, it's actually a big surprise."

"A big, big surprise."

"Will you two stop it," she said. "I don't need any more surprises."

"Maybe we'll take it back."

"Okay, tell me," she said.

"Keep your eyes forward and march," said a female voice.

Katie turned in surprise to see her friend Elizabeth Cromwell—a tall, thin brunette she had been in boot camp with, standing in the doorway of her guest room. "Lizzy!" she cried with joy.

"Yep, it's me," replied her friend. "Katie, you look awesome! Well, maybe not the torn shirt…"

The women hugged.

"How did you get here? Why are you here?" said Katie.

"Well, I was transferred to Monterey Presidio at the Defense Language Institute. And I had a week off before I begin my new assignment to visit you."

"But how?"

"Well, Sarge had a bit to do with that."

"I figured. Oh, it's so great to see you."

"C'mon, there's snacks and beer," yelled McGaven. "And Katie, I see some presents that need opening."

The noise level raised as everyone talked, laughed, and began preparing the food.

"This is a perfect time to catch up. C'mon," said Katie to Lizzy, leading her out to the backyard and around the property to a circular trail. The air was chilly but they didn't mind.

As Katie and Lizzy walked the trail, Cisco caught up and padded along easily, keeping them in sight.

"I can't believe you got to keep Cisco. I'm so happy for you," said Lizzy, smiling and watching the dog. "You two were the best team—at least in my opinion."

"I don't think I could have made the transition without him."

Cisco did a spin around the women and trotted up the trail, checking out various bushes.

"I hear that from a lot of us soldiers about coming home. But you're doing okay?"

"Getting there. It's a process and I'm not going to lie, there are days that try to break me," said Katie.

"I bet Chad helps."

Katie couldn't help but smile. "Definitely."

"What a cutie, and a firefighter too. Good for you, girl."

They laughed.

"So tell me all about heading the cold-case unit. That's amazing, Katie. But knowing you, they're lucky to have you working those cases."

"I wouldn't be able to do it without a great partner."

"And he's quite a looker too!" Lizzy laughed.

"What about you?" asked Katie. "Anyone special?"

"Yes, but long-distance relationships don't really work. We'll see what happens…"

"I thought you'd be in some exotic place by now. You've decided to go into intelligence?"

"I've been in training for a while. I was offered a job that will eventually take me to DC, but for now I'm going to be working in Monterey here in California. It's beautiful, by the coast."

"You better come visit again," said Katie.

"Same for you! When you get tired of all the fabulous mountains and forest, come to the beach."

"Deal."

Cisco barked, and took off towards the smoking barbecue on the deck just outside the kitchen.

Katie laughed. "I guess he wants his steak."

The women went back inside to the party. Katie introduced Lizzy to John and the two hit it off. Everyone was having a great time.

Katie had been exhausted when she arrived home, but now, surrounded by all her friends and family, it gave her a boost of energy and a much needed recess from the homicide cases. For a few hours, she didn't give a thought to the little girls, the spooky old house, or the strange town.

After almost everyone had left Katie's house, the two couples, Katie and Chad, McGaven and Denise, sat in the living room with Lizzy.

Cisco had used up all his energy and was sleeping peacefully on the floor.

"The look on your face was absolutely priceless," said McGaven to Katie.

"It was really funny," agreed Lizzy.

"Well, I wasn't expecting my friends and family to be hiding in my guest room."

Chad hugged her tightly. "We don't get to see enough of you."

"The work schedule is rough."

"And bumpy," said Chad. "Look at your new scrapes and bruises."

"My bad, I really stepped into this one…" Katie said, laughing in spite of herself.

"Yep," said McGaven. "But right now it's your birthday… for another hour and half."

"Technically, it's not my birthday, guys."

"Hey, I have an idea," said Denise. "Let's go for a nightcap at the Star Chamber."

"Great idea," said Chad. "You up for it, babe?"

"Sure," she said. "Lizzy?"

"Count me in."

CHAPTER SEVENTEEN

Wednesday 0835 hours

Despite her unexpected birthday celebrations, Katie had made her usual early start and had spent the last forty-five minutes updating her lists on the Mayfield double homicide. She wrote down everything they knew to date, and what they didn't. The killer's profile was beginning to take shape. It was a good start—better than most.

While she waited for McGaven to arrive, and for the results from forensics, she kept digging to try and locate Whit Mayfield, and find about more about the abandoned house in Rock Creek.

She turned back to her laptop as a thought occurred to her. Since she was getting nowhere with the house, why not get up to speed on the town and the police department? Something about that place really bothered her, like it was a backdrop in a play and nothing was real… the abandoned house, the police department that used to be a grocery store. Just as she was typing in the details, her cell phone rang. An unknown number.

"Scott," she answered.

"It's Chief Osborne here."

"Yes, Chief. What can I do for you?" She hoped for some good news.

"When we talked yesterday, you asked about someone here that was friends with Whitey—I mean, Mr. Mayfield."

"Yes."

"I have a name and address for you. Darren Rodriguez. He lives at 261 Pine Street, apartment number 3."

Katie quickly wrote it down. "Was he a good friend?"

"I don't know about good. But those boys would hang out and sometimes cause a disturbance once or twice. They've been buddies for years."

"Thank you, Chief," she said.

"Oh, and sorry about my boys getting the jump on you and your partner."

"Not a problem."

"You know, we're all on the same side."

"Of course."

"Do you happen to know when you'll be coming back out here?"

"Not sure, we're evaluating our evidence and priorities right now."

"I see," he said with a sigh, just as McGaven entered.

Katie made a gesture that she was on an important call. "Would you like for us to let you know when we're on our way?"

"That would be fine. Again, I hope our little town didn't discourage you."

"No, of course not." She rolled her eyes in frustration so McGaven could see her reaction. "Thank you again, Chief."

"My pleasure. Bye now."

Katie ended the call and put down her cell phone.

"So what did the chief have to say?" asked McGaven.

Katie smiled and leaned back in her chair. "Good morning to you too. We got a name."

"You mean the police chief wants us back?"

"Well, he gave us the name: Darren Rodriguez at 261 Pine Street."

McGaven immediately flipped open his laptop and began searching through the police database. Files and background information scrolled down his screen.

"Anything?"

"Yep."

"That was fast."

"Well, Mr. Rodriguez here has had some bum luck. Quite the change from Mr. Mayfield, where I can't seem to get any real information besides a prior, but nothing substantial like work history or places of residence."

Katie rolled her chair next to McGaven. "What do you have?"

"Drunk and disorderly… quite a few of those."

"That fits what the chief said," she said, reading over her partner's shoulder.

"Trespass, low level assault… shoplifting… and it looks like he did eight years for vehicular homicide from ten years ago."

"It shows he drinks and drives, and gets angry," she said.

"Our killer?"

"Can't rule anyone out at this point. For now we need to talk to him about his buddy Mayfield."

McGaven looked at Katie's desk, which was covered with steno pads and several small sticky notes. "You've been busy."

"It's mostly notes, but 3 7 2 has been bothering me. In fact, it's a bit of an obsession right now." She flipped through her notes. "What are the odds of three numbers showing up in two different places that I happened to visit?"

McGaven shook his head.

"It's more than one hundred thousand to one… could be more. So," she said. "I've done the usual rundown of what these three numbers might mean. Like birthdates, addresses, locker combos and such. It's not enough for favorite lotto numbers."

"And?"

"Nothing," she said.

"Aren't there a million things that these numbers could represent?"

"You have to remember, Gav, these numbers may have something to do with the killer. It means something to him."

"You're thinking that the parents have something to do with it."

"We can't rule it out. Statistically speaking, someone being murdered by a family member occurs in approximately seventy-five percent of cases, leaving a friend or stranger to make up the other twenty-five percent. But there are also associates through family and friends, people in town. We have to keep alert. We've been fooled before."

She pulled a small notebook and started scribbling.

"What now?" asked McGaven, studying his partner closely.

"Could be a reference, like a verse from the Bible," she said.

"Killers have done that before, you know."

"Of course," she said. "The difference here is that these numbers are branded onto a child's *scalp* and scratched into the wall of the basement of that house. This is the pivotal clue, Gav—outside the forensic evidence, of course."

"So, something about wrath? The end of days?"

"My Sunday school days are a bit behind me and I haven't read the Bible recently, sorry to say. But..." She shuffled her notes. "I've come down to a couple possibilities."

McGaven moved closer.

"Okay. It's 3 7 2, right?" she said.

He nodded.

There are sixty-six books in the Bible—the King James Version. So, the way I see it, it could be book 3, 7, 2, 37, or 72."

"What about 32, 23, 73?"

"I think the order is key—in fact crucial. In the same order is what they are about. I read through several books and one stood out to me – the Psalms." McGaven remained quiet, with a blank expression.

"Okay, I won't bore you with details, but if I had to guess I would say the numbers possibly refers to Psalm, chapter 37, verse 2."

"What does it say?"

Looking down at her notes, she finally found what she was looking for. "It says: '*For they shall soon be cut down like the grass, and wither as the green herb.*'"

"And that means?"

"As best I can understand, it refers to the evil in the world. As in, why do the good suffer, while the evil prosper? That was the way professors explained it as it was written by King David."

"Wow," said McGaven. "You researched all this last night, didn't you?"

"Once I got into it, I just kept digging, but I'm not sure if this is just wishful thinking. It's possible that whoever wrote those numbers on Tessa's head and the basement wall felt discouraged, never getting what they think they deserve, and are tired of seeing everyone around them getting something that they want."

McGaven took a moment to think about it. "So, your theory is that the person we're looking for – the killer or just the person responsible for the numbers – felt inferior to everyone, or hated a type of person."

"Something like that. There's some deep-seated hate."

"Good versus evil."

"So I think we need to have a plan and be ready."

"Ready for what?" asked McGaven.

"Scrutinize everything in Rock Creek. We need to talk to Darren Rodriguez and re-interview Mrs. Mayfield."

"Road trip… to hell." He looked at his watch. "And we have plenty of time today."

"It is where it all began and where the girls were abducted from," she stressed.

"I'm going to change clothes," he said.

Looking at her text messages, she said, "I have a stop first and then I'll pick you up at your house."

CHAPTER EIGHTEEN
Wednesday 0930 hours

Katie hurried to the main forensic examination room and found it empty. John wasn't around. Probably at a crime scene or stepped out for a break. Glancing up and down the deserted hallway, she entered the large high-tech room on the pretext she would leave him a quick note that she came by and would be gone for most of the day.

She still hadn't figured out John completely. He was ex-Navy Seal and seemed like the type of soldier that would be in the navy for life. He had studied forensics, chemistry, and biochemistry sciences before landing the supervisor job at the Pine Valley Sheriff's Department Forensic Unit.

Katie hadn't really spoken to John since the autopsy. At her birthday party, she barely spoke to him because he had seemed quite taken with her friend Lizzy. The thought of John and Lizzy together brought a smile to her face.

The DNA for Tessa Mayfield was always in the back of Katie's mind. She needed to know who she was and why the Mayfields had her. Most of all, what the numbers 3 7 2 really meant.

Katie looked around John's desk area for a small piece of paper to let him know that she had come by looking for him. Everything was in its precise place—all the paperwork, file folders, pens, steno pads had a specific spot, usually exactly perpendicular to the tables and desks.

Interesting.

There was one piece of paper that stood out. Tossed on the table rather than neatly tucked away. It was a crumpled bar receipt, and on it was Lizzy's name and cell number.

Katie wondered if John had called her, since she was going to be in the area for about a week. Searching around again, she saw a couple of folders with the names *Tessa* and *Megan Mayfield*. After listening for a moment, Katie opened the folders and read the preliminary report from the medical examiner's office. There were brief notes in pencil pointing to DNA, California soil and vegetation, and some type of debris mixed on Megan's skull fragments.

Katie then realized that she needed to forward a photo of the picture of Tessa wearing the necklace so that John could examine it and confirm whether it could have been used to strangle her. She retrieved her cell phone, found the photo, and emailed it to him.

Knowing that she would probably hear from John tomorrow or the next day, she had decided to leave the exam area when a stack of printed photos of the Mayfield crime scene caught her attention. She picked them up and quickly thumbed through them.

It brought her back to the moment she went over the edge and into the ravine, and the almost debilitating fear she felt that day. Her hands shook. Her pulse heightened. Her mouth went dry. She wanted to put the photos down, but she was mesmerized by them. Until she saw a photo of her amongst them, taken as she began to climb back out of the ravine. In fact, there were several photos of her. She didn't know what they had to do with the crime scene... Had John taken the opportunity after they had searched and documented the scene to take photos of her? Two were close-ups of her face as she focused on her ascent, while another was a pretty picture of her turning towards him, smiling. She didn't remember smiling much, but he managed to capture one.

Katie didn't know what to think. Or feel. She put the stack back down on the desk exactly as she had found it and left the forensic area, without writing a note.

CHAPTER NINETEEN

Wednesday 1030 hours

Katie picked up McGaven from his house so that they could keep an early start on their drive to Rock Creek—both dressed in jeans and layered sweaters. It would take them more than an hour to get there—it wasn't the distance, but the windy roads that slowed them down. She thought it was prudent to take her Jeep so that they might blend into the town more easily than in the sedan.

"You okay?" asked McGaven.

Katie glanced at her partner. "Yeah, just a bit tired. As you know my mind wouldn't shut off last night so I didn't get much beauty sleep."

"Just checking. This case would pull apart the strongest amongst us," he said, as he looked out the window at the countryside.

As Katie eased onto the narrow road leading over the mountain to Rock Creek, she tried to let her surroundings calm her. Watching the sun on the horizon was one of the best parts of living in the country. Heading northeast, the brilliance of the reddish-orange colors lighting up the hills and valleys took her breath away. Even the dense trees alongside the road glowed in the heavenly light.

"You alert the chief that we were coming?" asked McGaven.

"Yep."

"Think that was wise?"

"What do you mean?"

"Well, maybe he might tell Mr. Rodriguez or one of the officers."

"And?"

"I just don't quite trust anything in that town to be at face value," he said.

"That's true. But I also didn't want him to think we were snooping around behind his back." She thought about it. "I hope I won't regret that decision."

McGaven gave her a curious look.

"Let's just be cautious and alert to everything," she said.

"And did you report in to our sheriff?"

"Of course. I'm not putting us through another one of *those* meetings again."

"It's like going to the principal's office."

Katie laughed. "I bet you were sent there more than once in your school years."

"Once or twice."

The traffic had dwindled to zero cars, making it easier to navigate the narrow road as the Jeep came to a tight set of turns. Katie slowed to take the first, then the second… and then slammed on the brakes, bringing them to a screeching halt in front of a fallen tree branch around the third turn.

"Crap!" she exclaimed. "I would have been really upset if I'd dented my new Jeep."

She maneuvered the vehicle as best she could in case someone came around the corner. "There are some road hazard sticks in the back. We should put them a ways back to alert anyone coming. I'll put one up in the other direction."

McGaven grabbed the flares and headed back down the road.

Katie assessed the branch. It didn't seem too big, just awkward, with smaller pine branches jutting out at all angles. Between the two of them, they could ease it out of the way and clear the road. The hillside at the edge of the road was very steep, so, with a couple of flares in her hand, she climbed over the branch and spaced them ten feet apart on the other side to warn drivers.

Returning to the Jeep, she located the pine tree where the branch must have fallen from, and stopped in her tracks. Carved into the trunk were the numbers 3, 7 and 2.

"What the…?" she said softly to herself.

McGaven came around the corner and saw her expression.

"What's up?" he said.

"Look." She pointed.

"Is this some kind of joke?" He moved closer to get a better look at it. "It's been carved recently, look at the shavings on the ground. They aren't even wet from the overnight moisture."

"That would suggest that someone knew we were coming, and made sure this branch blocked the road. But who? And why? How could they have timed this so perfectly?"

"It doesn't look good," he said.

"Somebody knows what we're looking for—but is it a clue, or a threat?"

"C'mon," he said. "Let's get this tree limb out of the way."

Katie shook off the shiver that ran down her spine, and pushed up her sleeves. It took less than ten minutes for them to heave the branch off the road and send it down the hillside, out of harm's way.

Before getting back in the Jeep, Katie took several photos of the carving on her phone.

"We'll have to leave it for now. There's no way to process it or look for fingerprints. We don't have the equipment, but there probably isn't anything to process—except for the numbers themselves."

"Oh, I'm so looking forward to going into town again," McGaven said sarcastically, as Katie drove them down the other side of the mountain and back into Rock Creek. Today, there were more cars and people milling around than on their last visit, which made the town seem more ordinary.

"We're looking for 261 Pine Street, apartment number 3," said Katie, searching, then making a sudden turn off the main road.

"There's an apartment building," said McGaven. It was a small white building with two levels.

"That looks to be it," she said, and parked across the street next to several other cars.

They got out of the Jeep and looked around. The building was in an older area of the neighborhood, and in need of repairs. No broken windows, just a bit of work to update the peeling paint and freshen up the front yards.

They walked across the street to the main entrance—apartment number 3 was on the ground floor to the left. Katie led them to a door with a gold number 3, knocked and waited. No answer. Knocking again, there was no noise from inside. Noticing that the doorknob wasn't completely engaged, she pushed and it popped open.

Katie turned to McGaven to give the go-ahead, and then leaned forward and called out, "Mr. Rodriguez? Anybody home?" No answer, just a strong smell of cleaning products.

Katie pulled out her cell and looked again at the photo of Darren Rodriguez. He was in his early forties, long dark hair, medium build, scar on his left cheek, and a grim expression on his face.

"You looking for that good for nuthin' Darren?" asked a feeble-sounding old woman. "I loved him like family, but he was good for nuthin', leaving the way he did."

Katie turned to see a very short, heavy-set woman wearing a long floral nightgown. She held a ginger and white cat clutched tightly against her breast. The crinkles on her face were mostly caused from frowning.

"Darren Rodriguez?" Katie asked.

"That's him. He skipped out late last night."

"What do you mean?"

"He left, moved out—well, not everything, there's still some stuff left."

"Did you talk to him last night?"

"Yeah. He owes me two hundred bucks. I'm the apartment manager, so I ain't ever going to get it back."

Katie moved closer to the woman. "Cute cat." She scratched behind his ears, inducing a loud purr in response.

"His name is Arnie, after my late husband."

"Hi, Arnie," said Katie, hoping to get the woman to trust them.

"You cops?" she blurted out.

"Detectives," said McGaven. "And you are?"

"Sissy. Everyone calls me Sissy." She stepped forward and looked up at McGaven. "You're a tall one."

"That's what I've been told."

"Have you ever shot anyone?" she said, as she started her interrogation.

"Yes. And I've been shot at."

"Did the bullet hit you?"

"Yep."

"Does it hurt as bad as they say it does?"

"More."

"You married?"

"I want to be."

"Were you a tall kid?"

"Very."

"Did other kids make fun of you?"

"Some."

"It that why you became a cop?"

"Maybe."

Katie waited for the dialogue to cease, but she was fully entertained by the two's interaction.

Sissy took a moment and then said, "Why are you here?"

"To talk to Mr. Rodriguez."

"About?"

Katie interrupted. "I'm Detective Scott and this tall fellow is Deputy McGaven. We're from Pine Valley Sheriff's Department and we're working on what happened to the Mayfield sisters."

Sissy looked down. "Horrible. Those two little girls. Nuthin' like that should happen to the innocent. So you're from Pine Valley."

"Yes," said Katie.

"Good. They need your help here."

"We wanted to talk to Rodriguez about his friend Whitney Mayfield, the girls' father."

Sissy made a sarcastic noise. "I never trusted him. He seemed shifty to me."

"You knew him?" asked Katie.

"Everybody around here knew him. What do you want to know?"

"We're trying to locate him," said Katie.

"That I can't help you with, I'm afraid. Have no idea where he is, or went, or is going…"

Katie leaned in to look inside Rodriguez's apartment.

"Go in," Sissy said. "He's gone for good, so have a look around all you like. Nuthin' wrong with that. I was going to have everything hauled away anyway. Take what you want."

Katie looked at McGaven and then pushed the door open. "Why does it smell like bleach?" She covered her nose and then moved slowly inside.

"Cleaning up, I guess—at least that was decent of him. He lived like a pig," said Sissy. "Horrible. He never took out the trash." She shrugged in revulsion.

Katie looked around the small living room. The carpet had deep indentations where a couch, table, and chair had been removed—leaving the rest of the area dark and dirty.

"How long did he live here?" she asked.

"Almost eight years. And who knows where before that."

Katie scrutinized the walls and saw that only some of the artwork had been taken, with a few cheap reproductions still hanging in place. There was a large built-in bookcase littered with a few old newspapers and magazines and the odd old VHS video and DVD left behind. Some were labelled as home recordings and others were reality TV shows and a few documentaries.

"Huh," muttered McGaven, leaning closer to read the headings.

Katie looked at what he was scrutinizing. "What?"

"Did you read the titles?"

She shrugged, not paying close attention to them.

"*The Diamond Mines*, *History of the Boston Tea Party*, and *The Disappearing Polar Bears*."

Katie didn't understand what the titles meant. "And?"

"The film crew who you babysat filmed all of these."

"You mean those guys with Wild Oats Productions?"

"Yes. I recognize the DVDs of their work from when I did a brief background on them."

Katie was shocked. "What would their documentaries be doing here?"

"Unlike us, people who have spare time *do* watch films and documentaries."

Sissy had walked into the apartment. "Yeah, he always had those boring docu-films blaring in the background, day and night."

"What about Whitney Mayfield?"

"What about him? Sure, he watched them too. I think it was him that got Darren into them."

Katie turned to Sissy. "Did you ever see the Mayfield girls over here with their dad?"

"Um, a couple of times, I think, when they were really little."

Katie took a tour of the rest of the apartment looking for any personal items that would indicate where Darren had gone. The kitchen was mostly empty, though the refrigerator still had old food inside. The heavy cleaner had been poured down the drain and in the kitchen trash can. Several mouse traps were scattered on the floor.

Katie went into the bedroom where a bed frame remained without a mattress. The closet was a graveyard of empty wire hangers. It was clear that he had left in a hurry, taking only what he needed and wanted.

"Sissy, what kind of car does Darren drive?"

"One of those big trucks with enormous wheels, a monster of a truck. Black with that extra chrome stuff. He had to park it across the street because it wouldn't fit into our designated parking spots."

"So, he could have moved everything he could fit in there himself…" said Katie. "Everything else, he left behind." She pondered. "I wonder if he missed anything?"

"Let's see what we can find out…" said McGaven.

Both Katie and McGaven spent twenty minutes combing the apartment, but found nothing more.

"What do you think?" he said.

"I think we should take all of the DVDs and documentaries," she said. "It's just too… coincidental, that someone of interest in the Mayfield homicides has films from the same crew that just came to our town."

"Agreed." McGaven pulled some evidence bags from his pocket and filled them with DVDs, stooping to pick up a slip of paper that fell from the sleeve of one. "Look, it says 'Property of W. Mayfield.'"

Katie looked at it to confirm. Turning to the old woman, she said, "Sissy, is there anything else you can tell us about Darren Rodriguez?"

"Like what?"

"Like anything you remember about him. Strange. Unusual. Anything you've seen that would stand out in your mind." Katie watched the woman think hard, and waited.

"Darren and Whit always seemed to be working on something."

"What do you mean?"

"Like they were always plotting something… that no one else knew about. It was weird if you ask me, that's all." Petting the cat, she continued, "What's that they say? Thick as thieves."

"Something like that," said Katie. To McGaven, she said, "Call in for an APB for Darren Rodriguez and get his vehicle license number on that black truck. Find out if he has a warrant. We need to talk to him as soon as possible."

McGaven nodded and made several calls.

"Sissy?" said Katie. "Did Darren have family, or a partner somewhere?"

"The only thing he ever told me was his mom lived in Vegas."

Katie whispered to McGaven, "He could be heading there—include those instructions on the APB."

McGaven nodded.

Their search was interrupted when Katie's cell phone rang. As she took in some news her face momentarily crumpled before she regained composure. "Yes, we know where it is. Thanks for the call," was all she said before she hung up.

"What?" said McGaven.

"That was the chief. Mrs. Mayfield has been found dead in her home—apparent suicide."

CHAPTER TWENTY
Wednesday 1215 hours

After loading up the DVDs from Darren Rodriguez's apartment, and thanking Sissy for her help, Katie drove them straight to the Mayfield residence on Sandstone Way. When they arrived, there was already a city SUV, one police cruiser, and a dark navy van parked on the road. Two inquisitive neighbors were hovering in the driveway next door, and a couple more two houses down.

"Do you think Chief Osborne and his boys are capable of running a crime scene like this?" said McGaven.

"In a word, no," she said with a quiet tone, as McGaven vocalized her biggest fear: that this was actually a homicide, and that the local police would potentially trample all over the evidence before they'd had a chance to look.

Katie grabbed a couple pairs of gloves and booties, giving McGaven one set of each, and they entered the yard through the small white picket gate. The ghosts of the Mayfield girls danced all around her.

"Detective Scott," said Chief Osborne, as he hurried out through the front door allowing the screen to slam behind him.

"Chief, what do you have?" she said.

"We're pretty sure it's a suicide."

"You know you can never get the crime scene back if you're wrong," said Katie. "It's always good to operate on worst-case scenario."

He turned, checking behind him as if to see if anyone was listening. "That's why both of you are here—and perfectly timed, I might add. We have limited resources here, but do the best we can. I spoke with Sheriff Scott and he agrees you are the best around and should work the scene—whether it's suicide or not. So this is your scene…"

"Okay," said Katie, quickly realizing they didn't have all the equipment they needed to properly work the crime scene, but knowing it had to be done now. "I want everyone out of the house. Has anyone touched the body or any of the evidence?"

"Just the first responder, Officer Mason, to see if she was alive."

"I see," she said. "Who called it in?"

"No one."

"Why was Officer Mason here?"

"Mrs. Mayfield called the police herself."

Katie felt her stomach drop, like she was on a helter-skelter. She glanced at McGaven. "Make sure everyone is out." Turning to the chief, she said, "Do you have someone that can document the scene? A photographer?"

"That would be Wendell," said the chief.

"Good. Get him here now, please."

The chief moved toward his SUV and made a call on his cell phone.

Katie slipped on her gloves and booties, waiting for McGaven to escort Officer Mason and the morgue technician from the house.

Officer McKinney arrived and parked behind the other police car just as Katie was about to enter the house. She turned and said, "No one else is allowed in here until the search is complete. Except for Wendell—let me know when he gets here." McKinney nodded. He stepped aside and scanned the area. His expression wasn't somber, but rather, angry.

She and McGaven progressed inside, careful not to touch anything unnecessarily.

The interior of the Mayfield house looked just as it had when they were there the day before. The house was neatly organized and the large vintage couch had the same bright throw pillows carefully placed. The small table with four simple wooden chairs sat in the corner of the room.

Nothing seemed out of place, and there was no evidence to suggest a struggle. In the kitchen, there were dishes in the sink from breakfast—a plate, fork, glass, small skillet, and spatula. Crumbs were scattered around the counter and in the sink. Everything suggested that Mrs. Mayfield had been alone when she woke this morning.

There was a little desk in the corner of the living room, painted turquoise with a lacy scarf over the top, and a small backless white stool. A closed laptop sat on top on the left-hand side next to a yellow steno pad and a black pen. Lying next to the stool, face down on the floor, was Mrs. Robin Mayfield wearing a simple cotton dress with an apron tied around her waist. She was barefoot, her shoes neatly paired under the desk. Her head was turned to the left, hair neatly combed, eyes staring aimlessly, mouth parted, torso flat against the carpet. Her arms were bent at right angles, one up, and one down. A halo of blood circled her head—dark in color against the light carpet. On the right side of the body lay a 9 mm Smith & Wesson handgun. Leaning forward, breathing deeply, Katie could tell that it had been fired recently. The familiar smell was a bit sulfurous and a bit metallic… but mostly sulfur. The odor can linger up to a day.

Katie knelt down and carefully inspected the body. It bothered her how neat everything seemed, more like a stage play than real life. She was half expecting Mrs. Mayfield to get up from the floor and take a bow for her performance. Whether a suicide or homicide, or even a bizarre accident, it was usually very messy when a gun was involved; clothes stained, bodies in awkward positions, and blood spatter everywhere.

Mrs. Mayfield's skin was a sick gray, with purplish undertones of rigor mortis, meaning that she had been dead for no more than two or three hours.

Katie stood up and thought for a moment.

"Suicide?" said McGaven.

"It appears."

"But?" he said.

"Everything is too neat."

Moving closer, McGaven said, "The gun is where it should be…"

"Could be." She turned to McGaven. "You've seen suicide victims before, right?"

"Yes, unfortunately."

"How many women have you seen use a gun?" she said.

"I can't think of any, in my experience, but there have been female firearm victims."

"Of course." She gestured around the living room and desk. "And where's the blood spatter? Nothing on the floor, furniture, walls, or carpet."

"Hello?" said a quiet male voice.

"Yes?" replied Katie, turning toward the entrance.

A short stocky man in his fifties, with a digital camera lassoed around his neck, stood at the door waiting.

"Are you Detective Scott? I'm Wendell."

"Hi, Wendell. Don't come any further, please. I need you to go back outside and get some gloves and booties from the chief or officer."

He hesitated a moment and then left.

Katie rolled her eyes.

"Be nice," said McGaven, with a smile on his face.

"We need him to take this seriously," she said. Everything about this scene seemed suspicious.

"Hello?" said Wendell again, now wearing his gloves and booties.

"Wendell, come in," she said. "Thanks for coming at such short notice. I need for you to take shots of the interior first. You've seen a dead body before, right?"

He nodded.

"Okay, then once you've got the interior, take close-ups of the body, her head, her hands – everything. You good with that?" she said.

With confidence, he said, "Yes, ma'am, I am." He stepped over the threshold awkwardly in his paper booties, and began snapping.

"Did you read this?" McGaven said.

"What?"

"It looks like a suicide note."

"Where?"

McGaven carefully lifted the first sheet of the writing pad and revealed part of a letter—handwritten in neat cursive. It wasn't addressed to anyone in particular, but the sentiment was clear.

Katie read it aloud:

I'm sorry for what I'm about to do. But I couldn't save the fragile ones. The ones that needed protecting the most. I cannot live with myself for not keeping the girls out of harm's way. I cannot live a lie. The truth will come out. Please don't feel sorry for me, and don't be sad.

All my love, Robin.

Katie took a quick photo with her cell phone. "Wendell, can you photograph this letter, please?"

"Yep," he said, as he made his way over to the desk. Spotting the body at last, he stopped, swallowed hard, and then continued with his work.

"Wendell, did you know Mrs. Mayfield?"

"Not really. Just from around town. That's the way with most people here, everybody knows everybody, but not many are close friends."

"What about Mr. Mayfield?"

He frowned. "Run into him from time to time, but hadn't seen him in years. He was always with that guy… Darren something."

"Rodriguez?"

"That's it," he said.

"When Wendell is finished, we need to get the evidence collected and tagged properly," said McGaven with a concerned expression.

"Absolutely," said Katie. "It's imperative that the chain of custody stays intact."

Katie steered McGaven into the kitchen while Wendell finished shooting the rest of the scene.

"How do you want to handle this?" asked McGaven. "Does the evidence come with us to the sheriff's department? And the body?"

"I'll have to speak with the chief."

"What about Mrs. Mayfield's family?" said McGaven.

"When I checked her background, there wasn't much to find. Her parents are both deceased. She has a sister in Nashville that I can try to get in touch with. From everything I've uncovered about her, she kept to herself. She used to work at a diner in town, but that was more than a year ago."

"How did she earn money then?" said McGaven.

"Good question."

"Detective?" asked Wendell. "I'm done here."

"Gav, can you assist him with getting the photos to John?" she said.

McGaven led Wendell outside.

Katie took another moment looking around the small tidy house that so much care had been given to. Her eyes finally rested on

Mrs. Mayfield, so neatly arranged on the floor. She remembered the mother's grief and resilience, her refusal to keep from falling apart in front of her and McGaven. She had endured more than one person should. Now, she had ended her life without anything more to live for. The tragedy kept building around this family.

Katie finally left the house and went outside to find Chief Osborne.

"Chief," she said.

"Everything done inside?" he asked.

"Who usually collects evidence from your department?" said Katie.

"Either Officer Mason or McKinney."

"Okay, well, Wendell has finished with the photographs now so I want Mrs. Mayfield's hands wrapped and protected. All the evidence bagged and tagged properly with ID numbers for the chain of custody. That means the gun, the notepad, the letter, and anything surrounding the body in and around the desk area. Usually all of these items would be marked with small cones. Do you think you can make sure everything gets taken care of?"

"Yes, ma'am."

"The body needs to be transported as well."

"Sheriff Scott informed me on that. Our morgue technician will transport the body and evidence directly to the sheriff's department—there will be someone from forensics and the medical examiner's office waiting to receive them."

"Good," she said. Although she was concerned about the efficiency of the local police officers, it was the best they could do under the circumstances. "Did anyone hear the gunshot?"

"We canvassed the immediate area and no one heard anything until we arrived."

"Were there any visitors?"

"Nope. No one saw anything unusual."

Katie was frustrated, but didn't let it show.

She took the extra time to go back inside the house and scrutinize everything once more, before she watched the two officers collect and bag the evidence, zip Mrs. Mayfield inside a body bag, lift her onto a gurney, and wheel it out of the house.

When Katie was satisfied that everything was completed, she walked back out and conducted a final search around the property. Nothing presented itself and before long, she and McGaven were on their way back to Pine Valley.

"What do you think?" asked McGaven.

"I'm not sure."

"Of what?"

"This case…" She hesitated. "This case keeps getting more sinister as time goes on."

CHAPTER TWENTY-ONE

Thursday 0835 hours

Katie had received word that Mrs. Mayfield's body had arrived at their morgue, and the evidence collected from the crime scene was safe in John's lab. After interviewing the mother of the murdered girls only the previous day, yesterday had been shocking—and thrown up more questions than answers.

Katie stood at her whiteboard and moved around maps to make space to think. She cocked her head to the side and considered the killer as she wrote.

Stepping back, her mind spinning, she considered the previous day and the many strange clues—all revolving around Rock Creek. Just thinking about the town made her turn cold. But why? What wasn't she seeing?

Katie leaned against the side of her desk, thinking about everything they knew. The clues seemed to be telling her something, and that something was from Rock Creek. It was where everything had started, with the abduction of the girls—and now everything seemed to be unraveling there.

With a thought, Katie picked up the phone and pushed an extension.

"Records, Denise," said her friend after two rings.

"Hey there."

"Katie, hi."

"Are you swamped with work?"

"Just the usual. What do you need?" she said.

"I have a fun assignment for you."

"Bring it on."

Katie smiled. She really liked Denise and her spunky enthusiasm. "Yesterday, Gav and I went to Rock Creek, and we found numbers carved into a pine tree on the side of the road—3 7 2."

"I'm with you so far."

"We were about three miles from entering into the main part of town on Highway 9 going northbound."

"Okay."

"Someone seemed to have carved those numbers early yesterday morning. The tree shavings weren't wet from the overnight storm. And I have a sneaky suspicion that person drove a big black pick-up truck."

"Let me guess… you want to know if anyone saw that truck within the vicinity."

"You got it. And…" continued Katie, "I want to find out anything you can about Rock Creek, people who live there, strange things that have happened, or anything that doesn't seem right. I know it's a big ask, but it's a small town and we need to get to know its secrets."

"I can get on that Neighborhood program for the area and poke around. I'll use names of local folk on there to search social media and see what else I can find. As for the tree, let me check the aerial maps online. They update every four to eight hours or so—maybe we'll get lucky. I can also see if there are any CCTV traffic cameras in the vicinity."

"Great, thanks, Denise. That would be great. Oh, beers Saturday with Gav and Chad at Third Watch Bistro?"

"Wouldn't miss it!"

Denise hung up and Katie listened to the high-pitched buzz of the disconnected line. Slowly replacing the receiver to the cradle, Katie's mind returned to the numbers tattooed on Tessa's scalp. It was horrifying, yet she was convinced it was the key to the investigation.

Reading her lists on her notepads and glancing at her boards, Katie ran ideas. She decided to search the Internet to find out if there was any research into the psychology behind people who tattoo themselves and others excessively. Maybe there was some terminology for this, or a condition she wasn't aware of—that would give her something to go on.

Several results came up, but nothing that pinpointed what she needed. Katie made a tighter search using the words: tattoo, compulsive, identification, people, trafficking, children. A couple of researchers came up, including a Dr. Simone Halverson, an adjunct professor at the local university, who was published on the topics of excessive tattooing and branding of others.

Katie made an appointment for the next morning, which was the only time Dr. Halverson had available. Immediately after, her cell phone buzzed.

Preliminary results on Mayfield cases are in.

Katie hurried to the forensic lab, leaving her notes spread out all over her desk and part of McGaven's too. She hoped he would arrive soon to hear what John had to say firsthand.

She slowed her pace and took a breath before entering John's exam lab. He was at the far corner, on one of the new computers with a screen as large as a TV.

"Have you been avoiding me lately?" said John, never averting his eyes from the computer.

That stopped Katie dead, rattled her a bit. "Not at all," she said.

He looked at her and smiled, which was unusual for such a serious guy. "Sorry I had to leave your party early. I had quite a bit still to do here."

"It was nice of you to come."

"I love your place. It reminds me of my folks' house growing up in Tennessee."

Katie was taken aback—that was the most personal information that John had ever expressed about himself. She didn't know how to respond.

"Looks like you've been busy. We received a lot of stuff for processing from Rock Creek PD last night. I was wondering if you would check this list to make sure," he said.

"I know it's a bit sketchy how they handle things." Katie walked over to his workstation.

John grabbed a couple of papers and turned on his stool. "Here you go."

Katie began to read down the list. Everything appeared correct, except…

"What's the matter?" said John.

"This small photo album."

"What about it?"

"It wasn't at the house when we searched and documented everything. I saw this album when I visited with Mrs. Mayfield the day before. It was in the girls' room. But it wasn't there yesterday. I remember noticing as I'd asked her to ID the people in it… What do the notes on it say?"

John found the evidence bag. "It says it was photographed and collected from the top of the desk in the living room."

"That's not possible," said Katie.

"What's the timestamp?" he asked.

"It says it's at the same time everything else was collected." Katie reread the list carefully. "I don't understand. That's not true. It wasn't there when I looked around the crime scene."

"Who collected the evidence?"

"The local police officers, but I directed them and I'm telling you, I know what was at the house." Katie looked around the room as if an answer would materialize. It didn't. "Someone must have put it in with the rest of the evidence. Either the morgue technician, one of the two police officers, or the chief."

"Anyone else have access?"

"No. Just me and McGaven."

John put his hand on her arm. "I know this is weird. Let's move forward for now and then come back to the photo album later, okay?"

Katie looked at John. He had always been a good friend and held her in high regard—they shared the fact they were military vets. There was some type of chemistry between them, but neither had acted on it. It was simple. Katie loved Chad. He was the love of her life.

"You okay, Katie?" he asked.

"Sorry. This case is taking some unexpected turns. That town, Rock Creek, is really bothering me. Things are strange…"

"Spooky," he said, and laughed.

"I know… something is off." Katie pulled herself together and focused on the evidence. "Okay, what do we have?"

John stared at her for a moment longer, and then suddenly rolled his stool to another workstation, pulling up what looked like a magnified photo of a rope. "This is a magnification of the photo of Tessa Mayfield wearing her necklace. Luckily, in terms of the comparison to the wound, it's a thick chain and has a distinct pattern."

Katie leaned in to get a better view. "It's a heavy 's' pattern."

"And look at this," he said, as he flipped to a split screen with a close-up of Tessa's neck wound. Even though her small neck was bruised, the skin partially missing, there was a clear and definite pattern.

"Wow, that's a perfect imprint of the chain."

"Just about perfect," he corrected.

"I know you can't say it's 100 percent, but that's remarkable," she said. "She was strangled with her own necklace, or it was ripped hard from her neck… It wasn't found anywhere at the crime scene. It's probably lost, but I can't help but think—"

"Think what?" said McGaven as he stood in the doorway, eyes wide with curiosity.

"Hey, Gav, glad you're here. I was saying… I can't help but think the killer might have taken it as a souvenir."

"It's possible," he said.

"I'm curious about the fabric in Tessa's hand," said Katie.

"Actually, it's not fabric. It's a heavier material that's consistent with something like a tarp—industrial strength. Sometimes you can find this type of fabric on all-weather gear made for skiing or extreme snow sports. Pricey stuff."

Katie's mind ran through a few different scenarios of tarps for cars, boats, the back of a flatbed truck, or pick-up trucks. Then an idea struck her on how the girls could have been transported.

"So you're saying it has more plastic qualities than regular fabrics, such as upholstery or faux leathers?"

John nodded.

"Would the plastic of a body bag fit that description?"

"It's possible, but the density is different."

"But it's possible?" she asked.

He nodded. "Definitely."

John quickly searched through his computer file folders and opened one with several chemical compounds. He enlarged the specimens. "From the fingernail scrapings from both girls, Tessa was the only one that had anything that could be studied." He angled the computer screen towards Katie and McGaven.

"What is it?" said Katie, scrutinizing the image.

"Dirt."

"Dirt?"

John laughed. "I'm sorry, that's a forensic joke."

Katie stared at him blankly. He wasn't usually one for witticisms.

"The local soil broke down into three major categories of pine trees: gray pine, foothill pine, and ponderosa pine."

"We're loaded with pine trees up around here," she said.

"True, but the gray and foothill pine trees are thirty-six to forty-five feet high and are located in the eastern part of the mountains. And the standard ponderosa pines are huge. They grow over a hundred feet, sometimes two hundred feet tall, and spread out significantly."

Katie thought about the trees and wasn't sure if it was significant. The dirt and debris could have been embedded underneath Tessa's fingernails from when she was at the swing, or even before. "Was there anything else on the girls, fluids, DNA, or anything that would guide us in the right direction?"

"Just the remnant of the pine trees, I'm afraid. I know you were hoping for more. Sorry."

"What about Tessa's identity through her DNA? We know that she wasn't Megan's biological sister."

"It's been difficult to track down—I've even made calls as well as emails. What we know is that she was reported missing when she was barely six months old. But since it was more than ten years ago, the information is vague. Jenni and Brad Homestead were the parents that filed the report from Austin, Texas from the First Memorial Hospital and Austin PD. But…"

"I knew there would be a but…"

"After a child stays missing for so long, the information goes into a larger database and updates the missing and abducted children computer catalog as well. And sometimes these large databanks don't get updated properly, which is why we weren't able to find any information until now."

"Okay," she said.

"The record for the parents, and the actual report, is missing."

"What do you mean, missing?" Katie couldn't believe it.

"Missing… gone… nowhere to be found."

"What about Austin Police Department, or the hospital?"

"They have no record. Austin PD said they would continue to look through their files, but the hospital had some issues with their computer systems around that time."

"Wait," she said. "This is like running in circles and never finding a way out. How can this be? How can we have information from a DNA databank, and not the PD and hospital?"

"That's all I could find, I'm afraid—or couldn't find," said John.

"From speaking to Mrs. Mayfield, she seemed to be defensive about the girls' records. Maybe she knew—or didn't. We'll never know now."

"The only thing we can do is track down Jenni and Brad Homestead by name, and see what they have to say," said McGaven.

"That's one for you," Katie told him.

John moved to another workstation and pulled up a computer image of a skull. "Now, here's Megan's skull. I've been trying to piece it together in order to figure out what made the impact that killed her." He looked from Katie to McGaven before continuing, "We have this new re-enactment program that fully stands up in court. So, I can hypothetically show you what a wound from various types of murder weapon would look like."

"Great." Katie kept her eyes glued to the screen.

"I first wanted to show what a fall would look like, but nothing remotely appeared to simulate this injury," said John.

Katie watched with interest.

"Then I tried a baseball bat, or something in similar size, but look at the result."

The computerized depiction showed a baseball bat smacking the small skull area, but the actual damage was too immense to match the damage on Megan's skull.

"By a long process of elimination, I got this result from a standard size tire iron." The screen showed the simulated impact, which was very consistent with the injury Megan received.

"Tire iron," she said.

"Well, consistent with a tire iron or something with that approximate size and density."

"Thank you, John," said Katie.

"Sorry I couldn't be of more help."

"No, it's been very helpful. There's always something to be learned from evidence—or even the lack of it."

"I'll email over a copy of that album, okay?" John said.

With so much in her mind, Katie had momentarily forgotten about the photo album she'd found in the girls' bedroom, that had mysteriously turned up in the evidence. She needed to know who the people in those family shots were.

"That would be great, thanks."

Katie turned and walked slowly out of the large exam room. McGaven followed her back to the office. There were maps newly taped on the wall showing Rock Creek, with small dots designating places of interest.

"This is great," she said.

"You like it?"

Katie marveled at the display, looking at it from different perspectives. McGaven had put little pins where they got a flat tire, the girls' home, the swing where they were last known to be, the police department, and the house on Sandstone Way.

"It's beautiful. A story is emerging—a dark story."

CHAPTER TWENTY-TWO

Friday 0945 hours

Katie drove solo to the university to meet with Dr. Simone Halverson, an expert on the psychology behind excessive tattooing and physical branding. She left McGaven in the office working on the locations of Darren Rodriguez, and Jenni and Brad Homestead, as well as searching other jurisdictions in California for cases similar to the Mayfield double homicide. Her hope was to find a link from other cases—but mostly, it was conducting due diligence.

Before Katie had found Dr. Halverson's research, she would never have believed that people could inflict such horrible and degrading brandings on themselves and others. It was a taboo subject, but some researchers had been learning more about why a small portion of the population want to brand themselves—the opposite of using tattooing as a means of expression and art.

Katie ran all the events in Rock Creek through her mind once again, trying to make sense of it all. She felt as if someone was pulling her strings, dragging her through a maze of unrelated incidents.

Then, out of nowhere, it happened. Driving through the main entrance of the university, a strange uneven vertigo hit her from nowhere, skewing the lines on the road and sending her off course.

Frantically, she wiped her hands on her thighs. Why was this happening now? Was it the pressure of the case? Was it because she felt backed into a corner? Whatever the trigger, Katie couldn't continue to hammer the anxiety head-on. She had to stay in the moment and let it relinquish its hold on her. She realized too late that she hadn't been working on the assignments that Dr. Carver had given her—in fact, she hadn't been thinking about her panic attacks at all, and now she was running into problems again.

Pulling into a space, Katie sat straight with hands still on the steering wheel, engine running, and contemplated whether or not to leave or continue with her assignment. Breathing deep and slow, she began to feel her pulse slowing and returning to normal—at least close to it. Her head and vision felt better. But the incident left her realizing that she had underestimated herself. How many panic attacks had she been through? And every time she had managed to overcome it. She could, and would do it again.

Glancing in the rearview mirror, she smoothed her hair and stared at her reflection for several seconds before readying herself to interview Dr. Halverson. Color had returned to her cheeks and her eyes had cleared from their glassy appearance during the attack.

Katie grabbed her notebook and exited the car. The cool fall air sent a welcome chill through her overheated body, and the invigorating scent of pine was like medicine for the soul.

Breathe.

Katie hurried up the leafy walkway to the social sciences building. The campus was mostly deserted but for a few tardy students hustling into buildings at the last minute before class. Inside, Katie took the stairs, not feeling at ease enough to be trapped in an elevator. At the end of a long corridor, rounding a corner, she found a door labeled 'B13 Halverson'.

She knocked three times and waited.

The door was opened by a striking woman in her thirties with dark hair slightly curled at her shoulders. She wore a beige suit with a vibrant jungle print blouse.

"Hello. Detective Scott?"

"Yes," Katie replied. "You are Dr. Halverson."

"Please call me Simone. Doctor sounds so clinical, like I belong in a hospital." She opened the door to allow Katie to enter.

Katie found she liked her immediately, which was uncommon for her. The doctor was warm and friendly, and there was a caring quality about her. Her office was small but stylish and put Katie at ease.

"Please, Detective, have a seat," she said, gesturing to one of the oversized comfortable chairs.

"Thank you," said Katie, as Simone joined her in the other.

"I have to say, I was intrigued when I received your call."

Katie quickly gathered her thoughts and began, knowing that time was running out on this case. "Everything I'm about to tell you is in the strictest confidence. Much of it isn't public knowledge and I'd like to keep it that way for as long as I can. I need your help to solve a very unusual case."

"Of course," said Simone. "And I would never share what you're going to tell me."

"I'm looking for the killer of two little girls."

Simone's easygoing demeanor changed in an instant as her eyes filled with dismay.

"I won't distress you with the details, but the reason why I'm here is that one of the girls has a series of numbers branded onto her scalp... 3 7 2. I've never seen anything like this before. Tattoos, yes, but not actual branding—numbers burnt into the skin, similar to cattle branding."

"Where is it?"

"It's above the ear on the left side of her head."

"I see. Would you have a photo?" she asked somberly.

"Uh, yes." Katie pulled out her cell phone and searched her crime scene photos, handing her phone to Simone.

Dr. Halverson studied the image, enlarging it and moving it back and forth across the three numbers. After a few moments, she handed Katie back her phone.

"Have you ever seen anything like this before?" asked Katie.

"I have," she said slowly.

Katie was taken aback.

"There are cultures, or rather sub-cultures like underground sex trafficking and prostitution, that use this branding method either to identify the child, or to brand them with something specific—meaning it represents something important for them. Mostly sex workers and Satanists."

"The medical examiner estimated that the numbers had been there since before she was two years old. Is that typical?"

"Unfortunately the answer is yes, but that doesn't mean they won't brand an older child or woman. Detective, you have to realize that the people who do this feel strongly about it—it's important. It's how they identify themselves in their sub-culture. The act is taken very seriously and often seen as an honor." She shifted in her seat before continuing, "You see, the numbers not only identify who that child is, or belongs to, but also give the brander power by adding another person to their sect, group or collection."

Katie took a moment to comprehend what Simone was saying. "I've been trying to think what the numbers might represent. I came across a Bible passage that talked about death. Would that be something worth branding on a baby?"

"Absolutely. It may mean something different to them than it would a Sunday school teacher or a scholar, but it could represent their mission, or point of view."

"Wow," Katie said. "These are psychopaths?"

"I know many people want to put the title of 'psychopath' on any individual who does cruel and heinous things, things that you or I wouldn't do, but they don't see it that way. They are technically a partial psychopath." She studied Katie for a moment. "I know you run into more than your fair share of psychopaths, Detective. But people from all walks of life can find solace in labeling in this way. Yes, they can be controlling, cruel, and overbearing, but they can also be extremely loving, caring and family-oriented. Now does that sound like any psychopath you know?"

"No, not at all."

"That said, obsessing about ownership in this way can be extremely dangerous and is usually well hidden. The only advice I can give is to be very cautious when pursuing someone like this."

"Thank you," said Katie. "It's not completely clear to me yet, but some things are beginning to fit into place." She stood up. "I won't keep you any longer, thank you again for your time."

"My pleasure. If you have any more questions, please don't hesitate to reach out."

Katie stood up and shook Dr. Halverson's hand.

"And I hope you find your killer."

Katie was still digesting what Dr. Halverson had told her when her cell phone rang. She saw that it was McGaven.

"Hey, what's up?" she said.

"Two presents for you."

Katie stopped walking and waited to hear what her partner had to say. "Hit me."

"The Vegas PD found Darren Rodriguez at his mom's house and are preparing him for transport for questioning in a double homicide."

Yes...

"Things are getting interesting."

"And, Denise, my lovely, my super-intelligent girlfriend, some day to be my wife..."

"Tell me," she said rolling her eyes.

"Denise was able to get a photo of his truck en route to the area where the branch was in the middle of the road, right next to the carved tree."

"How'd she get that?"

"Turns out that one of the locals is on the new neighborhood software – I-Neighbor, or something like that – drove up in the early morning and asked him if he needed help. The back of the truck was filled with all his stuff. They moved the branch out of the road, but when he drove away he saw Rodriguez moving it back. And… drumroll, please… Our townie had his dashcam running. Great photos—black and white, but good nonetheless."

"That's fantastic. When will he be arriving?"

"Not sure. Probably sometime tomorrow. Just wanted to brighten up your day as soon as possible."

"You certainly did. See you in a few." She hung up.

All the pieces of this strange puzzle were finally starting to fit.

CHAPTER TWENTY-THREE

Friday 1145 hours

As soon as Katie stepped into the forensic division and shut the world out, she felt at home. The quiet. The calm. Peace.

"Katie?"

She stopped and turned to see John standing there. "Hi."

"I have duplicates of the small photo album pages that ended up in the evidence from Rock Creek," he said, and turned back into the exam room.

"Oh." She moved closer to the entrance and waited.

"Here you go. I thought it might help with things."

"Yes, thank you," she said, taking the manila envelope.

"See ya," he said, and disappeared into the forensic lab.

Suddenly revived, Katie burst into the office, tossing her stuff on the desk. She tore open the envelope and pulled out photocopies of the pages in the album.

"Hello is usually acceptable," said McGaven.

"I'm sorry, hi."

She opened the file inside, tossing the folder to the side.

"What is that?"

"John gave us copies of the photo album. Grainy. The brightness and contrast are okay."

McGaven moved closer.

"I knew it," she said.

"What?"

"Look at this." She put the paper flat on the desk so he could see. "It appears that Mrs. Mayfield wrote on the photos the names of the people she recognized, just like we asked."

"Yeah. And?"

"It's all in capital letters, but her suicide note was in cursive and with a different slant to the letters."

"You're assuming that *she* wrote on these photos."

"I am. Look at the letters neat, orderly, almost exactly identical. That's how she dressed and kept the house. It just fits her." She looked at McGaven then sighed. "You're right, we need to have this writing compared to something else that she had written. Okay." She got up to pin the photos to the board.

There were four photos with Mrs. Mayfield's writing:

1: *Tessa & Megan Mayfield* (smiling sisters)
2: *Mr. & Mrs. Mayfield 2009* (the couple looked happy but Mr. Mayfield turned his face towards Mrs. Mayfield to give her a kiss making it difficult to see him clearly)
3: *Mack and Cyndi Mayfield 1992 (grandparents; since deceased)*
4: *Housewarming Party Guests (ten years ago) Me, Chief Ricky Osborne, Brad Mason, Darren, and ?(unknown).*

Katie strained to see Whitney Mayfield clearly, but it was tricky. When they ran his background, nothing came up. Mayfield was clearly an alias, not his real name.

"Does it bother you that the chief is in this photo?"

"Maybe it was him who moved the album and had his officers include it as evidence?"

"But why?" she said. "To cover something up? Throw us off the trail? Or to help us without others knowing?" Frustration filled Katie.

"Is that Brad Mason, the local police officer?" he asked, looking closer at the photo.

"It's difficult to tell. He's much thinner in the photo. But I believe it is."

"Wasn't he the first to arrive at the scene of the apparent suicide?"

"Yes, he was."

"Coincidental?"

"I'm not one to believe in coincidences," she said.

"I always hesitate asking this but… what are you thinking?"

"They all have secrets," she said, staring at the housewarming photo. She let out an exasperated sigh. "What aren't you telling us? It's like everyone in Rock Creek has a part to play in this complicated whodunit. There is someone behind the scenes orchestrating everything, but no one is talking." She sat down at her desk and thumbed through her notepad. "Do they all know each other? The chief didn't make it sound like that."

"I guess we'll find out tomorrow when we have a chat with Mr. Rodriguez."

"Knock, knock."

Katie looked up and saw Denise in the doorway holding a beautifully decorated oversized chocolate cupcake, with a lit candle. John stood next to her with a grin on his face.

Everyone broke into a birthday song as Katie waited, embarrassed.

"Happy Birthday, Katie," said Denise. "Make a big wish and blow out the candle."

Playing along, Katie paused and blew out the candle.

"Yay!" everyone chimed together. "The birthday girl!"

"Okay, thank you so much, guys. I appreciate it," said Katie, blushing. She wasn't used to people making a fuss over her and it made her uncomfortable.

"I think you've made my partner blush," said McGaven.

"Alright, alright, get back to work," she said.

"Happy birthday," said John, whistling the tune as he went down the hallway.

"Oh, here you go," said Denise as she handed Katie several photos of Darren Rodriguez pulling the branch across the road.

"Great," said Katie, quickly flipping through them. "Really great. You can see everything. Thank you."

"My pleasure. I'll email you some screen grabs and conversation about the town that you might be interested in."

"Thanks."

"And happy birthday, Katie," said Denise, smiling before she left.

Katie looked down at the chocolate cupcake.

"I want a piece of that," said McGaven.

"Split it?" she asked.

"I'm in."

Katie found a plastic knife and sliced the cupcake.

McGaven took his half and gave Katie a peck on the cheek. "Cheers to you, partner."

"Cheers," she said, laughing.

"Let me see those photos from the road," he said, with cupcake remnants in his mouth.

She handed him the photos to study. "I had an interesting conversation with Dr. Halverson earlier on—the professor at the university I told you about."

"And?" He took another bite, waiting to hear.

"She's heard of people who brand children. It can happen in instances of cults, sex traffickers and extreme religious organizations, but it fits with a certain psychology about ownership and cataloging—either by numbering an individual as an item, or by branding them with something that embodies their beliefs, no matter how twisted."

"So you think this could be part of something bigger? A serial case?"

"I don't know. Right now, it looks like a double homicide, and then another murder made to look like a suicide."

Looking at his laptop he said, "How about I start looking for any other cases with branding involved?"

"You read my mind, Gav."

McGaven's cell phone rang. "McGaven," he said. Turning to Katie he pointed at the phone indicating that it was important. "Yes, Mr. Homestead. We'll be there." He paused. "Thank you."

"What?" said Katie, her interest piqued.

"That was Mr. Brad Homestead, the father of the missing girl we know as Tessa Mayfield. Her name was Brianna Homestead. They are flying in from Austin this afternoon to speak with us immediately."

"Thank goodness."

"They will be staying at the Highland Sierra Hotel and want us to meet them there."

"Excellent. Finally we should get the real story about Tessa."

CHAPTER TWENTY-FOUR

Friday 1745 hours

Katie and McGaven arrived at the Highland Sierra Hotel in Pine Valley early for their meeting with Mr. Brad Homestead, a real estate broker, and Mrs. Jenni Homestead, a stay-at-home mother. They had had three children since the abduction.

The road leading up to the resort was narrow and with the frequent rain storms they wanted to make sure they had plenty of time to get there. Katie drove in silence as McGaven stayed in his own world as well. She had memorized the abducted child report from Austin, Texas and was quite disappointed that it was more like an overview or a basic outline. The investigating officer at the time had since moved to another state and retired. It was clear that they thought it was going to be an open-and-shut case—and finding the child would be easy. No case was ever easy. The report stated that the child was in a stroller and taken from the park. There were no eye-witnesses that could identify who took the child—except that it was a man between the ages of twenty and fifty-five years old.

Realizing that they had made great time, Katie was relieved that soon they would hear first-hand from the Homesteads what had happened that day. It was going to be a difficult interview for her; she didn't have anything positive to report to the parents yet, but at least they now knew what had happened to their daughter.

They passed the valet parking, lined by palm trees, where several impeccably dressed employees waited for the next vehicles to drive up. Katie drove on and parked in the visitors' area.

"Wow, some place," said McGaven.

"Yeah, out of my pay scale."

"Ever been here?"

"Once for a friend's wedding," she said. "It was nice."

"Well, now for a second time," said McGaven, trying to sound upbeat.

Katie suddenly felt conspicuous in this opulent setting, and tugged at her gray suit jacket to smooth the wrinkles from the car ride. She grabbed her notebook and a manila envelope before shutting her door. McGaven was already patiently waiting for her, a big smile on his face.

"What?" she said.

"You are funny, you know that… I can tell that you think you're not dressed well enough for this hotel."

"Yes, well…"

"Detective Scott, you could be in torn jeans and a raggedy T-shirt and still people would be smitten with you and not even notice what you're wearing."

Katie couldn't help but smile, releasing the tension.

After one final straighten of her clothes, they walked into the hotel, the soft noise of a waterfall greeting them. For a moment, Katie found herself thinking about her own wedding.

They approached the front desk where a tall smiling woman greeted them.

"Welcome to Highland Sierra Hotel. How may I be of assistance?"

"Hi," said Katie. "I'm Detective Scott and this is Deputy McGaven. We're here to meet with Mr. and Mrs. Homestead."

The clerk punched in a few keys. "Oh yes. They are here and expecting you… in the Sierra Conference Room."

"Thank you," said Katie. "Where would that be?"

"Take the elevator up to the fourth floor, make a right, and follow the signs until you reach the Sierra Conference." She said everything with a permanent smile fixed on her face, her eyes casually glancing over Katie's badge and gun.

"Great. Thank you," said Katie.

McGaven smiled and nodded as they walked away to the elevator.

Once the doors eased shut and the car began to move, Katie turned to McGaven.

"Remind me again how we end up at nice hotels?"

McGaven chuckled. "And we're brave enough to take an elevator."

Katie remembered her daring climb out of a malfunctioning elevator working another case.

"You okay?" he asked.

"I'm fine. This is a difficult interview, that's all."

The elevator doors opened and they stepped out, taking a right as instructed. The hallways were extra wide and the plush carpet felt spongy beneath their feet.

Katie slowed her pace, reading the gold signs on the door. Finally reaching Sierra, she paused before pushing open one side of the double doors. It revealed a large conference room that had been cleared of tables, except for one, where a striking couple sat waiting.

Katie entered with McGaven behind her.

"Mr. and Mrs. Homestead?" she said.

The man stood up, "Yes."

"Hi, I'm Detective Katie Scott and this is Deputy Sean McGaven."

"Detectives," Mr. Homestead said, and extended his hand. He was tall with an athletic build and dark-blond hair.

"Nice to meet you both," said Katie as she shook their hands.

"Please, take a seat," said Mrs. Homestead. It took Katie by surprise to see her striking resemblance to Tessa—blonde hair with subtle curls around her face and a petite frame.

"Thank you."

"I'm sorry for such a large room, but it was the only place we wouldn't be interrupted," said Mrs. Homestead. Katie couldn't help but notice the two very expensive diamond rings she was wearing, and her perfectly manicured fingernails. She was dressed in a designer pantsuit. It was obvious the couple was affluent and she wondered why they hadn't pursued the case further.

"We're going to the medical examiner's office tomorrow. Our friends have already told us that we shouldn't, but we've decided to see her..." His voice trailed off.

"First," Katie began, "on behalf of the Pine Valley Sheriff's Department, we offer our sincerest condolences for your loss. I don't claim to know how you've dealt with this terrible situation, but I hope that we can help with closure." She cringed inside, thinking of the condition their daughter was in lying on a steel gurney. It would be something that the Homesteads would remember for the rest of their life.

"Thank you, Detective, that means a lot to us," he said, squeezing his wife's hand.

Katie opened the manila envelope and slid out a photograph of Tessa and Megan. It was the last photograph taken of them. "I thought you'd like to see a recent photograph of Tessa—apologies, I mean Brianna."

Mrs. Homestead stared at the photo, immediately sucking in a breath and putting her hand to her mouth. Tears welled in her eyes. "Oh, she was so beautiful." It was obvious she knew which girl was her daughter. She turned the photo to her husband. He remained stoic, but it was clear the deep hurt would never heal.

Katie's stomach tied in knots as she watched a mother begin to grieve over her abducted and murdered daughter. It was heart-wrenching—so Katie concentrated on anything she could glean from the Homesteads that might help the case. Glancing at McGaven she began.

"If you feel up to it, could you tell us what happened that day?"

The mechanical hum of the heating system above their heads turned on as if on cue.

"Yes," said Mrs. Homestead, as she cleared her throat and pulled herself together. "It was almost ten years ago. But I can remember it like it was just this afternoon." She paused. "Brianna was being fussy and taking a walk in the park would always settle her down. It was this time of year, in Austin, and that day was particularly chilly so I bundled her up and we went out."

"Did you notice anything unusual? Like a car, or someone that you'd never seen before?" said Katie.

"Uh, no. It was like any other day. And that day there were even less people we passed or came across." She began to get upset.

"Please, Mrs. Homestead, take your time. I know it was a long time ago, but we just want to try and fill in the pieces."

"Of course. I'm fine."

"Had anyone taken an unusual liking to Brianna?" said McGaven.

"Like?"

"Well, someone that seemed just too eager to talk to her? A bit clingy?"

"No, not that I could think of. And believe me, I've had plenty of time to think about this."

Katie took a breath and gently prodded. "What happened next?"

"We arrived at the park. Like I said, there were less people than normal, but it was still nice to get out. I sat down on a bench with the jogging stroller next to me. Brianna kept fussing with her knitted cap and it fell to the ground a couple of times. And then, a wind picked up and blew the cap. So I got up, looked at Brianna and she was smiling…" She took a moment to compose herself; it was clear she was right back at the park that day. "I walked over to get the cap and rounded another bench with some bushes. When I turned back… she was gone. The stroller was empty. I looked in every direction, calling her name, but there was nothing. I ran one way and saw a young couple, but no Brianna. I ran another way that led out of the park and there was a mother of two little girls—I asked them if they had seen my daughter, or someone with a baby. And they said no…" She began to cry.

Mr. Homestead tried to console her as best he could.

Katie waited patiently and didn't say anything as the distraught woman relived her worst nightmare.

McGaven cleared his throat as he too was moved by the woman's story.

Katie pushed herself to remain impartial, but she watched the couple's interaction with one another and studied Mrs. Homestead as she recounted her story. There was nothing that seemed rehearsed or disingenuous. They were parents and victims of a horrible abduction.

Finally Mr. Homestead spoke. "We spent the entire day and night searching for her with the police. We answered questions from who might have wanted to hurt us, to what types of projects I was working on."

"Were there any leads?" asked Katie. She didn't see anything mentioning it in the Austin PD report.

He shook his head. "There were a few, but they always fell through. You have to understand, this went on for days, then weeks, and then months. We'd get some information about a lead and then found out it was nothing. We went on every news show we could and loaded our information on every missing child website, but nothing."

Katie made a few notes. "I'm sorry but I have to ask this… did Brianna have any birthmarks or scars?" She wanted to ease into the fact that she had been branded because they would see it firsthand soon enough.

"No, she didn't. She was so perfect," she said.

Perfect.

Katie didn't say anything right away.

"What? I know there's something you're not telling us."

"There's no easy way to say this. We found numbers on Brianna's scalp."

"Like a tattoo?"

"The forensic team has determined that they were branded when she was very young."

"Branded?" she said, looking at her husband.

"Are you sure?" he replied.

"Yes, I'm afraid so."

"Why? What were these numbers?"

"Three numbers: 3 7 2," said Katie. "Does 3 7 2 mean anything to you?"

Barely taking a breath, Mr. Homestead said, "No. I don't understand this." It was clear he was disturbed by the news.

"We're trying to run this down, but I wanted to let you know before you saw her."

"Of course, thank you, Detective," he said.

The room felt stuffy and confining, even though it was large enough for a banquet.

Katie focused her questions carefully. "Has anyone ever contacted you that seemed out of place? Or have you noticed anyone after the abduction following you or watching you?"

"No, nothing. We're very careful with our family now—in fact, almost to the point of madness," she said with sincerity.

"We appreciate you meeting with us today. If you think of anything you might have forgotten, please don't hesitate to call me," said Katie, leaving a card on the table.

Katie and McGaven stood up to leave.

"Detective?" said Mrs. Homestead still clutching the photo.

"Yes?"

"Let us know when you catch my baby's killer."

CHAPTER TWENTY-FIVE

Friday 2005 hours

Still drained from her moderate panic attack earlier in the day, Katie headed straight home from the hotel. Chad had dropped by her house to keep Cisco company for the afternoon and would still be there if she got back in time.

As she drove up her driveway, she saw Chad's SUV parked on the right side. Relief flooded through her. Chad and Cisco were her lifeline, and the fact they were waiting for her to come home was all that really mattered at the end of the day.

Katie got out of the Jeep and hurried to the front door, which flung open before she was able to get there. Cisco ran out to greet her, doing circles around her accompanied by whines of joy.

"Hi, boy," she said, petting and ruffling his heavy fur.

Katie looked up to see Chad standing in the doorway, with his mischievous smile and hometown good looks. Even though they had grown up together, spending endless days and summers in each other's company, she knew the first time she saw him when she returned from the army that she would be with him forever.

"Hard day?" he said. "You looked so far away just now."

"Just thinking about stuff." She entered the house and closed the door behind her. "Crazy week."

"I know." He pulled her close and kissed her. "Now, I couldn't very well do that with both our departments looking on."

"Not very professional," she laughed, returning his lingering kiss.

"Oh, the sheriff came by and left you something."

Katie shed her jacket and went to the counter. "He couldn't stay?"

"No, he said something about a Homeowners' Association meeting at the golf course."

"Of course."

There was a small box on the counter with a card. Katie read her uncle's neat print.

Happy Birthday, Katie,

You've been the sweetest addition to my life as my niece. I loved your parents more than you know, but I cannot imagine my life without you. Enjoy your birthday and every day to follow with love, courage, and happiness.

With love always,
Uncle Wayne

"Oh," she managed to say, as her eyes welled up. Since she lost her parents, her uncle and aunt had been her only family. The tragic murder of her aunt earlier that year had made her realize even more how fragile life was, and her uncle's love meant more than he would ever know.

"You okay?" he said.

"Yeah, everyone sees him as the tough sheriff, but he's still my uncle." She picked up the box and opened it, gasping in surprise. Inside was the gold necklace that her aunt had always worn—but her uncle had added a German shepherd charm.

"Nice."

"He's so thoughtful." Katie put the necklace on and took a moment to remember her aunt.

"Okay," said Chad and he clapped his hands. He went into the kitchen dramatically, where there was a plate covered with a silver lid. "Why, what do we have here?"

"What are you doing?" she said, smiling at his silly performance.

"I was thinking that we could go out to dinner, but that's so boring and predictable. So… I decided to surprise you with your favorite meal of all time."

"My favorite meal?"

"Yes," he said and put the dish down in front of her. "I remember this well. You told me it was your favorite." He dramatically removed the cover to reveal two peanut butter and banana sandwiches with corn chips. "Tada!"

"PB and banana." She laughed. "I told you that was my favorite meal when I was *thirteen*."

"And now?"

"Okay, I still love it." She grabbed half a sandwich and began eating. "That's still so good. I haven't had one of these in a long time."

Chad went into the kitchen to open a bottle of wine.

"I'm going to change, is that okay?" She went to her bedroom with Cisco in tow. The dog seemed more clingy than usual.

"As long as you're still going to be Katie when you get back," he called, accompanied by the pop of a cork.

Katie quickly changed from her work suit into comfortable sweats and hoodie. She found some thick socks and was about to leave the room when she stopped for a moment to look at a photograph of her parents.

"I love you, Mom, Dad," she whispered. "Let's go, Cisco." She flipped off the light.

Katie returned to the kitchen but Chad wasn't there. She saw the sliding door was open and could see him sitting on the swing on the deck, even though it was chilly.

She grabbed a blanket off the couch, wrapped it around her and joined him.

Cisco wasn't going to be left out and ran outside doing his rounds before quietly taking position on the deck near Katie.

It was cool but being outside was worth it, the best relaxation possible. She snuggled up against Chad as they drank wine and enjoyed the evening.

"You haven't asked me what I got you for your birthday," he said.

"Okay, what did you get me for my birthday?" She played along but closed her eyes and listened to the sounds of the evening.

"Katie?"

"Yes?" She snuggled against him closer.

Chad put his hand under her chin and kissed her. "I have something for you, but you don't have to accept it."

"What do you mean? Like, I can take it back?"

"Katie…"

She opened her eyes and looked at him. His face was serious, which made her sit up. "What's wrong?"

"Nothing is wrong. I love you, Katie Scott. Everything about you. I know you've been fighting your experiences from the battlefield, but I love you. I've come to the conclusion that I will always love you, no matter what."

Katie couldn't say anything, she just stared at him.

"That's why… if you'll have me… I want you to be my wife," he said, pulling out a ring and holding it up to her. "Katie, will you marry me?"

Katie sucked in a breath. She always knew it might happen, but she wasn't prepared for it. She had thought about it—more nights than she cared to admit. Pushing out all the noise in her head, she whispered, "Yes, I'll marry you."

He put the sparkling solitaire diamond ring on her finger. "I love you," he said.

"I love you too," she said and kissed him.

CHAPTER TWENTY-SIX

Saturday 0830 hours

Katie took the turns on her familiar back road faster than she should on her way to work—she knew every curve of the road and could probably drive it blindfolded. A good night of sleep had given her the energy she needed to find Tessa and Megan's killer—nothing was going to stop her, even if she had to stay in Rock Creek until she did.

Her life had taken a positive turn for once. She was overcoming her anxiety, and the love of her life wanted to spend the rest of his life with her. The buzz flooded through her veins and lit a fire inside her to get justice for those two little girls who would never grow up and fall in love.

Her cell phone rang and she flicked on the hands-free setting.

"Scott," she said.

"Are you on your way?" said McGaven, his voice anxious.

"Yep, about ten minutes out."

"You got your wish."

Katie waited for the news.

"They're bringing in Darren Rodriguez as we speak. And it appears that he also has a warrant in Sequoia County for assault in a bar fight. Aren't we the lucky ones?"

"Yes!"

"They'll bring him up from holding and you'll be interviewing him in about an hour. We've impounded his truck at the police garage. John will be all over it."

"Great news. Thanks, Gav. See you in a few minutes."

Katie and McGaven stood in the general area of the detective division waiting for the correctional officers to bring up Rodriguez. Katie gripped the file folder and notepad in her hand as she felt her jaw constrict. She had a lot riding on this interview and she needed the interrogation to go her way.

"You okay?" he whispered.

"Yeah, why?"

He shrugged.

Crap.

Katie realized that if McGaven had noticed her jitters and stress, then Rodriguez would too. She loosened up her shoulders and neck, breathing deep, and readied herself. This was her moment to shine and to move the investigation forward.

A correctional officer with "Bush" printed on his ID tag motioned for Katie to go into the first interview room. It was the largest room, and had the best facilities to restrain detainees with potential for violence. She thought it odd for Rodriguez, so she stopped and said to the officer, "Is there a problem with him?"

"He's clever. Tried to escape twice. Be on your guard when you interview him. If you need anything, holler."

She nodded and moved toward the door. The correctional officer stood at attention outside and waited.

Katie stepped into the room as McGaven shut the door behind them. She had never used this room before, but it had built-in cameras and microphones. The atmosphere upped her angst, but at the same time, she felt energized and wanted to get to work.

Darren Jonathan Rodriguez, thirty-nine years old, with a mixed bag of offenses and a live warrant, sat at the table in the traditional California orange jumpsuit, head down, wrists shackled and attached to metal loops. His jet-black hair, greasy and over-long, hung down around his face. He clenched his hands into fists and then released them on an endless loop.

McGaven slowly pulled out the metal chair, the legs screeching a horrible high-pitch scream. He paused, and then sat down staring at Rodriguez without saying a word.

Katie glanced to the left where there was a two-way mirror and saw her reflection.

"Mr. Rodriguez," she began.

There was no movement or response from him. He didn't raise his head or look at her.

Katie raised her file and notepad and slammed it down on the table to get his attention.

Rodriguez slowly lifted his head. His dark brown eyes, almost black, stared right through her. He was in desperate need of a shave.

"Why are we here, Mr. Rodriguez?" she said.

He finally spoke. "You tell me."

"Oh, but what fun would that be? I want to hear what you have to say." She remained standing so that he had to look up to talk to her.

"How long have you lived in Rock Creek?" she continued.

"A while."

"Eight, nine years?"

"Something like that."

"I like Sissy," she said, letting him know they had been in his apartment.

He looked away.

Got him.

"She talked a lot about you—even though you annoyed her, she liked you. You owe her two hundred bucks."

"I told her I would send it in a couple of weeks."

"Did you tell her where you were going?"

"No."

"Is that because you didn't know where you are headed? Or were you waiting for your orders?"

He didn't answer.

"Well, let's just get to the point, shall we? How about the easy stuff first?"

Katie removed the eight by ten photos of him dragging the tree across the road and dropped them one by one on the table in front of him. "Can you explain these?"

"Grainy. Not very flattering."

"You know, Mr. Rodriguez, how things are going to go depends mainly on you—and your cooperation. You understand me?"

He let out a breath. "What do you want me to say?"

"The truth is always a good place to start."

He looked at the photos.

"Why did you block the road with the tree branch?"

He shrugged.

"Why did you carve 3 7 2 on that tree?"

He remained quiet.

"Look!" said Katie as she slammed her fists on the table. Both Rodriguez and McGaven startled. "Did someone tell you to carve 3 7 2 into that tree?" She spat out the words.

Rodriguez leaned back in his chair. "I always do what I'm told."

"Who ordered you?"

"I always do what I'm told… *always.*"

Katie walked around and stood close to him. She leaned on the table. "Is it Mayfield? We're going to find out anyway. You might as well tell us now."

His demeanor changed from tough guy in the slammer to victim in less than a minute. But Katie remembered what Dr. Halverson told her about partial psychopaths and their emotions.

"Tell me," she said.

He nodded.

"Does that mean Whitney Mayfield told you to carve the numbers and block the road?"

"Yes," he said quietly.

"Why?"

"Because… so you would see it."

"You mean me and my partner?"

"Yes."

"Why?"

"He does things. I don't know why he does it—just stuff."

Katie felt a text buzz on her phone. She quickly glanced at the message—it was from John.

Mrs. Mayfield's gun has Darren Rodriguez's fingerprints all over it. Thought you needed to know.

"Well, Mr. Rodriguez, you certainly have some explaining to do."

"What?" he said. It was the first time he looked scared.

"Did you kill Robin Mayfield?"

"What? She's dead? I didn't kill her or anyone else." He kept Katie's gaze.

"That's not what forensics says. Your fingerprints are all over the gun that shot her in the head."

"What gun? I didn't know she was even dead. When?" He tried to stand up.

"Sit down," said McGaven.

"Did you kill her daughters, Tessa and Megan?" she said.

"What? No!"

"Too messy to use a gun. So you strangled Tessa and bashed Megan in the head, right?"

"No. I would never kill anyone, especially little girls." He put his head down.

"Is that what Mayfield told you to do?"

"No, he never told me to kill anyone. Ever!"

"Why were your prints found on the gun at Robin Mayfield's crime scene?"

"I..." he said, shaking his head.

"Killing women and little girls. It's not looking good for you."

He began to cry. It was unclear if it was sincere, but it appeared to be.

"Look," said Katie. "If you didn't kill Robin Mayfield, who did?"

"I don't know."

"Who killed Tessa and Megan?"

"I don't know."

"I think you do."

"What's my motive? I didn't kill anyone."

"You said you do what Whitney Mayfield says."

"Yeah, well. You don't know him. I've known him a long time and you don't argue with him."

Katie sat down in a chair across from Rodriguez and pulled up closer. "Tell me."

"He's actually a nice guy... like any other guy, but when he sets his mind to something... That's it."

"Like what?"

"It's when he goes into this... strange state... he has a thing with numbers... he doesn't think like you and me."

"Explain it to me." Katie softened her approach and he seemed to respond. She had guessed from his relationship with Sissy, and the fact that he ran home to his mom, that this might work.

"I don't know for sure. It's like he's a cult, or something."

"What cult does he belong to?"

"No, *he's* the cult."

"What does 3 7 2 mean?"

"I'm not sure. He has a weird thing about numbers. Like they're telling him the future, or what he needs to do."

Katie glanced at McGaven who kept his stare on Rodriguez. She picked up her notebook and began to read, "… *For they shall soon be cut down like the grass, and wither as the green herb…*"

"Where did you get that?" He changed. Tensed. Terror flashed across his eyes.

"A guess."

"He's here, isn't he?"

"What are you talking about?"

"You've been talking to him."

"Calm down, Mr. Rodriguez."

"He's here. I know he's here." He slowly turned to the mirrored glass. "I know he's here watching." He began talking to the glass. "I did everything you ever asked me to do. *Everything.* Please."

Katie knew she was losing his focus. "Mr. Rodriguez, who killed Robin and the girls?"

He shook his head.

"Please, it will help you if you cooperate with us. Who killed Robin, and Tessa and Megan?"

He began writhing in his chair and making gurgling noises of distress.

"Who killed them? Was it Whitney Mayfield?"

"I can't talk to you."

"Who. Killed. Them?"

He turned his head slowly, almost mechanically, looking up at her. "You don't understand. You have *no* idea what you're up against."

"Try me," she pushed.

"I didn't kill anyone. I didn't kill anyone. I didn't kill *anyone…*"

"Mr. Rodriguez, you're going to be charged with the murder of Robin Mayfield if you don't start explaining things."

He slammed his hands down. "I didn't do it! But I did everything he asked me to do!"

Katie realized that she wasn't going to get anything more from him.

"Where is Whitney Mayfield?"

"I wouldn't know."

"Meaning?"

"He comes and goes as he pleases, does anything he wants. Sometimes, he would show up at my apartment looking different."

"Different how?"

"Shorter hair, clean-shaven, sometimes with a beard."

"Where does he work?"

"Don't know. Don't ask. He seems to have money."

"You've known him all these years and you don't know where he works?"

"He said he did some odd jobs, like me. And that's all I know." He suddenly turned again to the mirror window and said, "See, I did good. *Really* good."

Katie turned to McGaven, making a gesture to go outside. They both stepped out the door, shutting it quietly. They could hear Mr. Rodriguez saying he could hear them talking to Whitney.

"He needs to be evaluated," said Katie.

"I agree. They will probably put him on a seventy-two-hour watch."

"Do you think it's possible he's faking it?" she asked.

"Can't make that call, but anything's possible with this case."

Katie motioned to the correctional officer. "You can take him back."

He nodded and went into the interrogation room.

Katie and McGaven retrieved their guns from the small vault and went out the back door, descending the metal stairs. They continued down the secured parking way, passing the prisoner transport van, and walked around the corner to get to the police vehicle compound.

"I want to have a look at his truck," said Katie.

"I'm curious too."

They made towards the compound but the crack of two gunshots stopped them dead in their tracks. Without hesitation, Katie and McGaven turned and sprinted back to the secured area with their guns drawn.

CHAPTER TWENTY-SEVEN

Saturday 1115 hours

Katie made it to the corner of the building first, with her gun directed out front. Back pressed against the wall, she peered around the corner seeing the scene from behind. At the back of the prisoner van, Rodriguez had the correctional officer held with a gun pressed against his head, and the officer driving the van was lying on the ground bleeding. No one saw her. She could only see their backs.

Katie pulled back and whispered to McGaven. "Rodriguez shot one of the correctional officers and has the other at gunpoint."

Voices boomed, telling Rodriguez to put the gun down and that he was surrounded.

Looking again, she saw two detectives and a deputy coming down the stairs with their guns aimed at Rodriguez, yelling, "Drop your weapon now!"

"No!" yelled Rodriguez. "I'll only talk to her—that woman detective. Get her! I'll only talk to her!"

Katie froze. She was right in the middle of a meltdown and there was already one officer down. She made ready.

"No," said McGaven. "It's too dangerous. There will be twenty officers in another minute."

"I'm not going to let another officer get hurt... or killed. We don't know how seriously that officer is injured. He needs help *now*. I seem to be the only one that can disarm this." She knew what she had to do.

Katie calmed her nerves as much as she could, then put her Glock in the waistband of the back of her pants and boldly walked around the corner. "Darren," she said, using his first name to keep things personal.

Immediately he backed up, turning slightly to the left of where she approached with her hands in the air. "I'm unarmed."

"Make them put their guns down," he said.

"I can't do that. You just shot a guard and you've got a gun to another guard's head."

"They will shoot me."

"Not if you do what I say," she said, trying to keep her voice from trembling.

More officers came out and she saw the sheriff with them.

"Let's just stay calm. Darren and I are going to have a chat. Okay?" She glanced around at everyone. "*Okay?*"

The officers, including the sheriff, remained in position. She stepped slightly to the side and assessed the injured officer who was on the ground leaning against the van. His shoulder and leg were bleeding heavily.

"Darren, what did you want to say? I'm here."

Sirens sounded as the fire department and ambulance arrived, along with any patrolling deputies. They were all heading to the department. It would soon turn into a circus and Katie had to do something before she had no control over the situation anymore.

"What's that?" he said.

"Just standard procedure. The fire department always gets dispatched when there's a shooting."

"Look. I'm telling you the truth. I didn't kill anyone."

"I believe you, Darren," she said, trying to sound sincere. "But this isn't the way to get our attention. Let Officer Bush go, okay?"

"I can't do that."

"Give us something, okay?"

"I'm begging you," he said. "I didn't kill anyone—ever." He tightened the grip on his hostage. "I've done bad things, but not murder. You understand? Please believe me."

"Okay, Darren, I understand." Katie realized that she was in way over her head—she wasn't trained or equipped to handle this type of situation. "Let's go back inside and talk."

"No. He'll find me."

"Who?"

"You know him. You know *all* about him. You can reach out and touch him."

Katie hesitated.

"He's not who he says he is…"

She looked at the wounded officer. "Let's go inside where we can talk away from everyone."

"I can't do that," he said slowly. "I'm sorry, Detective."

As if in slow motion, he turned the gun on himself and pressed it against the side of his head, allowing his hostage to break free. Then he pulled the trigger. Darren Rodriguez crumpled to the ground as blood poured from his head. He was dead before he hit the pavement.

"Nooo!" screamed Katie as a stampede of officers ran to him. But it was too late, the image was forever burned in her mind. She couldn't stop it—she couldn't save him.

Snapping back into the moment, she ran to the wounded officer. "Stay awake, okay?" She assessed his condition and saw that a vast amount of blood was coming from his leg. It was something she had been through many times on the battlefield. He was trying to stop it with both hands without much luck. She took her belt off and secured a tourniquet tightly, causing him to groan. "Don't move, okay? The paramedics are close."

She could barely hear him say, "Don't leave."

"I'm going to wait right here until they arrive, okay?"

"In case I don't…"

"Don't say anything," she said, remembering losing some friends and how she had sat with them when they died. Her arms and legs tingled. Her mouth went dry. She felt removed from the situation even though there was shouting, moving about, and the sounds of a fire truck gunning its engine. The distinct smell of expelled gunfire infused everything around her—at least in her mind. She kept seeing Rodriguez pressing the gun against his temple and pulling the trigger.

Not now.

"In case I don't make it, Rodriguez said that…"

"What?" she whispered.

"He kept saying that you can reach out and touch him…"

She stared at him and relived Rodriguez saying the same thing to her.

McGaven came to her aid. "Katie?" He looked worried.

"I'm fine," she snapped back, pushing past him, away from the scene to the back of the building to breathe.

The sheriff ordered everyone to move out of the way so that the paramedics could make their way to the transport van, followed by two firefighters from the main engine.

"Katie!" Chad yelled through the pandemonium.

The deputies let him through. He ran up to her, seeing blood on her blouse and pants.

"I'm okay," she whispered, holding back what was left of her emotions. "I'm not hurt."

"When I heard there was a shooting here from dispatch—my heart stopped. I don't ever want to feel like that again." He held her tight.

"I couldn't save him."

Chad just listened, and didn't tell her that everything was okay when it wasn't. He was there for her—her rock—and that was all that mattered.

Sheriff Scott ran over to her through the chaos.

"Detective, are you okay? You don't need any medical atten-tion?" He sounded professional and neutral, when Katie knew he was clearly upset by the entire incident. "Maybe it would be best if you go to the hospital and have the doctors check you out?"

"I'm fine. I just need to go back to my office. That's where I'll be if anyone needs to talk to me. I'll write my report and have it on your desk by the end of the day," she said.

"That can wait," said the sheriff.

"Can it?" she said with skepticism. "We're trying to solve a murder—three murders."

The sheriff looked at her and didn't reply.

Turning to Chad, she said, "I'm glad you're here. I'll call you in a little while, okay?"

"Okay. You sure?"

"Yeah, I'm sure." Katie forced a tiny smile to keep her com-posure, still walking away around the entire area, and decided to enter the administration building from the other side, staying away from the turmoil.

What was Darren Rodriguez trying to tell her?

You know all about him. You can reach out and touch him.

CHAPTER TWENTY-EIGHT
Saturday 1300 hours

Katie walked back to her office by way of the forensic division. It was mostly dark on the bottom floor, except for the main hallway which was always dimly lit. John and his technicians were out, making it a much-needed retreat for her. Her mind still raced and her legs were weak, but she moved forward as she always did, always trekking on through whatever life threw at her.

She was glad that she didn't run into John—he must have been at the auto impound, thrust into the commotion of the shooting.

Turning the knob and pushing the door open, she took in a deep breath and let it out slowly, wanting to stay in the darkness a little longer to let everything settle inside her.

Eventually, she felt brave enough to switch on the light. One of the bulbs flickered for a moment, but then ignited for another day. Katie stared at the investigation board covered with lists of what they knew and didn't know, photos of suspects and victims, and various maps.

You know all about him. You can reach out and touch him.

She couldn't get Darren Rodriguez's voice out of her head. What did he mean by that? Was he trying to let her know that the killer was someone she had already met? The killer was close by? Rodriguez clearly had some psychological issues, but he seemed lucid in the parking lot and like he knew exactly what was going on. He knew all too well that he would soon become lost in the system and he wanted to make sure that Katie knew he was innocent. But was he?

Katie couldn't ignore it, but was also smart enough not to pin her whole investigation on it. She decided to add his words to the list on the board and see where it all fit together.

Sitting down at her desk, she felt the weight of the world pressing down on her shoulders. There she stayed for ten minutes, her hands on her forehead, resting her eyes, trying to relax. And suddenly it came to her: if Megan was number 372 of a group that branded children for whatever reason, there had to be other cases. Katie opened her laptop and began to sift through the police database with keywords and locations for child murders and branding or tattoos. She had begun a search as soon as they discovered the branding, but didn't have much luck. Now she was determined to find out more information.

As she waited for some of her searches to complete, she noticed a neat stack of papers clamped together with a heavy black fastener. Denise must have left these for her to read through. It was a list of people she had gathered from the neighborhood app for Rock Creek. She had printed out conversations, posts, maps and anything she thought might be useful to Katie's search. There were also some photos of the townspeople. Katie began to read through it all, amazed at what people divulged to strangers in an open forum—mostly gossip about who was sleeping with whom, and complaints about what horrible color someone had painted their house.

The door opened and McGaven stepped inside, a look of relief washing across his face.

"It's okay, Gav, I'm not so delicate that I'm going to break any time soon."

"I didn't think that."

"Really, I'm okay. It wasn't the way I imagined spending my day, but I'm okay."

McGaven sat down. "It never is."

Her computer had stopped searching and delivered a list of potentially linked cases with a ping.

"What are you working on?" he asked, as he looked at the newest statements written on the board. "*You know all about him. You can reach out and touch him…* I don't remember Rodriguez saying that."

"The officer told me that he said that on the transport, and Rodriguez said it to me just before he killed himself."

"Do you think he was playing some sick game?"

"I don't know for sure, but I think he was telling the truth. Just like I think he was definitely afraid of Whitney Mayfield." Katie read over the lists of cases on her screen of information that wasn't available before. "Check this out. There was a case of a young girl, eight, Darla Denton, who was found murdered, strangled, in Rock Creek about eight years ago. And she had numbers branded on her scalp."

"Not the same numbers."

"It doesn't say. But we didn't have this information before—why?"

"Why didn't Chief Osborne tell us about this case? Why wasn't it initially entered into the database?" he said.

"And over in Huntington County, there were two girls, Ella Dixon and Mary Steinberg, around the same time, about seven years ago. Both strangled and both numbered." Katie was astonished. What else didn't they know?

"This is quite unbelievable and a huge discovery," he said. "Anything else?"

"No, that's all could find. I don't quite have your research skills. Request copies of those cases ASAP. And any others you find."

"I'll search for similar cases in surrounding counties." He immediately got to work.

"And while you're at it, this scavenger hunt to find Whitney Mayfield is driving me nuts. All we have are blurry photos and vague descriptions of him. We need current photos."

"On it. I know what I'm going to be doing the next few hours."

"Gav," she said.

"I was going to say why do I get stuck doing all this computer stuff—but I realized I love digging for more information..."

"Gav."

"...You never really know what you're going to find."

"Gav, you can't ignore me."

He turned his attention away from the computer and looked directly at his partner.

"Thanks." Katie didn't need to explain, she knew that he would understand.

He smiled and went back to work.

McGaven worked for almost two hours digging for information, while Katie made notes about exactly what transpired before the shooting while it was fresh in her mind—so that she could easily write a report before leaving for the day.

"I searched everywhere and for some reason I couldn't get a recent driver's license photo of Whitney Allen Mayfield, but here's one from about ten years ago," said McGaven.

Katie moved closer. Mayfield's license showed him to have shoulder-length curly light brown hair, a scruffy beard, and he was wearing glasses.

"Is it me, or does it look like he's wearing a disguise?" she said, closely inspecting the photo.

"You're right. Something seems strange now that you say that."

Katie pulled the photocopy of Tessa's small album over and pulled out the image of Robin and Whitney Mayfield. "It's difficult to tell if it's even the same guy."

"What was it that Rodriguez said about Whitney's hair and clothes?" said McGaven.

"That he would show up at his apartment looking different. He would change his hair length or clothes."

"Why would someone do that?"

"To fool people. To blend into a crowd," she said. "It's something criminals might do so that they aren't identified easily." She looked at the investigation board studying the killer's MO: *Overkill—level of violence exceeded what was necessary to do the murder; Knew or frequented the area; Someone the girls knew; Closest friend did dirty deeds for him; Many people in town were scared of him.*

"Why are you so quiet?" he asked.

"We're looking at this all wrong. Do you realize that everything reverts back to Rock Creek?" She stood up and went to the board. "Everything. The girls' abduction. Mayfield's home. Mayfield's previous home. Robin Mayfield's staged suicide. The addition of Tessa's photo album to the evidence. Whitney Mayfield's best friend Darren Rodriguez. The connection with the numbers 3 7 2. Another girl, Darla Denton, found murdered eight years previous. Everything points to Rock Creek."

"Except the Mayfield girls weren't found there."

"Point taken, but there has to be some significance to that area. I believe that Mayfield isn't far from Rock Creek and the crime scene area for any length of time. He seems to always come back. Chief Osborne has some serious explaining to do."

You know all about him. You can reach out and touch him.

CHAPTER TWENTY-NINE

Sunday 1030 hours

After Katie had gone to the sheriff's department that morning to catch up on paperwork and sift through all the case correspondence and reports, she was ordered by the sheriff to go home and rest—the usual protocol whenever there was an officer involved in a shooting. She tried to resist, but as she wasn't going to sway him she opted to take the paperwork home with her. Grabbing a box, she loaded up everything that wasn't nailed down and took a photo of her working investigation board as backup.

When she arrived home, Cisco was extra excitable and wouldn't calm down. He spun and whined and barked. Katie felt bad because she hadn't been spending any time with the dog. Like any soldier who had seen combat, Cisco needed to occupy his time in a productive manner; keeping him busy and exercised was essential.

Katie quickly changed into her running clothes and loaded Cisco, bursting with joy, into the Jeep. She drove to one of their favorite running spots. It was fairly secluded and he loved to run along the canyon trail.

While she stretched, Katie realized that she hadn't been on a run in a while and it would help to re-energize her—clear her head of what had happened the day before. She needed to refocus her mind on the case, get a fresher perspective.

A gray oversize pick-up truck entered the parking area and did a slow circle, coming close to the Jeep and pulling to a stop. Katie couldn't identify the driver due to the heavily tinted windows. There were no license plates on the vehicle, just a paper flapping on the back identifying the car lot it had been purchased from. She hadn't noticed the truck on her drive over to the park. Maybe it was her overactive imagination, but she preferred to stay on the cautious side. She looked down at the small, loaded .22 pistol she always carried in an ankle holster when she ran. It was a bit uncomfortable, but after all this time she had become accustomed to it.

"Cisco, here," she said, and he obediently trotted over. Making sure he was close, she readied for their run.

The clouds were moving fast, making the late morning darker than usual. A few rolls of thunder rumbled in the distance, but there wasn't any rain predicted. Katie took off down a narrow trail and then began to slowly climb in altitude along the canyon. She loved this run. The views were better than anywhere else in the county and she was able to feel the autonomy rise in her soul with every step. All her stress melted away into her rhythmic breathing, the clean air, and the lushness of the forest around her.

Cisco ran from her immediate view. She looked back when she heard him barking behind her to see his tail circling, tongue hanging out, and a look of pure joy on this face. His shiny black coat still glistened even though the sun wasn't shining.

Katie laughed. "You're a funny boy. Let's go."

After about twenty-five minutes, the dog following her at a fast trot, Katie came to a lookout area that had been well travelled. The soil was beat down and the surrounding foliage was pushed back. There was a camera affixed to one of the pine trees about twenty feet up. She had never noticed it before, but realized it must offer a wonderful panoramic live view of the valley for Internet viewing.

A thought occurred to her. There were increasing numbers of cameras installed, not only in the cities, but in the rural areas as well, especially well-travelled areas like this one.

It was clear that Rock Creek wasn't at the forefront of up-to-date technology, but she wondered if there were cameras scattered around town, the streets, and especially anywhere the children played—like the video camera they had discovered at the swing by the creek, which they hadn't heard on back yet. They would have all been checked when the girls went missing, but something told her that Whitney Mayfield might be the kind of killer who would return to the scene of the crime. He certainly seemed to circle Rock Creek like a vulture. If he often changed his appearance, as Rodriguez had said, he could be around Rock Creek even now.

The run had done her good. Her head was clear. Her muscles relaxed. Most importantly, Cisco was happy and exercised. Cooling down with a brisk walk for the last few miles, she headed back to the Jeep. About five car lengths away, the gray truck was idling. It was parked with the front facing her direction. Katie's skin pricked. Something wasn't right, whoever was in the truck was waiting for her and she was going to have to tackle this problem head on— even if it was just as innocent as kids making out, or someone looking for directions.

"Hey!" she said, walking toward the truck.

Cisco started barking incessantly.

Katie ordered the dog to stay down next to the Jeep. "Cisco, *platz* and then *bleib*."

She turned back to the truck. "Who are you?"

The truck revved its engine, readying to lurch at her.

Moving closer, she repeated, "Who are you? Why are you following me?"

The truck pitched forward about a foot. Then again, the engine revving even higher.

Katie kept her wits and was ready to dive to the side. She glanced behind her, making sure Cisco was in a safe place.

It was a matter of seconds…

The truck lurched forward and Katie sidestepped with ease as the gray vehicle continued to drive a circle around her.

"Who are you? You coward!" she yelled.

Finally, the truck exited the parking area leaving a huge cloud of dust behind it.

Katie ran to her Jeep and Cisco, and they jumped in ready to give chase. But the truck was nowhere in sight. It had vanished. There were two ways to leave the area and she didn't see which direction it had raced away.

Back at home, Katie changed into something comfortable and warm, glancing at the diamond on her finger—taking a deep breath and realizing everything was going to change for the better. Her life with Chad felt worlds away on days like these. The incident with the truck at the park had rattled her, but she needed to let it go and focus on the case.

When Cisco was sleeping peacefully, Katie took the opportunity to clear her coffee table and pull up another small table beside it. Then she covered both surfaces with pages of notes and pictures that made up her investigation.

Dr. Dean had sent over a preliminary autopsy report for Robin Mayfield, which indicated that cause of death, as Katie already knew, was from a gunshot wound to the head. The burning question was, was it self-inflicted? But Darren Rodriguez's fingerprints were on the gun—and when forensics tested Mrs. Mayfield's hands for gunshot residue, they got a negative result.

Katie grabbed a blanket and wrapped it around herself while she drank her second cup of hot tea. Looking at all the evidence, she whispered, "Speak to me."

Why would the killer leave the gun at the scene? It seemed too contrived—convenient.

Who put the photo album into the gathered evidence? Why?

Katie looked at a copy of the suicide note again—still waiting for the official handwriting results.

I'm sorry for what I'm about to do. But I couldn't save the fragile ones. The ones that needed protection and saving. I cannot live with myself for not keeping the girls out of harm's way. I cannot live a lie. The truth will come out. Please don't feel sorry for me, and don't be sad.

All my love, Robin.

To Katie, on the surface, it seemed like something that Mrs. Mayfield would say. But the more she looked at the note, several words jumped out at her.

Sorry

Fragile ones

Cannot live

Don't be sad

"Wait a minute," said Katie. She quickly shuffled through paperwork until she came to the copy of the photo album where Mrs. Mayfield identified the names of the people in the photographs. "Here we are…" The writing samples from the suicide note and the album photos weren't the same; she didn't need a handwriting expert to tell her that. They were clearly different—appearing to come from the hand of two different people. It bothered her. She looked closer at the letters and possible meanings behind them. The note was written in a stilted manner, with leaning letters trying to make each loop perfect. The printed names on the photos were perfectly formed and straight up in all capital letters.

Katie let out a breath. "If Robin Mayfield wrote on the photos, who wrote the note? Or if she wrote the note, who wrote on the photos?" She was assuming that Robin had written on the photos because that's what Katie had asked her to do—but what if it was someone else? The same person who slipped the album into evidence. And why would Robin write a suicide note if she didn't kill herself?

Katie stood up suddenly, dropping the blanket and pacing back and forth. "Because it's not a suicide note. We assumed that, because she was dead, but it was a note for something she was *about* to do. And that's what she was apologizing for." It helped her sometimes to speak out loud, even when no one was around.

Cisco chuffed in his sleep.

What was Robin going to do? What was she going to tell? Did she know who killed her girls?

Katie's phone alerted her to a text coming in: *You better be resting. That's an order.*

She laughed. Her uncle was hovering over her, even from afar.

She sent him a text: *In my PJs on the couch with Cisco.*

A smiley face came back.

Resting her hand on the necklace her uncle had given her she gently pulled it side to side, thinking about the marks on Tessa's neck from her pendant chain.

Where was her necklace?

Katie's brain was spinning and her vision was beginning to blur. She needed a break. Leaning back against the couch, she looked into the box of things she had grabbed from her desk and saw that she had thrown in the DVDs found at Darren Rodriguez's apartment. As she looked them over, she saw there was some writing on one of the DVD covers. It was small, almost missable and written in pencil, but it said, *For my bud, you'll get there*, with a strange squiggly character after the sentiment.

They were all DVDs made by Wild Oats Productions. Someone had given Rodriguez these DVDs and, according to Sissy, he watched them all the time. It was strange for someone to have a full collection of this production company's work, but it was the kind of thing that someone working there might do.

Did Rodriguez know someone on the film crew?

Katie snatched up her cell phone searching for previous numbers that had called her. She found the one she was looking for and pressed it. It rang. She wasn't sure what she was going to say.

"Hello."

"Is this Matt?" she said.

"Yeah, this is Matt Gardner."

"This is Detective Katie Scott."

There was a pause.

Finally, "What can I do for you, Detective?"

"I'm working the homicide case of those two little girls we found, and some of your DVD documentaries turned up in a search of a suspect in our investigation."

He didn't respond.

"There's a handwritten note on one of them and I was wondering if you guys ever send out sets of signed DVDs to fans or in competitions. Anything like that."

It was a few beats before he answered. "Yeah, we have before, but we all usually sign just the first one."

"Oh, I see."

"What's your interest?" he said sternly.

Katie was surprised that the director was gruff and unfriendly to her. It was possible that she had caught him at a bad time, but they had gotten on well on the trip to Silo—even in the storm. "It was kind of a coincidence that a local suspect in my investigation had a whole set of your DVDs."

"I don't see it that way."

"Well, we're all entitled to our opinions," she said. "So how's your scouting going?" She decided to change the tone.

"Fair."

"Any other areas you have questions about in Sequoia County?"

"Let's see," he said, and she could hear paper rustling in the background. "We're checking out Pine Valley, Cedar Run, and Rock Creek next week."

"I'm sorry, did you say Rock Creek?"

"Yeah, Butch said that there is supposed to be a haunted cemetery and one of the oldest buildings in the entire county there, that's worth checking out."

"Sounds great," she said. "Good luck. Let me know if you need any questions answered about those areas."

"Will do," he said and the connection went dead.

CHAPTER THIRTY
Monday 0730 hours

Katie stared at the large computer screen as the software compared the bullet that killed Robin Mayfield and the gun left at the scene side by side. The unique striations, or scratches, left behind on the bullet were similar, not 100 percent, to the rifling inside the barrel of the gun.

"It looks like a match," she said.

John turned to her. "Now remember, it's never perfect. I would say, in my opinion and in court, that they are a match by eighty-five percent."

"Eighty-five percent? More like ninety-five."

"That's your opinion," he said and smiled.

Katie remained solemn.

"What's wrong?"

"It's all very well that we have the bullet and the gun that killed Robin Mayfield, and only Darren Rodriguez's fingerprints on it, but he killed himself in our parking lot."

"That would be case closed?"

"No, I'm afraid not."

"I see."

"Was there anything in Robin's system?"

"All the toxicology reports came back negative," he said.

"Her clothes were so neat, positioned perfectly like dressing a mannequin," she said, more to herself. "Who would do that after they killed someone?"

"Family member, close friend, boyfriend."

"You're right, but…"

"You brought to my attention the writing on the photos and the writing in the note," he said. Moving the computer mouse, he pulled up more images. "You're correct. These were not written by the same hand." He looked at Katie's reaction. "I could consult a handwriting expert."

"No, that's only necessary if and when we go to court."

"Oh," he said. "Officer Davenport is going to be just fine, by the way. He's recovering at home. Thought you'd like to know that."

"That's great news, thank you."

"He also said thank you to you for being there for him."

Katie nodded. "It was like a battlefield out there."

John became somber and nodded in agreement. "Yes, it was."

Katie had just finished explaining her thoughts to McGaven about the letter not being a suicide note, and how strange it was that the DVDs from Wild Oats Productions showed up.

McGaven remained quiet, which was unusual. He finally said, "So you're saying that Robin Mayfield was going to spill the beans on something big—possibly the identity of the person who killed her daughters. But the killer actually got to her and tried to make it look like suicide."

"I couldn't have said it better myself."

"Well, that's a great theory, but now we need proof, evidence, a confession… you know, those things."

"I never said it was going to be easy."

"That reminds me," he said, turning towards his computer. "Remember when you asked me to run background checks on the film crew?"

"Yes."

"Well, I did."

"And?"

"And nothing."

"Why do you do that?" she said.

"What?"

"Get my hopes up? Did any of them stand out?"

"Well," he said, "disorderly stuff, fights, trespass, assault."

"Assault, who?"

"It was…" he read, "Bryan 'Butch' Price. He's a bit of a hothead. Keith Cooper was arrested twice for bar fights."

"That makes sense with those two, but they don't strike me as the serial killer types."

"The other guys have zero issues or arrests."

"Not even Matt Gardner?"

"What does he do?"

"Director. He leads the group."

"Nope."

"He was strange on the phone, a bit hostile when I asked him about the DVDs."

"There are many reasons why he could be like that."

That was true, but it didn't sit well with Katie. Her phone interrupted her train of thought.

"Scott."

"Detective Scott, is McGaven there with you?" asked the sheriff.

Katie put the phone on speaker. "He's here and we're on speaker."

"Good. I want you both to hear this. I received an interesting call from Chief Osborne earlier. He has asked that both of you go up to Rock Creek to work the Mayfield cases."

"Why?" said Katie.

"McGaven had requested copies of the cold case of… a Darla Denton?"

"Yes, sir, that's right. She had the same type of branding as Tessa Mayfield."

"Apparently there's some history there and he worked the case, eight years ago, I believe."

"You want us to go there and look at his files?" said Katie.

"No, I'm saying that I want you and McGaven to go there and work *all* the cases."

"For how long?" she asked, feeling her stomach drop.

"For as long as it takes. The chief agrees with me. You're always saying that the different agencies never work together. Now's your chance."

There was silence from both Katie and McGaven. It was clear neither wanted to go to Rock Creek, much less stay there.

"Can I count on you?" asked the sheriff.

"Can I take some surveillance cameras with me?" she said, thinking on her feet. "And if I need help from John in forensics, do I have permission to bring him to Rock Creek?"

"Do whatever you need to do to close these cases. I've been getting letters about people wanting justice for the Mayfield sisters. I don't want this turning into a national media event. Do you both understand?"

"Of course," she said.

"Good. I look forward to your reports."

"Yes, sir."

"Oh, and Katie," he said, reverting back to his uncle voice, "be careful. Keep alert. Take Cisco with you. That's an order."

CHAPTER THIRTY-ONE

Monday 0945 hours

Katie gave Chad a quick hug beside her packed Jeep and ushered Cisco into the back seat. She couldn't believe that she had been ordered to do her job in another town over an hour away, but that was what needed to be done. The sooner she got to Rock Creek, the sooner she and McGaven could solve the case and come home.

"I can't believe I'm on shift for the next four days when you're going out of town," Chad said, stroking her hair. "After everything that has happened, I have to tell you that I'm a little bit—"

"What?" she interrupted.

"I worry, okay?"

"I'll be fine. I have Cisco and McGaven. Don't worry, okay?" She kissed him.

He gave her one more kiss and then smiled. "My soon-to-be bride."

Katie gave him a long look before she got into her Jeep. She didn't want Chad to see how difficult this case was becoming and the toll it was taking on her. She backed the SUV down her driveway, gave one last wave with a smile, and drove away.

"Well, it's you and me, Cisco," she said.

Cisco pushed his head between the seats.

"Yeah, buddy, we'll be seeing Gav soon." McGaven was going to meet her in Rock Creek, at the Oak Grove Motel & Cabins. They had two cabins booked. She had no idea what the conditions would be, but was promised there was a small kitchen, comfortable feather bed, clean towels and sheets, Internet access and a free breakfast every morning. Good thing she wasn't allergic to goose down. And of course, they were fine with an ex-military dog staying there too.

A light rain spattered across her windshield, forcing her to switch on the wipers. There was a heavy rain storm forecast that evening and it ramped up as she drove along Highway 9 all the way to Rock Creek. She instinctively slowed at the area where the branch had blocked them previously.

Just as she drove up to the highest point and began descending into the town, sheets of rain hammered her SUV, blowing in gusts across the roadway. Her headlights automatically illuminated the dark road, reflecting the standing water and making it difficult to see the dividing lines. Katie tapped the brake carefully to take the sharp turns. Her Jeep slipped from side to side—fishtailing even at her slower speed.

"Sorry, Cisco, we'll be there soon."

The dog ran back and forth across the back seats. He let out whines every so often to let Katie know that he was not happy with the car ride.

As if by a miracle the rain eased as the lights of Rock Creek came into view. It wasn't Las Vegas, but she was thrilled to see civilization again and realized that she was hungry. She wasn't sure if she ever wanted to live in a town where there was only one road in and out.

Her phone gave a chirp to indicate that she had signal again. There were three messages from the three men in her life: her uncle, Chad, and McGaven. She quickly listened to them. Her uncle just wanted to give support and remind her to keep in touch. Chad said he loved her and to be careful. Finally, McGaven said he was already in town and wondered where she was. He said he'd be at Joe's Diner until he heard from her.

Just then her phone rang and she quickly answered:
"Scott."

"Hey, girl, I finally got a hold of you."

"Lizzy, so good to hear from you. I thought you were down in Monterey hanging out at the beach by now."

"I'm going to be in town for another few days because of the storm that's coming."

"Oh, no," said Katie.

"What?"

"I'm on assignment out of town for a few days, maybe more."

"I can push my orientation till the end of the week, if that helps? Maybe the storm will give me more," said Lizzy.

"It might. I'm hoping that Gav and I can leave Rock Creek before the end of the week."

"Well, let me know, okay? We didn't get to spend enough time together."

"I'll do what I can, and call you when I know."

"Sounds good. Bye, Katie."

Katie drove through downtown. It was easy finding the diner with a 1950s neon red sign and McGaven's big red truck parked outside.

"I'll bring you some goodies," she said to Cisco, leaving him in the Jeep.

Katie jumped out and ran to the door of the diner, flinging it open. She stomped her feet on the large mat, and shed her jacket. Looking up, she saw McGaven sitting in one of the booths. His height, big smile, and the fact he didn't look like he belonged there made him stand out.

There were two other tables occupied by middle-aged and elderly patrons. It was the early-bird hour, so the crowd was light. Two waitresses were behind the counter. The restaurant was dated, but tidy. Silver accessories dotted the walls, accompanied by knick-knacks that patrons had given to the restaurant over the years.

Katie went straight to the red booth where McGaven was seated and sat down. "Hi."

"You made it," he joked.

After finishing their meals, Katie and McGaven found the Oak Grove Motel & Cabins, passing several boat storages along the way. The area reminded her of a camping motel, surrounded by dense trees and extra property with picnic tables and barbecue pits. Like the diner, it too was old in style but nicely kept up. The motel was unusual and divided into single-story cabins.

Katie and McGaven exited their cars to the sound of rumbling thunder and a few flashes across the sky. They hurried into the office to get their rooms. An older woman wearing a bright yellow turtleneck, with tightly curled platinum-blonde hair, greeted them. "Hello there, and welcome to the Oak Grove Motel."

"Hi," said Katie. "We're here to check in to our cabins."

"Let me guess, Detective Scott and Deputy McGaven, right?"

"Yes. We're that transparent?" she said.

Leaning forward, the woman said, "Yes, but don't worry the whole town won't know for a few days." She retrieved two electronic key cards and handed them to Katie and McGaven. "Detective Scott, you're in room number 4 and McGaven, you're in room number 3."

"Thank you," said Katie.

"It's just around back toward the end. I figured you'd want a quiet spot and there's a large enclosed grassy area for your dog."

"Oh, that's great."

"And I'm Betty, if you need anything. Breakfast is at seven in the dining area. Some of the best homemade biscuits around."

"Thank you, Betty," Katie said as they left the office.

After parking in front of their cabins, Katie quickly unpacked her things and let Cisco out to do his business. The weather appeared to be ready to rage for most of the night and she was eager to get inside and get her bearings. And most importantly, get to work.

Katie's cabin was nicer than she thought it would be—it even had a fireplace. The dark wooden furniture matching the equally dark walls was old but tasteful, with a comfortable beige couch, coffee table, plush rug and small functioning kitchen with bar seating for two. The bedroom was lovely with crisp white linens on top of a feather bed with two large pillows. A large overstuffed armchair with blue chintz fabric sat across the corner of the room. The bathroom was tiny with a narrow stall shower and small pedestal sink.

"Well, Cisco, this is home for a while," she said.

The dog immediately took his place in the comfortable chair in the corner of the bedroom.

"Nice choice," she said.

Katie moved her four work boxes into the living room, placing them on the floor next to the coffee table. She noticed a stack of file folders sitting on the kitchen counter. There was a note from Chief Osborne that read: *Here are those Denton files you requested.* She quickly flipped through them—it was the investigation into the murder of Darla Denton.

"Hey, can I come in?" said McGaven at the door as he peeked inside.

"Of course."

"Just checking." He looked around. "Your room is bigger than mine."

"Don't whine just yet. We'll be working here then." She showed him the files. "The chief, or someone from his office, delivered the Darla Denton files."

"That's efficient. It could only be one of three people."

"Did you get the copy of the files from Huntington County?"

"Yep."

"Good."

Katie turned to face her partner. "Did you notice something strange about Rock Creek? We've been here three times now and it suddenly occurred to me."

"Besides it's creepy? I feel like people are peeking out their windows and watching our every move."

"Did you notice that we haven't seen any kids? No kids running around, riding their bikes, none out walking, none in the diner, even here at the motel—no kids anywhere."

CHAPTER THIRTY-TWO

Monday 2130 hours

After a couple of hours, Katie and McGaven had the living room looking like a police command headquarters instead of a small cabin in the middle of nowhere. Katie had carefully removed the two landscape prints on one wall in the living room, placing them in the closet for safekeeping, and taped the maps, evidence photos and pictures of various people of interest on the wall. Their prime suspect, Whitney Mayfield, was right in the middle of it all.

She made a detailed timeline along the bottom part of the wall, from the discovery of Tessa and Megan Mayfield's bodies, including their investigative stops in Rock Creek, and ending with the suicide shooting of Darren Rodriguez at the sheriff's department.

"Have you read all the way through the Darla Denton case?" she asked McGaven.

Sitting on the small couch, McGaven had kicked off his boots and wore his casual running pants as he read through the reports. Cisco was curled up on the floor near him. "She lived with her grandmother who has since passed away. Her parents were derelict, homeless, on drugs. They weren't even able to find them to tell them the news."

It deeply saddened Katie. "What about her injuries?"

"Strangulation, and she had the same branding on her skin that appears to have been there since she was a baby. It shows the numbers 1 1 7 from the autopsy photos."

"Where was she found?"

"Looks like," he said looking at the map, "one street west of Sandstone in a vacant lot."

"Near the swing area?"

"Yep."

"Near the Mayfields' house?"

"Yes. I see where you're going with this."

"Looks like we have some serious questions for the chief tomorrow."

"No suspects. Not many leads, just town gossip that didn't pan out. Looks like they did a canvass, but nothing substantial."

Thunder boomed overhead, rattling the walls and flickering the lights.

"Maybe we should continue in the morning?" said Katie. Her energy was fading and she wanted to get comfortable, take a shower, and sleep on that fantastic feather bed.

Another cracking explosion was followed by heavy rain pelting the windows and door.

McGaven sat up and said, "I think you're right." He leaned down to pet Cisco.

"Seven a.m.?"

"Make it eight. I want to try those world-famous biscuits," he said, putting his shoes on.

"How about meeting for breakfast at eight?" Katie said.

"Sounds great," he said. "Oh, lock your door and be safe."

Katie could hear him walking away down the flooded path.

"C'mon, Cisco, let's go to bed."

It took Katie only fifteen minutes after a hot shower to be tucked into the most comfortable bed she had ever experienced. She started thinking about the case, but then fell into a deep sleep, lulled by the heavy rain and thunder.

*

Lightning filled the room. Flashes exploding all around her. Katie woke with a start; she had been dreaming about the battlefield in Afghanistan and was covered in sweat and breathing heavily. Cisco had climbed onto the bed to give her comfort and she stroked his head as he snuggled against her, her heart rate slowly returning to normal.

Another flash illuminated her room before it blacked out again. There was a rattling sound at the door; she distinctly heard it in a pause between thunder claps. Cisco sat up straight; he too had heard something that didn't have anything to do with the storm. His ears went back and, in the dark, his amber wolf eyes glowed as he fixated on the front door.

Katie quickly got out of bed. Cisco wanted to follow, but she commanded him to stay in his current position on a ready. She retrieved her Glock from the nightstand and prepared herself with the weapon strategically directed in front of her.

A huge crash tore the sky, the sound coming from all around her, taking the electricity out. Everything went black. Katie used the cover to creep barefoot toward the door before lightning lit up the room again. She could make out the outline of a figure on the other side of the red curtains, shorter and stockier than her partner.

Katie kept moving until she reached the door. She shifted to the left side, disengaging the lock, and put her fingers on the door handle, turning it slowly until it stopped. Then, she yanked the door wide open in one quick movement, immediately feeling the rain blowing against her face.

Before her was a man wearing a rain poncho with the hood pulled tightly around his face.

"Who are you?" she demanded training her weapon on the figure.

He froze.

"What are you doing here?" she said.

The man took a step back.

"I said, who are you?" The wind battered her face and she was getting soaking wet.

As a huge gust almost unbalanced Katie, the man turned and ran.

"Hey!" she yelled, taking off after him. The mud and gravel under her bare feet was uncomfortable, but finding out who he was was more important. Fighting the wind, with a wall of rain blasting her face, slowed her pursuit. She pumped her arms, trying to keep her eyes open.

The sound of a gunning engine roared to life.

Katie stopped and frantically turned in a three-hundred-sixty-degree circle—no sign of the man. Suddenly, the gray truck she had seen on her run zoomed out from behind a set of trees, headlights blinding. It swerved right, just missing Katie, and then sped out of the parking area.

Katie stood staring after the truck.

"Katie!" yelled McGaven. "Are you alright? Who was that?"

"Someone tried to break into my room."

"C'mon, let's get you back inside." He helped his partner as she started to shiver uncontrollably.

"Why didn't you tell me about the gray truck back in Pine Valley?" said McGaven after she recounted the events.

"Honestly, I had pushed it out of my mind until tonight." She had changed into dry clothes with a blanket wrapped around her.

Cisco wouldn't leave Katie's side.

"We need to call this in."

"To who?" she said. "Who can we trust in this town? Clearly someone doesn't want us here."

"Are you sure that they don't want us here?"

"Aren't you?"

"What if all these things are happening because someone is trying to get our attention?"

"You mean like the flat tire, the tree branch in the road, tampering with evidence and lurking outside my room in a storm? Well, I have news for them—they got our attention," she said.

"Get some sleep. I'll crash on the couch."

"No, you don't need to do that. I have Cisco. Besides…" she laughed. "That couch isn't big enough for you."

"Just for added protection."

"Thanks, Gav. I'll be fine."

After McGaven left, Darren Rodriguez came to Katie's mind. He used to do dirty jobs for Whitney Mayfield. Maybe Whitney found someone new. But who is Whitney Mayfield?

You know all about him. You can reach out and touch him.

CHAPTER THIRTY-THREE

Tuesday 0830 hours

Katie sat a small bistro table in the motel restaurant, with Cisco lying down underneath waiting for a crumb to fall. She ate a bowl of oatmeal with fruit as she waited for McGaven. The storm had cleared for now, but there was worse weather predicted.

Betty fussed around her. "You need any more coffee, Detective?"

"No, thank you. Please call me Katie," she said and smiled.

"Very well, Katie. My daughter-in-law is named Katie."

"How many kids do you have?"

"I have two sons who are in the military—one army and one navy."

"You must be proud," she said.

"Absolutely."

Katie didn't know what possessed her to share about her personal life, but she said, "I served two tours in the army as a K9 explosives handler. This is Cisco, my partner. I was lucky enough to bring him home with me." She sipped her coffee.

Betty turned around and studied Katie for a moment. "I knew there was something special about you when you first walked through that door."

Katie smiled.

"Where's your partner?"

"My guess? He's probably talking to his girlfriend." She petted Cisco as he gently begged for something off the table. "He'll be here shortly."

Two people came through the front door and Betty handed over pre-made breakfast packages for them to take with them.

"Betty, can I ask you a question?"

"Sure, spit it out. I had a feeling you wanted to ask me something." She pulled up a chair and sat down. Cisco seemed interested in her, sniffing her shoes and nudging for a pet, which she obliged.

"Why don't I see children around town?"

Betty seemed shocked by the question and thought a moment before she answered. "Well, I don't know. How much time have you spent here?"

"Enough."

Betty looked down. "People don't come to Rock Creek to raise a family."

"Why is that? It's nice and quiet here."

"Well, the school isn't the best. Hard to get good teachers and all. It's more of a town for tourism because of the fishing and hiking. And I guess people like me getting close to retirement age."

"Oh."

"C'mon, Katie. There's something else you want to ask me."

"How well do you know Chief Osborne?"

"Richard? I've known him a long time. He's a good man—as good as they get. I'd stake my life on it."

Katie watched Betty closely and it was obvious that she truly felt that way about the chief. But Katie wasn't so sure. "Does he have a family here?"

"No, his wife passed about ten years ago."

"How lonely."

"Not really, there are a lot of good folks here and it's like family."

"Oh, one more thing. Is there someone staying here that drives a big gray truck?"

"No, I haven't seen one. We are barely at half capacity, so I would have seen it if it belonged to a tenant. Why?"

"I just saw one late last night." She didn't want to divulge too much information or worry her.

"Maybe someone visiting?"

Looking at her watch, Katie thought it was strange that McGaven hadn't shown up yet. "You're probably right. I'm going to see what's taking my partner so long. He better not be sleeping in," she said with a wink.

"Okay. Good luck today."

Katie hurried out of the office area with Cisco in tow, back to where their cabins were located. The rain had stopped and a snippet of sunshine peeked through. She stepped up to McGaven's door and knocked.

"Hey, Gav, get a move on." She knocked again. "You around?" She saw his red truck parked on the side, so he had to be there—unless he'd gone for a walk. She tried the door and it was open so she went inside and looked around.

"Gav?"

Cisco bolted past her and ran around, jumping on his unmade bed.

"Cisco, let's go," she laughed. The dog loved McGaven and was clearly looking for him and had picked up his scent.

Katie walked back to the front door and Cisco squeezed by and ran outside.

"Cisco!"

She followed the dog as he appeared to know where he was going, nose low, tail down—he was on a scent. There was a long row of nicely manicured hedges on the side of McGaven's room. Two large trees were in the back, and lying on the ground between them was McGaven.

Cisco circled him, barking.

"Gav," said Katie as she ran to him and dropped to the ground. "Gav," she said again, pressing her fingers to his neck. His pulse was strong. She saw a cut across the side of his forehead that had bled but appeared to have stopped.

McGaven groaned and began to move.

Cisco nudged him and began licking his face.

"Gav, you okay?"

"Oh, my head. What the…?"

"Take it easy. I'm going to have Betty call an ambulance."

"No. Don't. I'm fine." He sat up awkwardly.

Katie pressed the palm of her hand against his forehead. "I don't think you'll need stitches, but you should have it looked at. You feeling dizzy or nauseous or anything?"

"No, I'm okay."

"What happened?"

"I was about to meet you… I heard a knock at my door and when I went to answer it no one was there."

"How'd you get back here?"

"I thought I heard something, so I followed the noise and walked around the side. I started to turn but before I saw anything, wham. I got hit, and then I stumbled and fell. That's the last thing I remember."

"Okay, sit here for a minute," she said. Katie looked on the ground around them and saw McGaven's footprints and another set of men's boots, average size—and then hers and Cisco's. She tried to track the unknown footprints, but puddles made it nearly impossible.

"Anything?" he said.

Cisco barked.

"Thanks, buddy," McGaven said to the dog.

"No," she said and took one last look around.

Katie remembered from a forensic teacher that most people never look up or any higher than their vision level. Instantly, she looked up and walked around the long hedge looking for anything out of place. Wedged in the rough trunk of a pine was a sliver of blue at about shoulder level. It looked like threads, but upon closer inspection it was actually a piece of heavy-duty material. She carefully pulled the threads from where they had hooked themselves.

"What's that?" he asked, straining to see.

Katie walked back to him. "Don't know if it's anything. It's a blue piece of fabric."

"Okay, I'm up," he said, struggling to his feet. Katie helped him the rest of the way.

"C'mon, let's get some bandages from Betty and some food for you too."

"Yeah, I haven't had my first cup of coffee yet."

"Gav?"

"Yeah?"

"I think I've seen this fabric before," she said slowly.

"Where?"

"It looks similar to what Tessa Mayfield was clutching in her hand."

CHAPTER THIRTY-FOUR
Tuesday 1105 hours

After Katie patched up McGaven with the help of Betty, they drove to the police station to see Chief Osborne.

"I don't see any cars," she said.

"Let's go check it out," McGaven said as he got out of the Jeep.

"Stay, Cisco," she said, leaving the back window slightly cracked. The rain was still holding out, leaving the humid air smelling of pine and some late-blooming vines.

Katie knocked on the door of the small police station, which was really more of an annex than a department. No answer. She tried the door, which was unlocked, and pushed it open.

"Hello? Chief Osborne?"

Still no answer.

"I sent him a text this morning, but I haven't heard from him," she said.

"Let's go inside and leave him a note," he said, but she knew in reality he wanted to check things out, just like her.

They stopped in shock as they walked inside. It looked as if someone had been looking for something: drawers were open, files strewn everywhere, the garbage can dumped over and its contents spread across the floor.

"What the hell?" said McGaven.

"What happened here?" said Katie. She slowly scanned the files, not wanting to touch anything.

"Think they found what they were looking for?"

"Hard to tell."

There was a clipboard hung on a single nail with a list of the names and events on it. Katie noticed one name in particular, Wild Oats Productions. "Gav, check this out. Looks like the film crew are scheduled to shoot some footage tomorrow."

He moved to her side and read the clipboard. "Interesting."

"Well, maybe not so much. I called Matt Gardner, the director, and asked about their DVDs and if they signed any for friends and such."

"What did he say?"

"They would only have the crew sign one DVD. But he did say they were scheduled to be here in Rock Creek."

"For what?"

"There's some old haunted cemetery."

"I can believe that," he said.

McGaven spotted a single piece of lined paper sticking out of a blank file folder. It had several names listed in order on it and was worn, looking like it had been in a file for a long time. He pulled the paper out and took a quick photo of it with his cell phone camera.

Katie found the cell numbers for both local police officers and took a quick photo of them. "I think we need to call one of his men." She punched the number for Officer Brad Mason and waited. "It went to voicemail." She ended the call.

Trying the other number, she waited again. Finally, there was an answer.

"Who is this?"

Katie was stunned. What kind of greeting was that? "Officer McKinney?"

"Yeah."

"This is Detective Scott and I'm at your police station."

There was a pause on the other end. "What can I do for you, Detective?"

"Your chief seems to be missing," she said. "Do you know where he is?"

"No."

"Can you tell us where we might find him?"

"Running down leads or errands."

"I see. If you see or talk to him, can you tell him that we're looking for him?"

"Of course."

The connection went dead.

"No luck there," she said.

"Let's go, and check back in here later," McGaven said.

Katie headed for the door and was surprised to find Officer Mason on the other side. "Wow, I just called your cell," she said.

"What can I do for you, Detective?" There was something almost accusatory about his tone and the look he gave Katie.

"We were looking for the chief. Have you seen him?"

"No."

"I haven't heard from him. Would you know where he might be?" said Katie.

"He could be anywhere, doing an errand, home, at the diner, whatever."

"Can you call him?" Katie pushed.

Officer Mason shrugged. "Sure." He took out his phone, dialed, and waited, "Sir, it's Mason. I'm at the office with the detectives. Call back when you can." He hung up. "Left him a message. Don't worry, he'll call back."

"Tell me, does he always leave his office in such a mess?" asked McGaven.

Mason turned and stared at McGaven. "He's always been messy. He had to leave in a hurry maybe."

"We have some errands to do. See you around," she said abruptly.

McGaven followed her, but after a few steps she couldn't help but turn back around. "Oh, Officer Mason. Thanks for taking care of Robin Mayfield's crime scene evidence."

He didn't say anything, but pushed his weight from one foot to the other.

"There was a piece of evidence that I didn't identify when searching the scene. It was a small five by eight inch photo album. Do you remember it?" She watched him closely.

He thought about it for a moment, for her benefit, she guessed. "No, I don't remember anything like that," he said, subtly shaking his head.

"Oh, okay. Just checking. Thanks."

Katie turned and walked to the Jeep. The windows were fogged up and Cisco's nose pushed out the top of the window. They both got back in and she started the engine. Setting the defroster on high, she turned to McGaven. "How's your head?"

"I'm feeling fine. Isn't this like a typical day for you?" he said, touching the bandages on his head.

"Very funny. But what was that back there?" She motioned toward the police office. "Do you think the chief is missing, or he's on some type of errand?"

"Let's wait a bit longer before calling in the troops for a missing chief. There is probably a logical explanation."

"You're right." Katie put the car into gear and drove away from the station. "There must be a logical explanation."

But she wasn't so sure.

CHAPTER THIRTY-FIVE

Tuesday 1745 hours

Katie kept looking at her watch and tapping her pen with growing impatience. She sat on the floor going over reports on her laptop and looking up information on ACE Visions Inc.

"Still nothing from the chief?" said McGaven, as he worked on his laptop from the couch.

"No," she said. "I'm actually worried. Too many weird things are going on here. That guy last night with the gray truck, and you being attacked. We need to talk to him."

"And there's not anyone else we can ask."

Katie dialed Officer Mason's number, but it went directly to voicemail. She decided to try Officer McKinney and waited. It rang twice and then nothing—just dead air. She tried the number again with the same outcome.

"No luck. How can this town function without any available police officers?"

The rain pounded the side of the building.

"I don't know, but did you notice how quiet the streets were on our way back here?"

"I know," she said. "I don't think there is anyone else staying here tonight."

"Well, it is a Tuesday and it's raining… Another storm is coming in for the next few days."

At that moment a crack of thunder rolled through.

"Ha! Perfect timing," he said, half grinning. "We're going to lose electricity again, no doubt. And there will go the Internet. I'm charging extra batteries…"

Katie tried to keep her mind on the job in hand. "This video camera company is actually really cool, they offer all types of services. I hadn't heard from them from my earlier message, so I left an email for them to call me telling them what we're looking for." She sat back and closed her eyes. "Should we call the sheriff?"

"I think we should wait." He swung his legs over onto the floor. "For all we know, the chief is out of town visiting someone."

"Well, first thing in the morning, if I still haven't heard from him…"

"We'll call the sheriff," he said.

Katie agreed. "And I think you should sleep here tonight."

"Well, Katie, I never knew you felt that way…" he said jokingly.

"Really? You can joke at a time like this?" she replied, half-smiling.

"You're afraid to be alone?"

"Yeah, right. I'm just looking out for you. Thought you might get scared or knocked out again." She smirked.

"No, you're right. This place is bigger and everything is already here. Did you know that this couch pulls out into a bed?" He pulled a cushion from the back.

"I'll ask Betty for some extra bedding."

"And food," he said.

"And food," she chimed, realizing that her stomach was grumbly.

Within a half hour, Katie opened the door to Betty carrying sheets, blankets, pillows, and a bag of food.

"Oh wow, let me help you," she said. "Thank you." Katie passed the bedding to McGaven.

"I feel terrible about what you two have been through," Betty said with genuine concern.

"Don't worry about us, we're police officers. We're used to it," said McGaven.

Betty put down a brown paper bag. "There are turkey sandwiches, some minestrone soup, assorted crackers, and something special for Cisco."

The dog's ears perked up when he heard his name.

"Thank you so much."

"If you need anything else, don't hesitate," the older woman said.

"Oh, Betty, I don't want to alarm you, but I need for you to be careful, especially after Gav got attacked. Please lock your doors to the office and your apartment, okay?"

"Of course I will. But I'm not scared."

"Just the same, please lock up tight tonight."

"I will. See you both in the morning." She smiled and let herself out.

Katie threw another log into the fireplace and it crackled and popped, catching Cisco's attention. "Okay, new suspects or persons of interest?"

"What about the chief?"

"What about him?" she said.

"He was the one that wanted us here, right, and now he's done a complete disappearing act."

"I see where you're going, but what about the two officers? Wasn't Mason acting a bit strange earlier?" she said.

"I agree. They all had access to the evidence and were the first to arrive at Robin Mayfield's house."

There was a chime on Katie's cell phone. "Yes!" she said. "Finally. Here's a link to the videos from the swing area in the week of the girls' disappearance. Let me send it to your email."

With a few clicks, McGaven said, "Got it." He began to run through the days, seeking the afternoon of the abduction.

"It's going to take a while to watch."

"Not really, it only records when there's movement. But a moth could set it off, too." He set some parameters and let it run its course. "While I'm doing that, here's this list I saw in the chief's office. It was really worn and sticking out of a plain file folder." McGaven showed Katie.

"What do you think it's for?"

"I don't know. It looks like it was written a while back and has been handled quite a bit."

Katie typed a few of the names and ran a search.

The lights flickered.

"C'mon, don't fail me now," she said. The first girl's name popped up in a news article, Mary Matthews, age nine. She had been murdered and her body was found just outside of town twelve years ago. Another girl, Cynthia Evan, ten, murdered, body found down in the creek four years ago.

"What is going on?" she said. "Why haven't we received this information before? Why didn't it come up in our searches?"

"What?"

"Your list. Three of them, including Darla Denton, are girls that had been murdered. The others were all reported missing."

"Where?"

"Here."

"What do you mean here? In *Rock Creek*?" he said.

"Why didn't the chief tell us? Better yet, why didn't these murders show up on the FBI's Uniform Crime Report?" Katie kept searching for more information. "The local paper, *The Pine Cone*, said that Mary Matthews went missing from her front yard. There was a massive search with half the town. Her body was found a week later on the side of the road on Highway 9. What do you want to bet her body was found at the same location where the numbers were carved into that tree?" Katie kept searching but she could only find reference to the three girls: Mary Matthews, Cynthia Evan, and Darla Denton.

"Alright, now the chief has some serious explaining to do," he said.

You know all about him. You can reach out and touch him.

"This is so much bigger than the murder of Tessa and Megan Mayfield." Katie bit her lip and began spinning possible scenarios in her mind.

McGaven glanced at his screen, seeing the back of a man walking down to the creek. Then he went out of view, and came back. "Katie, look at this."

She was immediately at his side viewing the movements of the man. "Who is that?"

"Watch his movements and his gait."

Katie shook her head. "I don't know, but it sort of looks like the build of Officer Mason."

"That's what came to mind."

"I can't tell for sure."

"What do you want to do?" he said.

"Now it's time to call the sheriff," she said. He picked up after two rings.

"Katie, everything all right?" There was stress in his voice, which wasn't typical.

"Well, actually, no," she said. "Sheriff Osborne is nowhere to be found. There's something very strange going on here in Rock Creek—and I don't think we can trust the law enforcement. We found a list of girls that have been murdered here over the past ten years, but there's no record of them in the system."

"Are you sure?"

"From everything we've managed to find." She steadied her breathing. "I think we need the sheriff's department to back us up. No one is talking. The chief and both of his officers have gone missing—we're unable to contact any of them."

"Has the storm hit you there yet?" the sheriff said.

"It's been stormy, but bearable. Why?"

"We're bracing for really bad weather here. High winds, possibly up to seventy miles per hour with major flooding. Highway 9 has already been completely blocked with several trees down… We're preparing for high flooding right now across the county."

"When do you think you could send someone here?" Her heart skipped at the realization that they were trapped. "Only way in or out is Highway 9." She tried to sound calm, but she wasn't.

"Just sit tight. There's not much you can do with a big storm. Stay inside and stay safe," the sheriff ordered.

"Okay, I'll call you in the morning…"

As if on cue, a horrendous triple boom of thunder accompanied by several close flashes of lightning bombarded them, and the electricity went out. The only light in the room was the flickering fire. It cast an eerie glow on McGaven's face as he stared at her.

"Uncle Wayne? You there?" Loud static was the only thing she heard.

"Gav, can you dial out?"

He tried. "Nope, there's no signal." He sighed with irritation.

"No signal on mine either. He said there is a massive storm getting ready to hit for the next two days. The road is out. Pine Valley is preparing for major flooding and they can't get here until maybe tomorrow. There's nothing we can do right now but sit it out."

He studied Katie. "What's wrong?"

"We're stuck here, and so might be the killer."

CHAPTER THIRTY-SIX
Wednesday 0430 hours

Katie tossed and turned the entire night, her mind racing. Was she missing the clue that would break the case wide open and expose the killer? Faces flashed through her mind as frequently as the booming above the rooftop. Sheriff Osborne. Officer Mason. Darren Rodriguez. Robin Mayfield... the faces just kept revolving.

Her mind wandered to the discovery of the bodies of Tessa and Megan. The film crew. Matt Gardner, the director who was so suspicious of her call. Butch Price, the grip and all around grunt, who was overly interested in the discovery of bones at Silo. And the others... Then Officer Mason, possibly moving around the swing area within the last two weeks...

Katie sat up in bed. It was useless to try and sleep. Her room was cold and Cisco had nestled into the other side of the bed to keep warm next to her. She flung back her bedding and wrapped a blanket around her. With her feet touching the icy floor, she hurried to the living room to discover that the fire had burned down to embers. She placed a couple of logs on the hearth, the flames beginning to spring up again as heat slowly filtered into the room.

McGaven was sleeping under several quilts on the sofa. He suddenly said, "Can't sleep?"

Katie turned in surprise. "You neither? The storm?" she asked, but knew it was the case.

"I love the storm. No. I keep going through everything in my mind—this town—everything since the discovery of the two girls."

Katie sat down, trying to warm up. "Me too."

"We need to find the chief," he said.

"And fast." Katie got up. "Grab something to eat from the fridge and let's go find him." They couldn't wait any longer, storm or not. She went to her room to change and get Cisco geared up.

After waking up Betty, Katie was able to get the location of the chief's home. She assured Betty everything was okay and told her to stay inside and not open the door to anyone—not even someone she knew.

They decided to take Katie's Jeep because it handled better in the conditions and was narrow enough to get through slim spaces. Cisco paced and kept his head in between Katie and McGaven—he was ready for anything.

"I like Betty," said McGaven.

"I do too. I hope she'll be okay."

"Did you see that .45 she had?" he laughed. "She'll be just fine."

It was still dark and most of the streetlights were out. The only light came from the Jeep's highlighting of the rain pounding the road.

Katie drove slowly, creeping down the street where Chief Osborne resided. Inching by the large homes with pretty gates and driveways, both Katie and McGaven scrutinized the houses and cars. About halfway down, they spotted a moderate-size home up on a hill with large manicured bushes giving almost complete privacy from neighbors. There was a mountain of dirt on the side of the house, indicating that there was some type of landscaping in progress, and in the driveway was a patrol SUV for Rock Creek, and a gray truck.

"I know that truck," said Katie.

"Is it...?"

"That's the truck that tracked me and Cisco and was here at the cabins, and the one I saw outside the hotel the other night. I'd know it anywhere." There were no license plates.

Katie killed the headlights and opted to park a couple of houses away.

Cisco whined.

"Sorry, Cisco, you have to sit this one out." To McGaven, she said, "You up for this? There's no backup. How's your head?"

"I'm fine. I'm ready." He checked his guns and made sure he had extra ammunition. He pulled up his hood and secured it against the wind.

Katie didn't say anything.

"What?"

She shook her head. "I'm sorry it's come to this."

"It's not your fault—and this is what we do." He squeezed her arm. "Let's go."

The rain had subsided and Katie led the charge with McGaven watching her back. She indicated for him to go around the back of the house as she crept up the stairs to the front door.

The house was dark and quiet.

She carefully peered into the windows and, as her eyes adjusted, could see the kitchen and living room were wrecked—cupboards open, contents spilled out, books and knick-knacks strewn everywhere. She pulled her gun out and had it ready.

The front door was locked.

Katie moved along the deck and found that a sliding door was slightly ajar. She felt the heat from the house escape. Leaning in, she listened. She could hear muted voices—escalating higher and then softer, perhaps a television on in another room, but the more she strained to listen, the more she believed it was two people talking—arguing.

She made the decision to enter. Pulling the sliding door open wider, she slipped through quietly. Luckily, the lower door pulleys were quiet as she rolled them closed. She carefully stepped over broken dishes and kitchen utensils scattered across the floor, and moved through to the living room where the light was gradually brightening enough for her to see clearly; a large sectional couch, coffee table, and two large recliners. There was also another set of sliding doors leading out onto a deck.

The voices grew louder, and she heard something shatter against the wall. She caught a few words, "You knew all along…"

Katie moved faster and reached an open door that led to a basement living area. There were carpeted stairs leading down. She began her descent, steadily tiptoeing down, one silent stair at a time, until she reached the bottom.

"No, I told you before. I had to… I had to…"

Katie recognized the voice as Chief Osborne's. He sounded weary, slurring his speech.

"I told you that I would find out the truth. Why did you do that?" said the other voice.

Katie crouched down and moved behind a large entertainment center that helped to keep her covered.

"Why? Why?" the voice kept saying.

Katie inched closer and saw the back of a man with a heavy windbreaker. He turned slightly and she saw the profile of Officer Mason. He had his gun in his hand. The chief was tied up in a chair.

"I don't want to do this—you gave me no choice."

Without hesitating, and before Katie could move, Officer Mason fired the weapon twice, striking the chief directly at close range. The sound was deafening and rattled the underground room.

"Drop your weapon!" ordered Katie.

Before she could say anything else, Mason instantly charged her, knocking her back against the entertainment center and sending it crashing. He was more agile than he looked. He bolted up the stairs but Katie managed to gather herself and ran after him, cutting him off from the front door.

He paused. Instead of attacking her again, he turned in the other direction and threw himself through the sliding doors with a crash and rolled off the deck.

"Katie!" yelled McGaven from the back.

She ran to the back door, unlocked it and met with McGaven. "He's running, he jumped from the front deck," she said breathlessly.

They heard the sound of the truck revving its engine and screeching down the driveway.

"It's Officer Mason," she said, giving him the keys. "Go get him. I'll see if the chief's still alive."

McGaven leaped down the stairs several at a time and ran across the street to Katie's Jeep. Katie hurried back to the basement, her heart pounding. So many questions plagued her.

Chief Osborne was lying on the floor on his right side, still strapped to the chair. She could see he was bleeding heavily, his breathing ragged.

"Chief," she said, and knelt at his side. Looking at his wounds, the two bullets had hit his shoulder and right rib area. "Can you hear me?"

He nodded, having trouble speaking.

Katie shed her jacket and frantically searched in the basement and adjoining bathroom for towels and anything to bandage him with.

Returning to the chief, she cut him loose from the chair with scissors she'd found, and pushed it out of the way. Then she cut off his sweatshirt to look at his wounds, before pressing the towels against the bleeding areas.

"Don't hurt him…" he barely whispered.

"What?" she said leaning closer to him.

"Please… don't hurt him."

"Mason?" she said.

"He doesn't know what he's doing… he will never stop…"

"Chief, did he kill the Mayfield girls?"

He closed his eyes in pain.

"Are you saying he killed Tessa and Megan Mayfield?" she repeated.

He barely nodded.

"Have you been protecting him?"

He stared at her, but she took his response as a yes.

"Why?"

"He's… he's…"

"But the list of girls murdered and missing we found…" Katie managed to say as she tried to stop the bleeding.

He winced. "I had to…"

"Why, Chief?"

"He's my… my son…" the chief managed to say.

Katie was shocked. "But…" Her mind reeled at how Mason was able to murder the girls, and how easily he'd moved around.

"We adopted him… he was eight…" The chief closed his eyes and his head flopped back. He managed, "There's… another girl… she lives with her… grandmother…"

"What? Who? Chief, can you hear me? What little girl? Can you give me a name, when, where?" Katie heard him breathing with difficulty; most likely his lungs were filling up with blood as he floated in and out of consciousness.

The last thing Chief Osborne said was, "Please don't hurt him…" and then he died.

Katie tried to resuscitate him for almost ten minutes, but she knew deep down it was too late.

She leaned back against the couch, exhausted, and let the realization sink in. It made sense that Mason followed her to try and scare her away, because they were getting too close. He'd killed his own father, the man who took him in—so obviously was very troubled. A bit of his psychological disposition began to come to light.

Katie sat and listened to the storm gaining momentum outside, and lost all sense of time until a cold nose nuzzled her cheek.

"Cisco," she said and hugged him.

"Hey," McGaven said, coming down the stairs. "Mason knows this area well and already had a head start on me. I lost him." He looked to Chief Osborne, the broken entertainment center, and back at Katie. "You okay?"

Katie nodded, not able to speak. The exhaustion of trying to bring a wounded man back to life—too many similarities to the battlefield—had left her emotions raw.

McGaven offered a hand and pulled Katie up. "Did he say anything that will help us?"

"Mason is his adoptive son and he didn't want us to hurt him. And he said there's another girl—no name or location. I don't know if that meant there was another kidnapping, or what."

McGaven gaped for a moment while the new information settled in his mind.

Both Katie and McGaven turned around to see Officer McKinney standing there, eyes fixed on his boss.

"What are you doing here?" McKinney demanded.

"Whoa, take it easy," said McGaven, keeping a keen eye on the officer's hands.

"What happened?" he said, looking at his boss. "Who killed the chief? Mason?"

"What makes you say that?" asked Katie.

"Did he?"

Katie nodded. "Yes."

"I knew it. With everything that has been going on. I knew something like this would happen." He turned and sprinted up the stairs.

"Hey, wait!" said McGaven, running after him.

Katie grabbed her jacket and slipped it back on as she waited for McGaven. Her cell phone was in the pocket; she pulled it out and dialed her uncle. It rang, but then the call went directly to voicemail. "It's me. Chief Osborne is dead inside his residence. Killed by his adoptive son. Gav and I are going to try and find him. There's the possibility another girl had been abducted…" The connection went dead. "Let's hope he gets his voicemail," she said to herself.

McGaven came back, breathing hard.

"Where is he?"

"He's gone."

"This investigation is getting even more complicated."

"Do you think that McKinney knew what was going on?"

"I think he suspected and now he's angry," said Katie.

McGaven looked around. "Let's see what we can find here that might tell us where he went."

"Okay." She didn't want McGaven to see that she was really shaken by the events, but the best thing to do was to forge ahead. It was what she always did in the middle of combat—and no doubt this was a battle—so she kept going.

Cisco circled and barked as he sensed the heightened energy in the room.

Katie walked around the basement room but there wasn't anything that stood out to her. She climbed the stairs with weak legs. Joining McGaven, she looked around, trying to make sense out of the chief's house.

There were several photographs sitting on a shelf. One of the chief with a woman, who Katie assumed was his wife, near a fishing area on a nice boat. There was another photo taken some years ago with Mason as a young teen. They were hiking up a trail near the historical parts of the town—it stood out—an old general store brick building that was near one of the oldest cemeteries in the county. Katie wasn't exactly sure where it was located, but knew it wouldn't be too far from Rock Creek because that's where the film crew was headed for one of their scouting locations.

"Anything?" asked McGaven.

"If I had to guess… People are creatures of habit—perps are no different. They tend to stay in areas where they feel comfortable. Rapists will stay within blocks of their very own home. Killers usually dump bodies in areas that they know well, residential, rural, state parks, anything like that." Katie looked at the photos. "John said that the blue fabric was denser and could be from a high-weather jacket or some type of bag. Like what about a tarp? Or a cover for a boat?" she surmised. "That blue piece I found in the tree where you were attacked may have been from Mason or from someone else—we don't know for sure. But a boat storage would be one place to look until we get more clues."

"Like the storage places on the way to the motel?" he said.

"If it's true what the chief said, that he abducted another girl, and if she's still alive, these would be perfect places to hide them until…" She couldn't finish the sentence.

Katie considered the new information about Mason as she looked around the destroyed house. Her mind reeled at the fact that the killer might not be Mayfield, but Officer Mason instead. His profile, as the killer, would indicate that he was also a person of habit. For whatever reason, and whatever defining moment in his life triggered such a horrendous urge to kill little girls, it didn't matter that he had been adopted by caring parents into a loving home. The psychological damage had already been done and he was like a ticking bomb ready to go off.

Was he Mayfield?

Were Mason and Mayfield the same person?

And if so, why had he felt the urge to brand his young daughter? To brand her his property? A reminder of something good, or bad, from his past? To keep her safe from what he had experienced? It wasn't clear. Most wouldn't understand his actions, but it was important to him, and Katie and McGaven needed to look at his movements to find out where he would go next.

But what really bothered Katie was the fact that Chief Osborne knew his son was murdering innocent children. How could he have lived with himself?

"Who can we call about Chief Osborne's body?" asked McGaven.

Katie had been so immersed in the killer that she had barely thought about the murder of the town police chief. "The chief and his officer are the center of the murder investigation. I can try Officer McKinney again, but I doubt he'd come back. The only other law enforcement that could lead this investigation would be the county sheriff."

She paced back and forth. "We can call the morgue and see if we can get someone out here, but this is a crime scene and I want it to stay intact so that it can be documented." She thought about it more until an idea sparked. "What about the photographer—Wendell?"

"I don't think we have much choice."

"Try to get everyone coordinated—and remember the entire house is a crime scene. I'm going to look around downstairs and take a few photos with my phone as a backup," she said. "Gav, we need to hurry. We have a killer on the loose."

"On it," he said, searching his phone for the town morgue's number as he walked into the living room. "Hope my cell signal holds."

Katie took a moment before heading down into the basement room. "Cisco, stay," she said and the dog immediately complied. She wanted to make sure he was in one area and not trampling anywhere he shouldn't be.

She was not pleased that the crime scene had to be handled like this, leaving the chief's body, but they had no choice. There was a killer on the loose and there was reason to believe that another girl had been taken.

Katie stood among the broken pieces of what was once the entertainment center. She moved in a complete circle to view everything, snapping photos as she did. She dropped her vision to Chief Osborne. With everything she'd done to try to revive him, he had still succumbed to his injuries. For some strange reason, he looked content. All the lies and demons were now quieted. His expression was soft, like he was quietly napping, and finally at peace.

On the floor, underneath part of the shelf of the entertainment center, she saw two framed photos. One was Chief Osborne standing on his boat, like the one upstairs. Katie couldn't see the name of the vessel, but it looked like a nice fishing boat. The other photo showed a young man, who Katie assumed to be Mason, in a dug hole excavating artifacts. She looked closer and realized that it appeared to be a class of some sort—with students in the background. It made her pause a moment to take in the new information.

There was nothing more she could do, she thought solemnly, and was climbing the stairs to the living room when she heard McGaven.

"Let's go," said McGaven. "Thankfully, I got hold of Wendell and gave him explicit instructions, and he was more than happy to help out—he knows several people from the morgue. I left a message there, but Wendell will keep following up."

"Sounds good," said Katie quietly. The case was beginning to take a toll on her.

Katie and McGaven hurried from the chief's house, with Cisco keeping in sync. As Katie drove away, she glanced in the rearview mirror, watching the house disappear from sight. How could anyone let someone they loved abduct and kill children—and cover it up? From everything Katie had studied, she had never encountered a person that would aid a serial killer in such a blatant fashion.

Katie followed the signs leading to a marina on the lake. The road was narrow, filled with chuckholes, debris from trees, and the water was beginning to rise. She maneuvered as best as she could, weaving around obstacles.

Lightning cracked across the sky in jagged strikes as if spelling out a message.

"I hope Pine Valley holds up to the flooding," she said.

The road finally ended in a deserted parking lot. There was no gray truck. They drove slowly, checking out slips and the floating deck areas. Nothing. No activity. No illumination from any of the boats.

Katie saw that many vessels were battened down with heavy tarps—and many were blue. "Gav, look at the blue tarps. They're made out of that heavy material."

He surveyed the area. "You're right."

Katie stopped the Jeep, letting it idle.

"I'm not sure, but it could be the same stuff. Here's my theory. What if… when the Mayfield girls were abducted, maybe subdued somehow, he hid them under the tarp so no one would see them in the car or being transported onto a boat… or…"

"Or what?"

"When we were driving to the Oak Grove Cabins we passed that boat storage yard. We should check it out."

"Let's go," McGaven urged.

Chad plowed through the crowds of people moving sand bags in front of their businesses and down the sides of streets to redirect the flow of water. The rain pounded harder and the wind blew with such powerful gusts that it made it hard for him to walk in a straight line.

He spotted Sheriff Scott directing some of his deputies to patrol streets that should be cleared of civilians and stray animals.

"Sheriff," yelled Chad.

"Chad, what are you doing here?" he barked, competing with the wind.

"Sir, I can't get a hold of Katie or McGaven. The road is out and, from what I'm told, there's no power."

"Yes, that's true. I received a partial voicemail from her—cell phone reception is spotty. Surprised there's any at all, quite frankly."

"I would like to take some help and remove trees to get there," he said.

"No way. We can't afford to take anyone away from the department right now." He turned somber. "They are having some problems there. The police chief is dead."

"More reason for me to get there."

The sheriff pulled Chad to the side. "Look, Chad, I know it's difficult to think about Katie being in the middle of something, but she has McGaven and Cisco. And they are trained for this. That eases my mind a bit—at least until tomorrow."

"Tomorrow?"

"I'm sorry, I can't afford to send anyone with you."

"Sir, what about John?" Chad said.

"From forensics?"

"Yeah."

The sheriff thought about it. "You might be running into danger, I can't okay that."

"What if… you didn't know that I was going… would that make a difference?"

The sheriff cracked a tiny smile. "It might."

"Sir, I made a mistake."

"Meaning what?"

"I didn't ask your permission to marry your niece," Chad said, as the rain poured down his face.

"And?"

"And Katie said yes!"

"Well then, you not only have my permission, you have my blessing."

"Thank you, sir," he said and turned to leave.

"Chad!" yelled Sheriff Scott. "Be careful, and don't let anything happen to her."

Chad nodded and hurried to get to the sheriff's department.

Pulling up in his large SUV, Chad made a quick call and stood at the entrance to the administration building where the forensic division was located, waiting impatiently for John. Within minutes, he opened the door.

"C'mon in," he said.

Chad followed him inside and into the forensic area.

Once they reached John's office, he turned to Chad and said, "So, you are asking me to help you clear Highway 9 going into Rock Creek?"

"I have all the equipment we would need. I just can't do it myself—it would take twice as long, if not more."

"I get the feeling that you're not telling me something."

"Katie and McGaven are working that double homicide case and… things are happening… the police chief is dead and the killer could be roaming loose. There's no power, no way in or out. They could be sitting ducks…"

"Sounds like we need more people."

"Yeah, another person would be great. Do you know someone?"

"I think I can get another person."

"Great. Let's do it," said Chad.

CHAPTER THIRTY-EIGHT

Wednesday 1300 hours

The sky was the color of an angry bruise, and thunder rumbled in the distance as Katie drove into the shipyard.

"No gray truck," she said, disappointed. She really didn't expect it to be that easy, but hoping wasn't a bad trait.

"You can't see the entire area from the parking lot. Let's go take a look," he said.

Katie parked, zipped up her all-weather jacket tightly, and left a very anxious Cisco behind.

The larger shipyard had boats in dry dock and motorhomes parked in numbered places—it was more than storage for boats; there were cars, motorcycles, and RVs as well. There was a chain-link fence surrounding the entire area, which was the size of a mall parking lot.

They went to the entrance which was securely padlocked.

After looking around to see if there was a security guard, or someone like a caretaker, Katie started to climb.

"Wait," he said. "Oh, never mind. Let's go."

They both climbed over the fence.

When Katie's feet finally hit the ground on the inside of the compound she immediately turned stiffly, expecting to have set off an alarm or woken a security dog, but all she could hear was the howl of the wind around her and the rain as it battered her face and body. It wasn't dark enough to need a flashlight, but still she wished that there was more light available to fill in the shadows that surrounded her.

"I'll take this side," McGaven said, pointing to the left.

Katie nodded and moved to the right.

There were several oversized RVs parked in a row and she checked inside the windows of each, looking for outlines of bodies, anything unusual, and making sure that no one was hiding in the dark. After the RVs she headed over to the boats, pausing at one in particular called *Sassy Suzie*. Katie looked at the tarp cover, blue with a tough weave similar to the fragment Tessa had clutched in her hand.

Katie climbed up on the frame of the metal trailer and untied a portion of the blue tarp. The knots were thick and complex, it took her a few minutes before succeeding. Flipping back the heavy tarp, she spied inside. There was nothing except maintenance items to clean and work on the boat. Looking to the corners, she made sure that there wasn't anything that might hold a child.

Katie searched two more boats but to no avail. There was no sign of criminal activity or that a child might have been held on one of them. She took another last look to see if any of the boats was Chief Osborne's, but none of them matched the photograph back at the house.

As Katie reached the end of the row of boats, she saw McGaven coming around the corner. At the same moment she noticed a large kennel just to his left, housing a German shepherd poking his head out. The big dog moved forward a couple of steps, sniffing the air outside of the doghouse. It obviously hadn't heard them enter with the blasting wind and rain, but had sensed their presence and scent all the same.

Waving her hands, she got her partner's attention and pointed at the doghouse—McGaven nodded. Both of them turned and ran back to the entrance as the German shepherd charged, barking and snapping at their heels. Close to one hundred pounds, he had trouble with traction on the wet pavement, giving Katie and McGaven enough time to hit the fence and climb.

Katie reached the top and swung her leg over just as the dog hit the fence line. She jumped down, coming face to face with the dog—the chain-link the only barrier, his teeth bared and bark incessant.

The rain poured into overflowing puddles, causing large splashes beneath their feet as they ran to the Jeep and clambered inside, out of the elements.

Breathing heavily, Katie said, "Don't think our guy was there or anything else."

"Big dog," McGaven huffed. "Big bark. Could have been a snack." The Jeep steamed up from their heavy breath as well as Cisco's continued panting.

Katie quickly engaged the defroster. "Next?" She was disappointed, and felt her energy dwindle as well as her sharpness.

A familiar chirp alerted Katie that her cell had picked up a signal. She looked at it and saw a voicemail from her uncle. She played it on speaker:

"Got your message. Everything is flooding here and I've enacted the county emergency alert protocol, calling for some evacuations in certain areas. I can't send anyone until tomorrow. Chad is trying to get to Highway 9 to remove the trees for access. I also got a weird call patched through from dispatch from Matt Gardner that one of his team was missing. They were supposed to shoot at Rock Creek today, but he left and never returned. I hope you're able to hear this message…" The message became garbled and filled with static, finally ending.

Katie looked at McGaven. "Chad is on his way, but I'm concerned for his safety in the weather and this town."

"The sheriff didn't say who was missing from the film crew?"

"I'll try to leave him another voicemail and see if he could text back or leave another message. The signal is spotty but at least messages eventually get through."

Katie's anxiety just took another leap—her chest was heavy, her legs weary, and she still didn't know where to find the abducted girl. There was more added to the mix with a missing person from the film crew, and Chad trying to clear the road.

Time was running out. The weather was going to be the biggest obstacle if it flooded the town completely.

"What now?" asked McGaven.

CHAPTER THIRTY-NINE
Wednesday 1430 hours

It didn't take Chad and John long to load up the gear into one SUV and a large truck. John had invited another person who was not only qualified to help, but loved Katie as much as a sister—her army friend Lizzy. John called her from the number she had slipped him, and she jumped at the opportunity to do something useful to help a friend.

John and Lizzy were in his truck and Chad drove his large Jeep with a winch on the front. They made good time getting to the first tree down on Highway 9. The three of them worked to get the smaller branches cut and cleared before attempting to break down the large tree trunk.

The rain and wind had died a little, making it easier to do their job.

"You okay?" asked Chad.

"Piece of cake," said Lizzy as she revved the chainsaw and began cutting.

They worked for an hour before they could move most of the limbs and pieces. Chad's Jeep did much of the heavy lifting and they managed to make a space big enough to drive through.

"The day is about gone," said John. "We have little light to work by except headlights and it's going to slow us down."

"I know, but let's get to the next one," pushed Chad as he got back into the SUV.

"Let's go," said Lizzy heading to the truck.

"Okay," said John.

The rain picked up momentum again, drowning everything and rushing down the highway. It would be like fighting waves as they took apart the trees.

Chad kept trying Katie's phone without luck. He hoped that she was safe.

CHAPTER FORTY

Wednesday 1530 hours

Katie fought the road conditions and the rain with all the energy and strength she had. Her shoulder blades and neck burned from keeping the steering wheel under control. The weather and road conditions were getting worse, but neither she nor McGaven wanted to admit it. She eased up the accelerator and drove to the side of the road, keeping out of the hazardous deep pools of water that funneled in the middle.

"I don't know where else to go. The cemetery area is a long shot, but there was a place that Mason and the chief would frequent near it. It's also where the film crew was headed. The sheriff said one of them was missing."

"Let's go. Otherwise the water will be flooding everywhere and we won't be able to do anything but sit and wait it out at the cabins."

Again, Katie tried to use her phone and this time wrote a text to Chad, telling him where they were going and where they were staying—just in case. Without knowing if he would receive the message, she sent it.

They neared the old hotel historical building; built in the late 1880s, it had been used as a tourist attraction ever since. It was undergoing some restoration and there were county negotiations about possibly opening shops and a couple of small eateries during the spring and summer months to bring more tourism to the town.

The large building stood ominous, strong, at the top of a hill, nestled in between tall trees, an excellent example of a time gone by. There was still a porch in the front. The land, building, and the old cemetery adjacent to it dominated the vista.

Katie felt uneasy, as if there was something that she wasn't seeing clearly. Darren Rodriguez's words still haunted her.

You know all about him. You can reach out and touch him.

Officer Mason wasn't someone Katie knew, and she had never met him before he came by the Mayfields' first house—and that was only fleeting.

Was she taking that statement too literally? Was it just a form of expression? Close enough to touch the killer?

Still, it bothered her.

Water rushed down the incline from where the historical building was located. Instinct told Katie to slow down and cut the headlights.

"What's up?" asked McGaven, looking directly at her.

"Something doesn't feel right. I know that sounds vague, but there's something not jiving here…"

McGaven remained quiet and stared up at the building.

As they inched to the top of the drive, they saw the gray truck parked at the main entrance. Katie's blood went cold. Officer Mason was inside the building—for sanctuary, waiting the storm out, or waiting for them. She turned the Jeep toward the far left side of the parking lot off the pavement, and parked. It was in an area where the trees would act as a natural cover.

"How do you want to do this?" McGaven asked.

"We have to arrest Mason and locate the little girl," she said. "We can't wait any longer."

"Agreed."

"We don't have any backup. If Chad doesn't get my message, no one will know where we are and no one will show up," she said, hating that she sounded so grim and without hope.

"I understand," said McGaven, still staring at the building and the gray truck.

"I'll go in first through the front. Go around the back to make sure he doesn't escape and… then we'll meet up."

Katie and McGaven, soaked and tired, stealthily made their way to their locations, each with their gun drawn but down at their side—for the moment.

After watching McGaven disappear, Katie was at the main entrance where a simple lock had been busted. She felt her adrenalin pumping and a surge of energy pulsating through her body. The low drive she had experienced earlier was replaced with an all-time high.

She pushed the door open slowly and was hit immediately with an old building smell, along with a whiff of mold, that made her wrinkle her nose in disgust. Stepping inside, Katie was on high alert. Any noise or movement could mean instant death. She looked around but there was no sign of anyone. Nothing moved. No sound.

Moving deeper into the old hotel, there were drips spattering on the floor as the storm leaked through cracks and crevices in the ceiling. Over the sound of the rain she tuned into something else—moaning, more like pleading. She stopped to listen, tilting her head and concentrating hard. It was a two-way conversation, with a man's voice and the high voice of a child.

Shivers went up Katie's arms and down her spine, making her hands tremble. Her immediate thoughts were of the Mayfield sisters, and what might have happened to them before they were discarded into the canyon. Then she fought the vision of them lying on the medical examiner's table.

Katie caught herself breathing shallow—typical of an impending panic attack. Focusing as hard as she could, she pushed herself to move forward, following the sound of the voices.

She made her way up a rickety staircase and down a long hallway. To the left there were construction areas with caution tape and piles of brick. As she continued the voices became louder and easier to identify. One was a little girl, pleading between cries, and the other was Mason. Katie was sure of it by his pitch and speech patterns.

She inched closer to a small room at the end of the hallway which she speculated was a storage room. As much as she dared, Katie kept getting closer, holding her breath every time she thought Mason would come out and take her down. But he didn't. It sounded like he was trying to coax the girl to go somewhere with him.

There was a noise at the bottom of the stairs—a scraping and then a bump. She slowly turned in the direction and listened intently. When she didn't hear it again, she moved forward, thinking that McGaven was going to be joining her shortly. There was no way to contact him or alert him to where she was going—and the little girl was her first priority.

Katie was determined to bring Mason in alive so he would have to explain everything he had done to those little girls. She wanted him to look their parents in the eye. As she reached the doorway, she stayed flat against the wall next to the entrance, waiting for the right moment to take a quick look into the room.

Inside, Mason was leaning over a little girl sitting on the floor who was dressed in jeans and a sweater with a favorite doll ironed on. Her wrists and ankles were securely tied, and she had on a blindfold that had slipped down toward her chin. She was clearly terrified, shaking and never taking her big dark eyes away from him.

"C'mon, I'm not going to hurt you. I'm here to take you where it's safe," he insisted.

"No," she cried. "You hurt me. *Please*… I want to go home."

"No, I'm here to save you."

"Hands in the air, Mason," said Katie in a clear voice, her gun trained at his chest. "Do it now." She prepared to shoot, noticing his heavy dark blue windbreaker with two greasy marks on the left sleeve. He turned to look at Katie, his face pale like he was sick, his eyes haunted and faraway.

"I knew you would figure it out," he said, forcing a crooked smile. "Very clever you are."

"Put your gun on the floor," she said calmly. "Take it easy. Nice and slow."

Mason put his gun down gently and stood up again. He made no move to go with Katie, but he seemed to want to get something off his chest. He was shaken. Shifting from side to side.

"I knew you would figure it out. I had given up on Chief Osborne. He wouldn't protect the little girls—he's just as guilty for doing nothing. He wouldn't protect the fragile ones."

The word *fragile* struck Katie like an arrow to the gut. It was the same word that was in Robin Mayfield's supposed suicide note. *Fragile.*

"Don't you believe me?" he asked, turning his anxious expression to a worried one—his eyes wide and brows tensed.

"About what?" she said. "You're a killer. You abducted and killed all those little girls and you made your own dad cover it up for you."

"My dad? What are you talking about?" He continued to shift his weight from foot to foot. "My dad is dead. You believe I killed these little girls? I'm *saving* them. I figured out what was going on. I knew there was something not right and that the chief was hiding something. I was right. See, I was right. He was hiding something for his son."

"For *you*," said Katie, taking a step closer into the room.

The little girl sobbed and cowered further in the corner.

"Oh, you... you believe that I'm..." His voice became a desperate whisper. "It's true I've done some things that I'm not proud of... I'm sorry if I scared you the other night, and I didn't mean to hurt your partner. But... I've been conducting my own investigation. I wanted to get to the truth."

"You murdered Chief Osborne in cold blood," said Katie, although there was something about Mason which seemed genuine. "Not a good way to get to the truth."

"I know that was wrong, but he was a bad man. An accessory. He always covered for him. Even Rodriguez is dead. He did all the dirty deeds. Everyone dies for him, some way or another."

"Mayfield?" she said trying mentally to piece together everything they'd learned so far.

He averted her gaze and ignored her.

You know all about him. You can reach out and touch him.

"Why did you pick this place?" she said, beginning to comb through the investigation in her mind.

"This place? I didn't pick it. I followed the clues—just as you and your partner did. I tried to help you when I put that photo album with Robin Mayfield's evidence. I knew I had to do it."

Katie strained to think. Something seemed amiss—muddling the investigation. She felt like she was at a funhouse where nothing was as it would seem, every surface distorted and uneven, not knowing what to trust.

Darkness draped across the building as the day faded into dusk. Katie had to hurry. Her pulse was racing.

"Put your hands behind your back," she said, stepping closer to him. "Easy." She took her left hand and pulled handcuffs out of her pocket.

"You're making a mistake. He's still out there... he's cunning... crafty... you won't win against him. No one *ever* does...."

Katie snapped the first handcuff to his wrist and then the other to a pipe in the room.

"You're wrong, Detective." His face was haunted, pale and seemed to contort.

"We'll see. I'm playing it safe." Katie didn't know what to think. But once Mason was secured and couldn't hurt anyone, she grabbed his gun and pocketed the weapon.

Katie knelt down to the little girl and spoke in a soft voice. "Hi, I'm Katie. I'm going to free you and get you out of here, okay?"

She slowly nodded, staring at Katie as though deciding whether to believe her or not.

"What's your name?" Katie asked.

"Maggie," she said weakly.

"Maggie is a beautiful name."

"It's short for Margaret."

"How old are you, Maggie?"

"Five."

"Okay, Maggie, we're going to get out of here."

"You won't be able to escape," said Mason. "You won't! He won't let you! Never!"

Katie holstered her weapon, glancing at the doorway. She had expected to see McGaven by now. She picked up Maggie and moved quickly, exiting the storage room and heading down the hallway to search for him. She took the staircase with caution, not wanting to fall or drop Maggie.

There was light coming in at the other end of the corridor from a window. Katie made her way there and peered out. There was an expensive white SUV parked outside. Staring at it for a long moment, accessing her memories, her thoughts then slowed. One of the last pieces of the puzzle seemed to fit. The walls skewed. Her heart skipped a beat.

Katie stumbled backward as the entire investigation flew through her mind—jumbled at first and then the pieces finally beginning to fit together—one by one. Everything. The film crew. The discovery of the Mayfield sisters. Robin Mayfield's death. Darren Rodriguez's shooting.

You know all about him. You can reach out and touch him.

She focused on the documentary DVDs from the Wild Oats Productions and everything came to her like a movie reel. Meeting the film crew. Driving to Rifle Ridge. The crime scene. So many images. An abundance of evidence.

Rock Creek…

Katie took in a breath and tried to keep her composure as she held Maggie tight. She felt the little girl shiver and her heart pound.

The killer had been right under her nose all along. More exact, he had sat right next to her in the Jeep on the ride up the mountain with the film crew. He had fiddled with a long necklace he wore with a type of charm. It was the exact necklace that Tessa Mayfield wore in her photograph, that had made the impression around her neck after she was strangled. The DVDs at Rodriguez's house. The driver's license photograph of Whitney Mayfield—if his hair was shorter, dyed blond with a clean-shaven face—it was *him*. The writer and researcher for the show. The man who scouted locations for each shot. He wanted to come back to where he had dumped the tiny bodies of his first victims—his daughters.

The call to the sheriff that one of the crew was missing was a ruse—he had laid a trap. It was him… He was in power. It was a perfect cover. Ty Windsor was Whitney Mayfield, not Officer Mason. It had to be him…

Katie turned back and ran as fast as she was able, carrying the girl. Maggie began to cry, sensing Katie's stress.

"Katie!" yelled McGaven. He sounded far away. "Katie! He's here…"

She turned the corner and taking the staircase as fast as she dared. Her legs were fatigued with the extra weight, and the sheer exhaustion of the investigation.

Heavy footsteps approached.

She was relieved that McGaven was close.

"Gav," she said, and ran right into a gun pointed at her face.

"Gotcha," the man said, in almost comic tone.

Katie stared directly at Ty Windsor, his hair wet and uncombed, so it hung towards his face. It was clear how he could play the many faces he needed to, and not be recognizable.

A chameleon.

"Detective, you look surprised, but not as surprised as I thought you'd be." He smiled. "You figured it out, didn't you? I knew you were special—smarter than you should be."

Mason yelled from above, muffled slightly by the walls and distance. "Uncuff me, Detective! I told you the truth!"

Ty laughed. "Nice job, Detective. You're making my job so much easier."

Katie went to move and he pushed the gun toward Maggie, making her cry harder.

"You kinda interrupted something here…" he said.

Katie gained her composure. "You don't have Daddy to protect you now. You're not going to get away."

"Why? Because of your partner? He's down there," he said in a creepy whisper and pointed to a deep ditch dug in the ground as part of the construction work.

"Katie," McGaven said faintly from down below.

The funhouse feeling attacked Katie even more.

"Now give me Maggie," he said and dragged her, screaming, from Katie's arms. To Katie's horror, Ty turned and dropped the little girl into the deep hole with McGaven.

"No!" cried Katie. To her relief, she heard McGaven saying she was okay.

"For you, I have a special surprise. I was saving it for someone else, but you'll do." He snickered. He searched her with force and put both weapons in his pockets as well as her cell phone. Then he lunged forward and gripped her throat violently, shoving her against the wall. "Now do what I say. Move!" he said, indicating toward a back entrance with the barrel of his gun.

Katie had to wait for the right moment to defend herself and take him down, but Ty was cunning and acted as if he had a sixth sense. She hoped that McGaven could get out of the hole; if not, she was completely on her own.

The thunder roared and rumbled throughout the brick building.

Katie stepped through the doorway.

The rain blew at an angle, whipping her hair against her face. The black sky crowed with angry thunder and lightning. The storm was upon them as Ty pushed Katie toward the cemetery.

CHAPTER FORTY-ONE

Wednesday 1730 hours

Chad and John were at the third downed tree on Highway 9. The work was hard and the weather remained miserable, but with the help of Lizzy it was just about do-able.

Winded from the physical labor and fighting head winds, Chad looked at his phone and there was a text from Katie. "Hold up," he said. John and Lizzy looked at him, waiting. "Katie left a message. They are either at the ruins next to the cemetery or at their cabin at Oak Grove Motel."

"That's good to know. Smart detective," said John as his voice trailed off in the wind.

"Let's keep going," said Lizzy, as she pushed her wet hair from her face.

John and Chad started up their chainsaws again and began cutting, chips dominating the air in the downpour.

*

Katie stood at the rickety gate leading into the cemetery. There were crumbling headstones and old trees with dead branches bending toward the ground, like tentacles waiting to grab the freshly dead. There were sections with extremely old headstones, simple and showing the results of time. Others had more modern headstones, some large, others with small statues.

What caught her attention were the small graves that appeared to have been dug recently. There were no markers. Each small gravesite was the exact size of the others in the cluster. Was this where Ty buried the bodies?

She stopped and looked up as the rain halted. She wouldn't play Ty's games.

"Move!" yelled Ty. "I finally found a perfect way to get rid of bodies where no one would ever think of looking." He smiled and stood up straight, as if it was something to be proud of.

"I'm not moving," she said.

Ty shoved her hard.

"How could you kill your own daughters?" she said.

"You have all the answers. Why do you think?"

"Because you're a coward and a freak, who nobody could love."

He laughed. "You have no idea what you're talking about. But that's okay. I was brutalized over and over again—but my beautiful fair-haired sister was treated like a princess."

Katie closed her eyes. There was so much violence and hate in the world. But she wasn't going to have pity for a monster that murdered his children.

"You wouldn't understand," he said.

"But why kill your innocent children?"

"No one is innocent."

"You even marked them. They had to be special to you in some way," she said, trying to bide some time.

"Don't waste your time trying to profile me, Detective. You don't know me. And you never will. I'm not like you…"

"The chief loved you."

Ty made a noise with his lips that indicated he didn't care.

"He adopted you."

"Oh yes, Richard and Rachel Osborne, what wonderful people. They gave me everything a kid could ask for. No boy could ask for anything more. Then Rachel had to go and die of cancer. Isn't that just great…"

Katie sensed sorrow in his sarcasm.

"Who did Tessa belong to? Did you kidnap her too?"

"I saw this woman one day, who I suppose was the mother of the most beautiful blonde little girl—she looked so much like my sister. I took her. Robin didn't ask questions—she never would, she kept her mouth shut—until she couldn't take it anymore. We already had Megan, but Robin wanted two children. So I solved that problem."

"Why not just have another baby?"

"Robin couldn't. At least she was good for something though. She took care of the girls."

"Why the branding?" she said, but things were becoming clearer the more she heard Ty talk about his life, childhood, and all the wrongs that he'd taken care of.

"Three seven two was three hundred seventy-two days that I thought about killing my little sister, and it was exactly three hundred seventy-two days later that I carried out my plan. Every three hundred seventy-two days I would find another girl. Now MOVE!"

Katie refused to move forward. Ty leaned close and pushed the gun against her head, but she didn't respond. It made him angry.

"You're not following the plan," he said, frustrated.

What Katie wanted to do was push Ty off balance so he would make a mistake. Give most people, especially killers, enough time and they would make a mistake.

He put his gun away, something dropping from his pocket as he did so, then he grabbed Katie by the neck, almost lifting her off her feet. Then, slamming her down in the mud, he let the water rush over her face and held her down as it continued to rise. Katie closed her eyes as the heavy wind blew fiercely and the rain continued to pour.

*

Chad and John kept the cars close after they moved the last tree and made it into the town of Rock Creek. Growing impatience and concern drove Chad and he needed to get to Katie as soon as possible. He felt something deep inside. Something was wrong—very wrong.

The roads were terrible, some completely flooded.

Chad took a turn too fast. He wasn't familiar with the town and his Jeep stalled as he hit a deep-water area. He kept trying to start it but the engine wouldn't turn over. His SUV bobbed and weaved, unable to touch down.

Chad rolled down his window, waving at John.

John maneuvered his big truck well and stayed to the left side of the road while Lizzy rolled down the passenger window. "Climb out!" she hollered.

Chad scrambled to push his body out the window and dove into the bed of John's truck. The truck roared ahead, shedding puddles like waterfalls. The rain pummeled Chad, but he didn't care. He'd been through rough rescues before. He saw signs for the historical area and hammered on the back window. "Follow the signs!" he yelled, gesturing to the markers. John turned and nodded. Chad gave a thumbs up as he sat down against the back of the cab.

*

Katie fought the grip that Ty had on her throat. His ruthless and even gleeful approach to death was more than disturbing. She could see his face as he tried to choke and drown her in the six inches of water—eyes wide, dark, with his mouth slightly parted. He wanted to kill her—life didn't matter to him.

Katie's body was completely immersed now, her arms and legs numb, but she managed to grab a breath when her mouth was out of the puddle before she was slammed back under.

She moved her lower body and shifted her pelvis so that she could get leverage with her legs. Finally, swinging her left leg around Ty, she pushed him away enough to be able to get up. Her move angered him. From his grunts and groans it was clear that he didn't have anything more to say to her. It was going to be a death match—to the end.

Ty kept coming after her like a monster that wouldn't die. Katie backed up, weaving around headstones as her feet were sucked into the mud. With one huge shove, Ty was able to push her onto her back again, but this time, she fell several feet and landed on something hard.

Dazed and gagging on the heavy rain funneling to her face, she was able to sit up and gasp for air. Looking around her, she realized she was lying in a freshly dug grave. Memories rushed back of when she had been sealed inside a coffin by Chelsea Compton's killer.

All the feelings, emotions, smells, and restricted vision slammed into her psyche. She had tried desperately to calm her anxiety during the investigation—but now it had led her to the place she feared the most. Her breath escaped her. Dizziness enveloped her. Shadows danced around in the graveyard, playing tricks on her.

Ty stood looking down at her with a grin, his wet hair covering most of his face, and a shovel in his right hand.

*

Chad leaned over the side of the truck bed, watching for the turnoff for the historical area of town, when John abruptly stopped the truck. Rolling down the windows, he said, "I don't trust that driveway up to the top. We might slide back down. It's not like a regular four-wheel drive vehicle and I won't have complete control."

"Let's run," said Chad. "We need to see if Katie and McGaven are there."

John and Lizzy glanced at one another.

"Let's do it. It doesn't look very far," said John.

The three of them trekked up the hill. It looked easier than it was. The rain continued to pour and the wind pushed them backwards. Each of them fell a few times, helped each other up and continued on…

*

Katie caught her breath and began to climb out. Ty swung the shovel at her with such speed that it clipped her arm, sending her back into the grave flat on her back. Instant pain shot up through her arm and neck. She flailed in the water at the bottom, slipping around on the mud and wiping it from her eyes. Water was filling it fast, causing more mud to tumble into the hole every second.

Ty's silhouette loomed above her, the shovel poised over his head. She didn't need to see the details of his face to know he was about to kill her—his body language said it all. She had never encountered anyone like him before, a killer who could act so normal and go completely unnoticed for so long. A quiet man able to manipulate people with such ease. People willing to do things for him.

Taking several deep breaths, she thought of the way he had left his daughters—beaten and broken in a mountain cavern. It was all Katie needed to give her strength. She turned and climbed up the back of the oversized grave, using her feet to dig divots into the side walls, making her way to the top and landing on her belly.

*

Exhausted and soaked to the skin, Chad, John, and Lizzy finally made it to the parking lot. Weary and weak, they moved toward the building.

"Hey, there's Katie's Jeep," said Chad, fighting to be heard through the wind. The vehicle was parked at the edge of the property.

John and Lizzy followed Chad into the building.

"Hey!" said a voice from nowhere.

"McGaven?" said Chad incredulously. "Where are you?"

"We're in a well, or part of a basement, I think." His voice sounded far away.

"Katie with you?" said Chad.

"No, he has her! She's probably in the cemetery. You have to get to her. Go! Hurry!"

Chad walked up to the brick hole and looked down. He couldn't see anything, but McGaven's voice echoed off the walls from the bottom. The well was deeper than he thought.

Lizzy ran over to the construction area where there were some tools. She found a flashlight and switched it on. Directing the beam down in the hole, they saw McGaven holding a small child.

"Who is that?" asked John.

"Maggie," he said. "That's all I know. She was abducted from somewhere in town. Her family was just visiting."

"We're going to get you both out, hang tight," said John. "Where are you going?" he said to Chad.

"To help Katie," Chad yelled over his shoulder, as he ran out the back.

Lizzy didn't hesitate for a second, running straight after him.

*

Katie crawled on her hands and knees, baiting Ty with her defiance, knowing it would enrage him. He yelled at her. He called her vile names. But that didn't stop her perseverance or focus. She had been through worse and now used it in her favor as she swatted away the anxiety that tried to envelop her.

Ty took his time walking around the grave area, careful not to get knocked off his feet.

Katie dug her hands in the mud as she crawled.

"Coward!" Ty yelled. "You may be a good detective, but you're the coward."

Katie kept moving slowly until she was back near the rickety entrance gate.

Ty took his gun, as though he had enjoyed the performance but now it was time to act. "Sorry, but your time has just run out," he said, as he aimed it at Katie and prepared to fire.

Katie found what she was looking for beneath the rain and muddy sludge, fingers feeling the curves and smoothness. She had seen it fall from his pocket earlier and now grabbed it, sat up on her knees, and spun in Ty's direction—firing the gun at the exact same moment Ty discharged his.

Both Ty and Katie slumped to the ground.

*

When Chad and Lizzy heard the gunshots, they sprinted in the direction of the cemetery.

Lizzy pulled her firearm and readied herself for whatever they would run into.

Chad ran as fast as he could—his breath caught in his throat as he saw two bodies lying in the mud near a gravesite inside the cemetery.

"No!" He finally reached the entrance and slammed through the wobbly gate. Within seconds he was on the ground holding Katie. Blood was seeping through her windbreaker near her shoulder.

Lizzy joined him. "Is she…?" She couldn't finish her sentence.

Katie groaned and her eyes fluttered open. She didn't say anything at first.

Lizzy stepped back in relief. "She's okay." She then went over to Ty, who was clearly dead. Katie's shot was a direct hit to the chest, blowing a hole right through him. His eyes were open, in a vacant stare.

"I'm okay," said Katie, feeling her shoulder burn, knowing how lucky she was that the bullet hadn't hit a major organ.

Chad quickly assessed her injury. "Looks like the bullet grazed you."

"It still hurts like hell," she said. "Lizzy, you're here. I thought you were a ghost for a moment."

"Not yet," Lizzy replied.

Let's get you inside," said Chad, as he helped Katie to her feet.

The three of them made their way back to the building to meet up with the others and decide what they were going to do next. There was Ty's body, where to hold Officer Mason, and locating Maggie's parents. It was important that they find medical assistance for both Katie and Maggie. They were stranded in Rock Creek for at least another day and needed to take precautions. They were all exhausted and there was still much to be done.

Katie glanced over in the parking lot to where her Jeep was parked—but it wasn't there.

"Where's my Jeep?" she said. "Did someone take it?" But how could they have? she thought, because she had the keys.

"Cisco… Cisco…" she said suddenly, and began running toward the end of the parking lot, which was just above a fast rising creek —barely feeling the discomfort of her shoulder.

From the continuous and heavy rainfall running across the parking lot, the vehicle had run off the edge, taking large sections of the soil with it—including Katie's Jeep.

"*No! Cisco!*" She ran up to the edge and peered down, seeing her Jeep on its side about twenty feet down.

"Katie!" Chad yelled, trying to catch up. "Wait! Katie, wait!"

She had to save Cisco before the rush of the creek below took the entire vehicle, with her beloved companion trapped inside.

Katie disappeared over the edge.

CHAPTER FORTY-TWO

Wednesday 1845 hours

Katie slid down the muddy waterfall that had formed out of rocks, gravel, part of a grassy area, and pieces of the asphalt parking lot. Sliding was more painful than she had anticipated; when she hit solid ground it jarred her teeth and rattled her ribcage as she dropped down to the Jeep.

"Cisco!" she yelled.

She put her hands on the Jeep as it lay on its side. The side window was open an inch. Smearing the mud, she could see inside but it was dark. She didn't see Cisco. Her heart broke. But then she saw him lying on the opposite interior door, and cried with relief. He perked up when he saw her and came to the window, pushing his nose and barking.

"It's okay, buddy. Hang in there." She frantically tried the doors as he continued to bark at her, but they were all locked. Eyeing the rising water, she knew she had maybe five minutes before the car would be washed away. She patted down her pockets, but realized her keys were gone.

Katie looked around desperately for something to smash the window. There were two fist-size pieces of asphalt, and she grabbed one.

"Cisco, back… back…" she instructed, to keep him away from the glass.

Katie kept battering the window until eventually it started to crack.

"Need some help?" said Chad, as he appeared, breathless, next to her. "Let me try." He hammered the asphalt until the glass finally gave way.

Cisco immediately hurdled through the window to get to Katie—he was a black flash of joy.

"Oh, Cisco," she said, petting and hugging him. "Good boy… I'm never going to leave you… never…"

Suddenly there was a bright beam shining down on them like an angelic light. John and McGaven were at the top of the hill, giving them some light to see by. Lizzy held Maggie as they looked down.

The rain tapered off a bit, helping Katie and Chad with their ascent back up to the parking lot—Cisco scrabbling in tow. With many misses and slides, they managed to climb the hill from the side where there still were bushes and shrubs capable of holding their weight. Hand over hand, fist over fist, they kept climbing. The pain from her shoulder had gone from excruciating to numb, but she managed to keep most of her strength through her good side to scale the hillside.

Katie made it to the top first as Chad followed with Cisco between them.

"Let's get inside," said McGaven. "C'mon, we need to get out of the storm."

"I've lost another car," said Katie.

"Join the club," said Chad. He hugged her close. "But I didn't lose you."

Just as the group was about to enter the building to escape the storm, they heard the grinding engine of a large vehicle approaching. A large black truck crept up to the top and drove into the parking lot. It slammed the brakes, the driver's door swung open, as Officer McKinney jumped out with his gun drawn targeted at them.

"Who is that?" asked Chad.

"It's McKinney," said Katie. She watched the officer approach as relief washed over her. She knew that he was on their side. It had been McKinney who began investigating the list that she and McGaven had found in the chief's desk. It made sense.

McKinney dropped his arm and holstered his gun. His look of concern was evident as he saw the group and hurried to them glancing at the little girl. "Is everyone okay?"

CHAPTER FORTY-THREE

Two weeks later...

Katie walked down the perfectly manicured pathway at the cemetery until she reached the headstones she was looking for, as Chad and Cisco waited for her up on the hillside—watching over her.

She carried three flowers. Stopping at the first headstone which read "Robin Mayfield, loving mother", Katie put a white rose on the ground. The next two were smaller headstones with the names: "Tessa Mayfield" and "Megan Mayfield". She put a pink rose on Tessa's headstone and a yellow rose on Megan's. Tessa's biological parents had had her funeral and burial in Austin, Texas under her birth name, Brianna Homestead.

Katie bowed her head for a moment of silence. "Rest in peace, little fragile ones, and may angels carry you under their wings to heaven." She said a private prayer, then sat in silence, gathering her thoughts.

Glancing up at the top of the hill where Chad and Cisco waited, she smiled and was truly thankful for everything she had.

*

Standing at the railing of the resort as the cool air refreshed her senses, Katie gazed out at the beautiful country club with its rolling green hills and landscaped gardens filled with vines, late-blooming fall flowers, and a waterfall. The sun was beginning to set, showing off its reds, oranges, and pinks. Katie watched as the light began to fade.

Dressed in a long black velvet skirt and a turquoise blouse, she gazed at the flowing waterfall, remembering everything that transpired in Rock Creek. Nothing would ever be the same. The town. The people. Or the police department. There was much healing needed. Everything had changed for one small town with so many secrets—even she had a difficult time accepting them.

"Hi," said Chad, dressed in a nice suit. He leaned in and kissed Katie, then took a deep breath. "Wow, fantastic sunset. I'll never get tired of watching them."

"Me either. No two are exactly alike. Did you know that?" She smiled.

"Well, we can watch them together for the rest of our lives."

Katie leaned into him and closed her eyes. "That sound heavenly."

"Hey, you two," McGaven interrupted. "Come back in and enjoy your engagement party. Your uncle is about to do one of his famous toasts. And I think John is hitting it off with your friend Lizzy."

"We'll be right there," said Katie.

"Okay, but don't miss all the fun," said McGaven, smiling as he went back inside.

Katie laughed.

"That's nice."

"What?"

"Your smile and your laugh. I want to see more."

"Don't worry, you'll have a lifetime to catch them," she said.

A LETTER FROM JENNIFER

I want to say a huge thank you for choosing to read *The Fragile Ones* (Book 5 of the Detective Katie Scott series). If you did enjoy it, and want to keep up to date with all my latest releases, just sign up at the following link. Your email address will never be shared and you can unsubscribe at any time.

www.bookouture.com/jennifer-chase

This has continued to be a special project and series for me. Forensics and criminal profiling have been something that I've studied considerably and to be able to incorporate them into crime fiction novels has been a thrilling experience. I have wanted to write this series for a while and it has been truly wonderful to bring it to life.

One of my favourite activities outside of writing has been dog training. I'm a dog lover, if you couldn't tell by reading this book, and I loved creating a supporting canine character for my police detective. I hope you enjoyed meeting Cisco.

I hope you loved *The Fragile Ones*, and if you did I would be very grateful if you could write a review. I'd love to hear what you think, and it makes such a difference helping new readers to discover one of my books for the first time.

I love hearing from my readers—you can get in touch on my Facebook page, through Twitter, Goodreads or my website.

Thanks,
Jennifer Chase

AuthorJenniferChase

JChaseNovelist

authorjenniferchase.com

ACKNOWLEDGMENTS

I want to thank my husband Mark for his steadfast support and for being my rock even when I had self-doubt. It's not always easy living with a writer and you've made it look easy.

A very special thank you goes out to all my law enforcement, police detectives, deputies, police K9, forensic, and first-responder friends—there's too many to list. Your friendships have meant the world to me, and allowed me endless inspiration. I wouldn't be able to bring my crime fiction stories to life if it wasn't for all of you. Thank you for your service and dedication to keep the rest of us safe.

Writing this series continues to be a truly amazing experience. I would like to thank my publisher Bookouture for the opportunity, and the fantastic staff for helping me to bring this book and the entire Detective Katie Scott series to life. Thank you, Kim, Sarah, and Noelle for your unrelenting promotion for us authors. A very special thank you to my editor Jessie Botterill—your incredible support and insight has helped me to work harder to write more adventures for Detective Katie Scott.